One True Thing

One True Thing

A novel by
Lynn Jermyn
from

Wisteria Publications

Wisteria Publications
507-4 Briar Hill Heights
New Tecumseth, ON
L9R 1Z7

One True Thing
ISBN: 978-1-988763-18-7
Copyright © 2018 by Lynn Jermyn

Published in Canada 2018

Layout and Cover Art by Taria van Weesenbeek

Please contact the author at lynnojermyn@gmail.com for any questions or comments.

Dedication

This book, my first novel, is dedicated to Kaarina Brooks. Kaarina volunteers for the CNIB and is my vision mate. She gave me the plot idea and challenged me to write the story. She is a published author of many books under the pseudonym Karen Rossi and of children's books under her own name.

From her own experience she passed on to me things I needed to know about writing a romance novel. I thank her for her patience and for the hundreds of hours she dedicated to helping me make the story better. Without Kaarina this book would not exist.

About the Author

Lynn is a visually impaired senior in her seventies and has had several short stories published in local magazines.

She lives in Alliston, Ontario, with her husband, Ron Smith.

Acknowledgements

I wish to thank my husband, Ron Smith for his unfailing support during the creation of this book. He also provided internet research when I needed it, and most of all, technical support which kept me from throwing the computer out the window.

I also wish to thank Doris McDonald, who was the entire trumpet section of my little band of supporters, and Pat Robinson, who listened to my ideas and helped me clarify my thoughts.

Chapter One

It was a cold, miserable, January night. Charlie was at home watching the Leafs game on TV and nursing a Neo-Citron. The phone rang.

"Hey Charlie, it's Tom! Let's go to the pub and watch the ballgame and have a few brews with the guys."

"I feel shitty. I'm coming down with a cold or something," Charlie complained. "I think I should just stay home and go to bed early."

"Oh, come on man, don't be such a suck. A few brews will make you feel better. Besides we didn't go last week."

Hearing the yearning in Tom's voice, Charlie gave in. "Okay, I'll pick you up in fifteen minutes, as long as you promise we won't stay late."

Because he was taking cold medication and felt a bit fuzzy, Charlie drank only coffee at the pub. The other guys teased him and called him a wussy, but he didn't care. His head was pounding from all the noise and the smell of beer was making him queasy.

As soon as the game ended, Charlie said, "Say good night, Tom. We're out of here."

They stepped outside into a blizzard, the snow driving straight into their faces.

"Holy shit, I wasn't expecting this," Charlie exclaimed. "I can't even see my car on the other side of the lot."

Slipping and sliding they reached the car.

"I hope the ploughs have been out or we're in for a tricky drive," Tom said.

"Don't worry, I'm used to driving in snow. We'll be okay," Charlie assured him.

Unfortunately the ploughs hadn't been out and the roads were treacherous. But luckily the storm had kept people home, so the traffic was light. Despite the conditions Charlie drove at his usual speed. He just wanted to get home and climb into bed.

"Slow down!" Tom yelled. "Can't you see that car ahead sliding all over the road?"

At that moment Charlie's car hit a patch of black ice and spun out. He slammed on the brakes. The car lurched to a stop on the wrong side of the road, half on the road and half on the shoulder, facing the oncoming traffic.

Charlie looked up and to his horror saw headlights bearing down on them.

"No-oo!" he screamed and blacked out.

When he awoke, Charlie didn't know where he was. He tried to move but found himself constrained, except for his left arm. In a panic, he began to struggle. His writhing set off an alarm that freaked him out even more. He couldn't see anything. Was he dead or in the middle of some ungodly nightmare?

"Help me!" he yelled. "Somebody! Anybody!"

"Stop moving!" said a stern female voice. "You're in the hospital and I'm your nurse. It's good you're awake because I need to take your vitals."

Charlie felt the squeeze of a blood pressure cuff and the nurse's cool hand taking his pulse. A thermometer was inserted into his ear.

"Turn on the light and unstrap me! " he insisted. "I want to get out of here."

"You're not strapped down," the nurse told him. "I'll loosen the sheets if you promise to stop moving."

As Charlie felt the sheets loosen around him, he tried to sit up.

"Stop that!" the nurse ordered. "You're attached to an IV drip and you're going to break the needle in your hand."

"Then take the bloody thing out!" Charlie shouted, trying to rip the adhesive tape off.

"Leave it alone," the nurse said. "I'm going to get the doctor and he'll explain everything to you."

Charlie heard her footsteps hurrying out of the

room.

"Can somebody help me?" Charlie shouted. "I can't see and nobody will turn on the lights!"

"Stop shouting," a familiar voice said. "There's no one here but me."

Charlie turned toward the voice. "Paul, is that you?"

"Yes, it's me," his brother said. "You had everyone scared. How're you feeling?"

"Why won't they turn on the lights?" Charlie asked. "Did that car hit us? Where's Tom?"

"Take it easy, bro. There was no accident, but you passed out and Tom called 9-1-1. They couldn't rouse you so they brought you here."

"Why aren't the lights on?" Charlie demanded.

"The lights are on," Paul said.

"Then why can't I see?"

"What? You mean you can't see anything?" Paul's voice was incredulous.

"No!" Charlie shouted. "That's what I've been trying to tell everybody. What have they done to me?"

"I don't know. Let me get the doctor."

Just as Paul was going out, the doctor walked in.

"Hello, Mr. Weaver. I am Doctor Strong. I checked you in on Tuesday."

"Tuesday?" Charlie said. "What day is today?"

"It's Thursday," the doctor replied. "You've been unconscious for about thirty-six hours."

"Unconscious for thirty-six hours?" Charlie yelled.

"And now I can't see! What the hell have you done to me?"

"You were unresponsive when you were brought in. We did a full body MRI and found no injuries," the doctor explained. "I don't know why you can't see. It could be post traumatic stress disorder but you would have to see a psychologist for a diagnosis. We can make an appointment for you. You should also see your ophthalmologist to be sure there's no damage to your eyes."

"Right. But when can I leave?" Charlie asked.

"You should stay for another day of observation to make sure everything is working as it should."

"You just said there were no injuries, so why should I stay?" Charlie asked belligerently.

"Stay or don't stay, it's your choice, Mr. Weaver," the doctor said brusquely. "If you're determined to go I'll have the nurse come in and remove the IV."

Charlie heard the doctor's footsteps leaving the room.

"Paul, are you there?" Charlie asked, turning his head. "Will you take me home?"

"Yes, I can take you home," Paul said. "But don't you think you should stay for another day?"

"No!" Charlie yelled. "I think being here's the problem. I'm sure I'll be able to see when I get out of here."

"Well, if that's how you feel, I'll go to the desk and check you out," Paul said. "I'm also going to make an appointment for you with a psychologist."

"A shrink? Forget it! I'm not crazy, and I don't need someone asking me about my sex life. I'm sure this thing with my eyes will go away once I'm out of here."

They left the hospital and headed for Charlie's apartment.

"What do you remember about Tuesday night?" Paul asked.

"I was driving Tom home from the pub when I hit a patch of black ice and spun out. I just remember looking up and seeing headlights right there. An image of mom and dad's smashed up car flashed before my eyes and I was sure we were going to die. I don't remember anything after that."

"How much did you drink at the pub?"

"Nothing. I was feeling lousy and the smell of beer made me queasy," Charlie said and kept looking around. He was expecting to see where they were, but nothing penetrated the grey wall of his vision. Seized with terror, he whispered, "God Paul, what am I going to do?"

"Why don't you come and stay with Ilene and me until we find out what's wrong," Paul suggested.

"No, I can't face anyone now. I'll be fine on my own." Charlie lowered his head, muttering to himself, "This isn't happening. I can't be blind. How'm I going to live?"

"I'm worried about you," Paul said. "I don't want to

leave you alone. Please come to our place so I can take care of you."

"Stop pushing me, Paul!" Charlie lashed out. "I need to be alone to think." He sat in sullen silence while his brother parked the car.

Paul led him into his apartment, holding him by the arm.

"Let me check to make sure you have enough food until I can shop for you on Saturday," Paul said. "Will you be okay?"

"Yes, I'll be fine," Charlie snapped.

"Well, okay, then. I have to get going but I'll call you tomorrow," Paul said. "But you call me if you need anything at all." He left, locking the door behind him.

Charlie stood where Paul had left him. "Fuck! Christ! God!" he raged. "Why are you doing this to me? I've never hurt anyone. Why am I being punished?"

Where was he? He put his hands out and took a step. Nothing. Another step. What was that? Table. Kitchen table. Okay, now to find the wall and follow it to the living room. Now forward to find his chair. Ouch! Shit! What was that? The coffee table. He moved sideways.

At last there was his chair. He collapsed into it, put his head in his hands and wept. He couldn't live like this, a cripple who couldn't even take care of himself. He'd be better off dead. Why hadn't that car hit him? He wished it had!

After a time, Charlie got up and felt his way to the drawer where he stored his liquor. He didn't bother trying to find a glass but simply tipped the whiskey bottle and drank, weeping and cursing all the while.

Eventually, stumbling and bumping into the walls, he found his way to the bedroom. He collapsed on the bed and passed out.

He awoke with pneumatic drills pounding in his head, a stiff neck from his head hanging half-off the bed, and a mouth stuffed with cotton that tasted like a sewer. He also had to pee like a race horse. Feeling his way around the walls and furniture, he found the bathroom. He relieved himself and then set about brushing his teeth. The toothbrush was easy enough to find, but getting toothpaste on the bristles was more of a challenge. His first attempt had the paste sliding off the side of the brush. The second attempt was more successful and he was able to get the job done. Fuck! Now he had to clean up the paste that was on the counter. If he could find it. And where the hell were those aspirins?

After a shower he felt his way back to the bedroom to get clean clothes. Then he remembered that he hadn't done laundry for a couple of weeks. Shit! Now he was going to have to ask Paul to do it for him. How could the most simple tasks of living be so difficult?

He was ravenous! When was the last time he had

eaten? What was there to eat? He found bread and a package of cooked ham and slapped together a couple of sandwiches. He wolfed them down with a cold beer, while standing at the counter.

What to do next? By the sounds of the traffic going by, he assumed it was still day, but he couldn't be sure what time it was. He could call Paul at work and ask him, but he didn't want to talk to anyone. He was just going to have to find an all-news radio station that announced the time every ten or fifteen minutes. Well, it was something for him to do. Then he remembered that messages on his cell phone always gave the date and the time they were left.

But where was his cell phone? He felt around the counter and found his charger, but the phone wasn't there. He must have taken it to the pub. Where was his coat? He found it hanging in the hall closet, but the phone wasn't there either. Fuck! He'd have to call Paul after all.

Then he had an idea. If the phone was in the apartment, he could call the number from his landline and when it rang he'd be able to find it. That was brilliant, Charlie!

He went into the living room and felt his way around the furniture until he got to the end of the sofa. There was the small table where he kept the phone. He sat down and felt all the buttons. Which ones did he need to push? He felt the small raised bump in the middle of the keypad which, he guessed, was number five. How clever! Why hadn't he noticed that before? He dialled his cell phone number and waited to hear it ring. Nothing. Then a message system clicked in but it wasn't his. Obviously he had misdialed.

He tried again. Success! The cell phone was ringing quite close to him. But where? The coffee table? He leaned forward and swept his hand over the surface. There it was, but in his haste he knocked it to the floor. By now, the message system had kicked-in and the phone stopped ringing. He hung up his landline and crawled on the floor on all fours to retrieve the cell phone.

He found it, but gave his head a sharp crack on the corner of the coffee table as he slid back onto the sofa. Fuck! That sure didn't help his headache. His next challenge was retrieving the message. That would be trickier because there were more buttons and they were much smaller. He envisioned the keypad and what he had to do. Three tries later he got the message and the time—one twenty-three, p.m.

He was now thoroughly frustrated with doing simple tasks that he'd never given a moment's thought to in the past. How much of life he had taken for granted! The fact that he had succeeded in doing what he wanted, should have made him feel better, but it only added to his frustration. Simple tasks shouldn't be this hard, and take this long to accomplish.

Charlie sat, wondering what to do next, when the phone in his hand began to ring. Without thinking he pressed the on button.

"Hello?"

"Hey, Charlie, it's me, Harry. Paul called and told me about your troubles. I guess you won't be working for awhile, eh?"

"Yeah, you got that right," Charlie said.

"You're going to need money to be going on with, so I'm going to pay out your vacation pay, along with your last two weeks in the next payroll," Harry said. "I'll also send you a Record of Employment, so you can apply for Employment Insurance. It's not a lot but it's better than nothing."

"Are you firing me?" asked Charlie, his heart sinking.

"Hell, no man. You're my best electrician. It's just that as we don't know how long you'll be out of commission, I want to make sure you have some money coming in. The minute you're ready to come back to work, your job will be here."

"Thanks, Harry. I appreciate you thinking about me."

"Keep in touch and let me know if there's anything else I can do."

After Harry hung up, Charlie felt thoroughly discouraged and depressed. Not only was he a useless cripple, he was now an unemployed, useless cripple.

He threw his cell phone across the room. Christ, he needed a drink! Was that bottle still beside his chair? He went looking for it and found it where he'd left it the day before. Thank goodness it wasn't totally empty. He proceeded to chug back the rest of the whiskey and soon was drunk. This time he didn't bother to try to make it to the bedroom, he simply fell asleep in the chair.

The next day was Saturday. Paul came, as he had promised, to do some shopping and to see how Charlie was coping. He found his brother in the chair, hung over and bleary eyed.

"Get up and get cleaned up!" Paul ordered. "I'm going out to get us some breakfast. When I come back I expect you to be showered and dressed in clean clothes."

"I don't have any clean clothes," Charlie whined. "I can't do laundry now."

"At least get showered. I'll do some laundry for you when I get back. We really need to have a talk about your situation, and how you're going to manage."

Paul left and Charlie felt his way to the bathroom. He stripped down and climbed into the shower. The water woke him up and made him feel a little better. He groped his way back to the bedroom, put on his robe and gathered up his dirty clothes so Paul could do his laundry.

Paul returned with three Egg McMuffins, six hash browns and two large coffees. When Charlie smelled the food, he realized that once again he had neglected to eat. The two sandwiches he had slapped together yesterday were the last food he had eaten.

Paul got two plates out of the cupboard and set them on the table. "Come to the table, Charlie, and eat this while it's hot," he called.

Charlie groped his way out of the bedroom, still feeling a bit woozy from the hangover.

"I put an Egg McMuffin and two hash browns on your plate," Paul told him. Charlie picked up the Egg McMuffin, tore open the wrapper and virtually inhaled it. Next, he gobbled down the hash browns and sighed. "Thanks brother, that was really good. I haven't had a hot meal for a few days."

"If you're still hungry, you can have the same again. I brought extras."

"Great."

This time Charlie ate more slowly, enjoying the taste of the food.

"What have you been doing since I left you?" Paul asked. "I've called a couple of times but you never picked up. Is there something the matter with your phone?"

"No, there's nothing the matter with my phone," Charlie snapped. "I just can't think of anyone I want to talk to right now."

"I talked to Harry, and he's going to send you a Record of Employment so you can apply for the sick benefit provided by Employment Insurance."

"Yeah, great guy, Harry. He fired my ass," Charlie grumbled bitterly.

"You know damned well he didn't fire you. He's just trying to make sure you have some money coming in. But, listen, more importantly, how are you going to take care of yourself?"

"Don't worry about me, big brother, I'll manage somehow."

"Yeah, drinking yourself into a stupor every day. That's really managing, isn't it?" Paul said sarcastically.

"It's my life and I'll live it the way I want to," Charlie snarled.

"That's my point, you're not living it. You're not facing up to the reality of your situation. Many people lose their sight and still manage to cope. Which reminds me, I made an appointment for next Friday so you and I can see a psychologist. It's one of the benefits provided by my work."

"I'm not crazy and I don't want to see a shrink," Charlie said adamantly. "All they're interested in is how many times I jacked-off when I was a kid. They can get their jollies somewhere else, but they won't get them from me."

"You've been listening to too many stupid stories.

Psychologists are professionals and, in your case, someone may just be able to help you get your vision back. Don't you want that?"

"Of course I do. I just don't think talking to a shrink will get it back for me. You can go and tell me what he says."

"I'm not going to fight with you," Paul said. "But think about it. It just might help. In the meantime, how're you going to manage? Have you thought about calling the Canadian National Institute for the Blind to see if they can offer some help?"

"Stop pushing me!" Charlie shouted. "I need some time to get used to being a cripple. I'll do those things later."

"Which of course means you won't. Have you talked to Tom since you've been home?"

"No!" Charlie exploded. "And I don't want to. He's the reason I'm in this mess in the first place. If he hadn't begged me to go to the pub that night, I would still be able to see."

"Stop blaming someone else. You didn't have to go to the pub. You could've stayed home. Just remember, Tom saved your life that night. He put out flares, and called 9-1-1."

"Yeah, that's another reason to hate him," Charlie snapped. "Maybe I would've preferred to die. It would be better than this half-life I have left."

"Oh, grow up and stop feeling sorry for yourself,"

Paul shouted. "Yes, you caught a bad break, but you haven't even tried to do anything to help yourself yet." He stood up. "But enough bickering, I have things I have to do. So let me get some laundry done for you, and you can think about what you want me to get at the grocery store."

Paul proceeded to gather up Charlie's towels, sheets, and dirty clothes and headed for the central laundry area in the basement. "I've put your clean sheets on top of the bed," he said over his shoulder. "While I'm getting the wash started, you could make your bed."

Charlie went into the bedroom and found the sheets on the bed. He was surprised at how neatly they were folded. Then he remembered that the last time he'd washed the sheets, Brenda had been there and they had folded them together. Was that only two weeks ago? It seemed like a lifetime. So much had changed.

He picked up the fitted sheet and proceeded to shake it out. Which way did it go? He figured out the length from the width and then tucked in all corners. The flat sheet was much simpler because of the fold down hem at the top. Next, the quilt, and he was done. That wasn't so bad.

Paul came back and announced he was ready to go shopping.

"Get some of those hungry man soups," Charlie said. "I think I can manage opening the cans and heating them up. For the rest, just get sandwich makings like sliced cheese, cooked meats, whole wheat bread, mayonnaise, butter, and peanut butter. Some milk for coffee and some cokes and ginger ale," he listed. "The liquor store is right beside the grocery store, so you could get me a couple of bottles of whiskey. That'll do me just fine. What are you using for money? Take my debit card."

An hour and a half later, Paul returned with the groceries. "Put everything away, while I go to transfer the clothes to the dryer," he ordered.

As Charlie put the groceries away, to his surprise he realized that Paul had actually got him a bottle of whiskey. Not two, like he'd asked, but nevertheless it was something.

When Paul returned he had a basket full of warm clothes. "I didn't fold anything. I figured it would give you good practice to do it yourself. I have to go now. I promised Ilene I'd get the paint and wallpaper for the nursery."

It was then that Charlie remembered that Ilene was pregnant. "How is Ilene doing?"

"She's good. The birth is still a long way off, but we're very excited and talk of almost nothing else these days."

"Well, you better get going then. I'll be fine," he assured Paul. "Thanks for breakfast and doing my laundry and shopping. And double thanks for the whiskey.

The days are so long and a drink really helps."

Paul saw himself out and Charlie proceeded to get dressed. It was nice to have clean underwear. He bundled up the sheets and folded the towels and clothes. Matching the socks was a challenge but it didn't really matter, since he wasn't going anywhere anyway.

Still feeling hung over he decided to have a nap. What else was there to do? He stretched out on his bed and instantly fell asleep.

When he awoke he was thinking about Brenda and the joy of female company. Should he call her? No. He'd only dated her a couple of times and didn't think she'd want to get involved with him now. No, he was just going to have to learn to be celibate.

He got up and groped his way around the walls to the kitchen. In the fridge he found a cold beer and thought he would make himself a sandwich. Just then, there was a loud banging on his door.

"Hey, Charlie, it's me, Tom. I've brought the guys with me. Let us in."

Charlie felt his way down the hall and opened the door.

"Hey, Charlie, how's it hanging?" Vic said as they all piled in. "We brought you some supplies, and thought we could watch the hockey game with you."

"Hey Charlie, how about a game of poker?" Jonesy said, "I could probably beat you now. Ha, ha."

Charlie could smell the pizza, and was instantly hungry. "Hey guys, thanks for bringing the pizza," he said.

"We've got cold beer, potato chips, popcorn, and peanuts as well," said Vic. "I'll put the beer in the fridge and grab a couple of bowls."

"Can't find the damned remote," Jonesy called from the living room.

"Check between the seat cushions" Charlie told him.

As he made his way to the living room, Tom touched his arm. "I brought you a bottle of your favourite whiskey. You look like shit. How're you doing?"

Charlie shook off Tom's hand. "How the fuck do you think I'm doing, asshole?" he snapped.

"What's that for? I'm not the one who pissed in your cornflakes," Tom responded angrily.

"Oh no. You're just the one who made me go out that night."

"You didn't have to go!" Tom snarled back. "Besides, you were the one driving. It's not my fault that you can't drive in snow."

"Stop fighting you guys," Vic said. "What happened is no one's fault. Come into the living room and have some beer and food, and watch the game."

Charlie made his way to his favourite chair, and Tom sat on the couch. The tension between them was palpable.

Charlie ate a few slices of pizza and began chugging down the beer. Nobody was talking and everyone was uncomfortable. To top it off, the Leafs were losing.

When the hockey game was over, Tom was the first to leave. "When you come to your senses," he said, "call me."

Vic and Jonesy soon followed.

Charlie was once again alone. He collapsed into his chair. Oh Christ, what had he done? Tom had been his best friend since high school. He put his head in his hands and wept.

When he ran out of tears, he found his way to the bedroom and got undressed. He climbed into bed but couldn't sleep. He lay awake thinking about all the good times he'd had in his life. Then his thoughts drifted to the future which looked totally bleak. Finally he slept.

Tuesday morning Paul dropped by before work, bringing Charlie a breakfast sandwich and a cappuccino.

"This place is disgusting," Paul snarled. "It stinks, and you look like hell. Your clothes are filthy, you haven't shaved in days and you're obviously not doing anything to help yourself. I have a full time job and can't look after you. Either you come and stay with us, or I'm getting you a housekeeper. Your choice."

"I don't need anyone to take care of me," Charlie

snapped.

"Oh, yes, you do," Paul rounded on him. "All you've done so far, is feel sorry for yourself and get drunk."

"Easy for you to preach, big brother. It's not your life that's just ended."

"Don't be so damn stupid. You're blind, not dead," shouted Paul, "And there's no point in regaining your sight and becoming an alcoholic in the process!"

"Just go away. This is my life and I'll live it the way I want."

"That's my point. You're not living," Paul shot back. "You're simply hoping to die. Pull yourself together and get some help. I have to go to work now. Why don't you clean up this place and yourself, too. That, at least, would be a start." Paul left, slamming the door behind him.

Once again Charlie was alone. How he hated the endless silence, but he couldn't bring himself to ask for help. He'd always been independent and needing so much help now depressed him utterly.

But maybe Paul was right. A housekeeper would at least mean he wasn't totally alone all the time. Fuck! Why was life so difficult?

Chapter Two

At the end of her shift at the grocery store, Natalie was chatting to Cathy, who was taking over the till.

"What's it like out, has it started snowing yet?" Natalie asked.

"Not yet," replied Cathy. "Did you see the picture of that sweet, little dog who is lost?"

"No, where is it?"

"Check out the bulletin board. I hope they find him soon. It's much too cold for a little guy like him to be outside."

Natalie went over to the bulletin board, spotted the picture of the dog and read the ad. But while she was reading, she noticed the one beside it.

"Housekeeper required to take care of a recent trauma victim. Duties include food preparation, laundry and light housekeeping. Please call Paul to set up an interview."

Natalie was immediately interested. Perhaps this

was the answer to her prayer. Since her father's death a few months ago she'd been feeling like she was marking time. Working at the grocery store was not enough. She wanted to feel useful and somehow make a difference in someone's life. Perhaps this was the answer.

By the time she arrived home, she had made up her mind. She would call and find out what the job was all about.

She dialled the number and a man answered.

"I am calling about the ad for a housekeeper," she said. "Is it still available?"

"Yes it is. Have you ever taken care of someone with a disability?"

"Yes, my father, after he had a stroke. I was his care giver for nine years."

"That sounds good. Let's meet and discuss this further. Why don't you pick a quiet place that's convenient for you and we can meet there on Saturday morning. Is 8:00 a.m. too early for you?"

"No eight o'clock is just fine. The Tulip restaurant at Coxwell and Queen is pretty quiet at that time of the morning. Do you know it?"

"Yes, that'll be fine. What's your name, and how will I recognize you?"

"My name's Natalie Monroe. I have short, dark curly hair and a purple birthmark around my left eye. How will I recognize you?"

"I'll be wearing an orange ski jacket, and a Leaf's cap. See you on Saturday," the man said and hung up.

Paul arrived at the restaurant a few minutes before eight o'clock. He looked around and saw a woman waving to him from a booth in the back.

"You must be Natalie Monroe. I'm Paul Weaver," he said, and sat down opposite her.

He noticed that she already had a coffee so he flagged the waitress and ordered one for himself.

"Yes, I'm Natalie," the woman said. "Your ad didn't give much information about the job. What kind of trauma was it, who did it happen to, and what, exactly are you expecting the housekeeper to do?"

"About four weeks ago, my brother, Charlie, spun out on an icy road," Paul told her. "He wasn't hurt but the shock of the accident has left him unable to see. There was no damage to his eyes so it may possibly be post traumatic stress disorder. Unfortunately, the experience has driven my brother into a deep depression. He doesn't even try to care for himself and so needs someone to make his meals, do his laundry and generally keep the apartment clean. My wife and I have full time jobs, and aren't able to give Charlie the support he needs right now."

"I'm not trained in any way to deal with emotional disorders," Natalie said. "I don't think I would be able to help your brother."

"No. That's not what I expect," Paul said. "I just don't have the time to do the housekeeping chores for him. The reason I told you about his depression is so you'll understand that he's angry, and it may not be easy to be around him."

"Is he violent?"

"No, he isn't. He's just morose. In fact, most of the time he's drunk."

"Wouldn't the easiest thing be to just take the liquor away?" Natalie asked.

Paul sipped his coffee and thought about his response. He decided to be forthright. "I've talked to a psychologist about Charlie. The psychologist believes that he needs time to grieve and come to terms with his situation. He has advised that I let Charlie be for the time being, and give him six months to learn to deal with his blindness. If there's no change after that, then more serious steps will have to be taken. But tell me about yourself and your experience in taking care of people."

"I left school when I was sixteen to take care of my mother who was very ill," Natalie told him. "She taught me how to cook and take care of the house."

"That must've been a very difficult time for you," Paul said. "But on the telephone you told me you had cared for your father."

"Yes, after my mother died I was going to go back to school, but the stress of my mother's illness caused my dad to have a stroke. It totally paralyzed him on the left side and so he needed constant care. I provided that care for nine years. He died last year."

As Natalie was talking, Paul studied her. He noticed that her eyes were hazel, but the birthmark around the left eye made it appear more brown than the right eye. He liked her voice. It was low and very soothing. He also detected her sincerity as she spoke about taking care of her parents. He was quite impressed.

"I'm sorry," he said. "You've certainly had your share of troubles."

"Yes," she said with a smile. "But as they say, what doesn't kill you, makes you stronger."

"Cooking and cleaning are not usually tasks that young women volunteer for. What made you apply?"

Natalie looked down and then back at Paul. "Since my dad died, I've been working at a grocery store. I don't find that very satisfying. I need to feel that what I do makes a difference to someone. Your ad appealed to me because it indicated that this person needs help."

Paul knew then that Natalie was the right woman for the job, though he would have preferred an older person.

"Well, I can guarantee that my brother needs help," he said.

They agreed upon the hours of work and the pay.

"The place is a real mess right now," Paul told her.

"But once you get it under control, I suspect you'll have lots of spare time."

"When do you want me to start?" Natalie asked.

"Are you able to start on Monday?"

"Yes, Monday would be fine. Where does your brother live?"

"He lives not far from here. Why don't I meet you here on Monday. I'll take some time off work and we can go over there together. I'll introduce you to Charlie and you can get the lay of the land."

"That's great. I'll see you here on Monday," Natalie said, getting up.

They parted, and Paul felt more hopeful about the future than he had for many weeks.

He then headed to Charlie's apartment. When he let himself in, he found his brother, as usual, hung over and in a terrible mood.

"Hey bro," Paul called. "I've got breakfast. Come and sit down."

Charlie stumbled into the kitchen and sat down at the table. "Thanks for breakfast," he mumbled. "I guess today is Saturday, if you're here."

Paul unwrapped the sandwich and placed it in front of his brother.

"I've got great news," he informed Charlie. "I've hired a housekeeper, and by the look and smell of this place, it's not above time."

I don't want some old woman hanging around here.

I can take care of myself," Charlie declared belligerently.

"She's not some old woman, and you're obviously
not taking care of yourself," Paul said, trying not to
sound disgusted. "Her name is Natalie, and she's going
to start on Monday. Please be sober at least for her
first day. What do you need me to do for you today?"

"I guess I need some clean clothes, if you have time
to do a load of laundry. My food supplies are also a bit
low and a couple of bottles of whiskey and some beer
would be appreciated," he mumbled. "I know I'm
drinking too much, but right now I need something to
get me through all the endless hours."

On Monday, Paul met Natalie outside the restaurant.

"So, are you ready to meet Charlie?" he asked.

"I must admit I'm a little apprehensive," Natalie told
him.

"I'd be surprised if you weren't, but there's really
nothing to worry about," he assured her as they got
into his car.

"Here's a key for Charlie's apartment," Paul said,
starting the car. "I'm sure you'll need cleaning supplies, so after you assess the situation, we'll go shopping."

They arrived at the apartment and Paul let them in,
praying that Charlie was showered and dressed but

most of all, sober.

"Hey bro, I've brought Natalie," Paul called.

Paul and Natalie advanced into the apartment, and found Charlie, half-asleep, in his favourite chair.

"Charlie, this is Natalie, your new housekeeper," Paul said, pissed off that Charlie didn't bother to get up to meet her.

"Hello Charlie," Natalie said.

"I don't need your services," Charlie growled.

"It sure smells to me like you do," Natalie responded, sounding non-plussed.

Paul was impressed with her handling of Charlie, and thought once again that he'd made the right choice.

Natalie immediately set to work, checking out the cleaning supplies.

"Paul, I have the list of what I need," she told him. "Do you want to go right now?"

"Yes, let's get it done," Paul said. "Charlie, we're going to get some cleaning supplies. We'll be back shortly."

Once in the car, Natalie asked, "Where is the laundry room, and what coins are required for the machines? Also, what are the rules about garbage, and where does it go?"

"The laundry room is in the basement, right beside the elevators," Paul said and told her what she needed to know about the machines. "There's a jar of coins in the kitchen cupboard. As for garbage rules, Charlie would know that better than me."

"What does Charlie like to eat? Does he have any hobbies? What does he usually do for entertainment?" Natalie was full of questions.

"When he came to dinner with Ilene and me, he always gobbled up whatever we served, without comment. On his own, he never cooked much and seemed to exist on fast food most of the time. So again, ask him what he would like. We weren't really that close," Paul confessed, "but I don't think he had any hobbies. For fun, I think he went to the pub, hung out with his friends and watched sports on TV. He dated girls pretty regularly, but I don't know if there's a current someone in his life."

They arrived at the store. Natalie took a shopping cart and set off. "I'll see you back at the check-out in half an hour."

When they met back at the check-out, Paul couldn't believe the number of things Natalie had in the cart.

"I know it seems like a lot of stuff," Natalie admitted. "But quite frankly I don't think your brother was much of a housekeeper. I couldn't find even simple things like tea towels and dish cloths, so I'm getting everything."

Silently Paul agreed with her estimate of Charlie's housekeeping habits.

At the apartment Paul helped Natalie carry in the

supplies. She immediately unpacked everything and put them away.

"Try and be pleasant," he warned his brother. "I don't want Natalie quitting after her first day. I'll drop by and see you in a few days. In the meantime, you know where to reach me."

He went into the kitchen where Natalie was starting to get things organized.

"I'm sorry this is such a mess. Just do the best you can with it. You have my number, so call me anytime you need something, but do call me tonight and let me know how the day goes," he said.

After Paul left, Natalie looked at the mess around her and sighed. She knew Charlie was blind and depressed, but this was really appalling. One had to be careful what one wished for.

She started with the pizza box on the counter and found stale pizza still inside. When she opened the cupboard under the sink, looking for a garbage pail, she couldn't believe her eyes. The garbage pail was full, and there were more pizza boxes and other fast food containers stuffed under the sink. Paul had told her it was a mess, but he didn't know the half of it.

As she worked, she could feel Charlie's brooding presence in the living room. It was so palpable she needed something to combat the nervous tension building up inside her.

She went into the living room and asked, "Do you

mind if I put on some music?"

"I like the quiet," he growled.

Natalie started humming to herself as an antidote to the oppressive quiet. She heard Charlie mumble under his breath, "Fucking cow."

Natalie ignored this and continued to hum.

By the time five o'clock arrived, she had made a good start on the kitchen. She would finish it the next day.

As she was leaving, she said, "There's a bowl of beef barley soup, and a ham sandwich on the table. I'll see you tomorrow."

Charlie gave no sign that he had heard her.

That night Natalie called Paul.

"How did it go?" he asked.

"Okay, but I think things are possibly worse than you thought." She described the mess under the kitchen sink. "It's going to take longer than I thought to get things under control," she concluded.

"How was Charlie during all this?"

"He was downright miserable," she said.

"I sure hope you're not going to give up," Paul pleaded.

"No, I took this job to help someone, and it's clear Charlie needs help. So I'll give it three weeks before I make up my mind."

After agreeing to talk the following day, Natalie hung

up.

Tuesday was a beautiful, sunny day. Such a warm day for March, Natalie marvelled. She let herself into Charlie's apartment, and found him still in bed, sound asleep. Good, now she could get on with cleaning this place up, without hearing him constantly muttering to himself.

She immediately went to the living room and opened the window right up. Next she went into the kitchen and was annoyed to see that Charlie hadn't eaten his soup. Well, she would just keep it, and give it to him again. No point wasting food. She tidied up the remains of the dinner and then continued cleaning where she had left off the previous day.

Having cleaned everything in the kitchen, she proceeded to the bathroom. She had noticed how disgusting it was, and had only used it herself once. She got the strongest cleaners she had and set to work.

She was just wiping down the sink when Charlie stumbled into the bathroom, totally nude.

Natalie looked at him for the first time. She saw a young man with a lean muscular body, sandy coloured hair pulled back into a ponytail, and bloodshot, blue eyes. He was a good five or six inches taller than she. It was impossible to tell if he was good looking or not, because his beard was hiding his face.

"Oh, good afternoon," Natalie said and squeezed by

him, backing out of the bathroom.

Charlie stopped short. "Who the hell are you, and how did you get in here?"

"I'm Natalie, your housekeeper," she said nonchalantly. "Don't you remember?"

"Of course, I remember, but I told you I don't need your services, so you can just leave," he snarled.

"May I remind you that you didn't hire me," she riposted. "So, if you have a problem, call your brother. And another thing, I would appreciate it if you would wear a robe when I'm here."

"What's the matter, you never saw a naked man before?" he sneered. "Besides, as I can't tell night from day, how do I know you're here?"

"Just wear a robe all the time," she snapped. "That way you won't have to worry about it. Also, be careful in the shower, I've cleaned the bathtub and it may be slippery."

"Bitch!" Charlie muttered, and closed the door in her face.

By now it was getting cool, so she closed the window and began her campaign on the living room. She found empty bottles, beer cans and snack food bags on the floor and tucked between the sofa cushions. Two more bags of garbage. She shook her head. Just what kind of slob was this Charlie?

An hour later, Charlie emerged from the bedroom, dressed in jeans and a heavy sweater.

"As long as you're here, you can make me some breakfast," he said in a churlish tone.

Natalie ignored his rudeness and went into the kitchen to see what she could make. There weren't a lot of options.

"How about some scrambled eggs, brown beans, toast and coffee?" she offered.

"Sure, if that's all you know how to make."

Natalie stifled her angry rejoinder, and set to work making his breakfast. When it was ready she called him to the table. Charlie ate with gusto, obviously very hungry.

She grinned, realizing that Charlie was much happier about his breakfast than he was letting on.

"Would you like anything else?" she enquired sweetly.

"No, I'm fine," he mumbled.

Natalie noticed that he didn't thank her. Were his manners so poor, or was he just being churlish?

She continued her cleaning until she realized it was time to go home. She set out the bowl of soup and sandwich from yesterday on the table.

"Goodbye Charlie, I'll see you tomorrow," she called at the door. "The bowl of soup and sandwich from yesterday are on the table for your dinner."

When she arrived home she went straight to the telephone to call Paul.

"How did it go today?" he asked.

"Charlie didn't get up till three, so I was able to get a lot of cleaning done," she reported. "However, he was pretty nasty when he did get up."

"I'll talk to him," Paul promised.

"Don't worry about it. I'm sure he'll come round when he realizes that it's not scaring me off."

"Still, there's no call for rudeness."

"I guess I agree with you, but then we aren't in Charlie's shoes, are we?" she said in a sympathetic tone.

"Yes, you're right," Paul agreed. "But I'm going there tomorrow before work, and will talk to him anyway. Call me again tomorrow."

Chapter Three

Wednesday morning Paul let himself into the apartment. He was immediately struck by the fresh smell of the place. He went to wake Charlie up.

"Hey, bro, I brought you a cappuccino. Get up and come to the kitchen."

Paul entered the kitchen and could not believe the improvement Natalie had made. The whole place sparkled. In all the years Charlie had lived there, Paul had never seen the kitchen so clean.

"Good morning, Paul, thanks for bringing the coffee," Charlie said.

"How are things going with Natalie?" Paul asked, sitting down at the table across from his brother.

"Okay," admitted Charlie, "She's a pain in the butt, but the place does smell a bit better don't you think?"

"A bit? Charlie, you've no idea the miracle she has performed on your kitchen. It's never been this clean in all the years you've lived here," Paul exclaimed. "But why do you say she's a pain in the butt?"

"I guess I resent her giving me orders," Charlie grumbled. "Like wear a robe when she's here. And she always seems to be where I want to be."

"Asking you to wear a robe isn't unreasonable, and once she gets the place in order I'm sure things will settle down. Why don't you cut her some slack?"

"Has she been complaining about me?" Charlie asked suspiciously.

"As a matter of fact, she was making excuses for you."

"Tell her I don't need anyone pitying me," Charlie snarled.

"Oh, for goodness sake, stop being so damned prickly!" Paul snapped. "Natalie is very empathetic. She nursed both her parents through debilitating illnesses, so she's no stranger to depression and anger. All she's trying to do, is help you. But, how are you doing, otherwise?"

"Surviving, as you can see."

"Do you need anything? I have to go to work now, but if you need anything I can pick it up and bring it over tonight," Paul offered.

"No, I don't think so. If I think of anything I'll give you a call

Paul left, hoping that Charlie would soon begin to appreciate the jewel that Natalie was.

Natalie arrived shortly after Paul had left and found

Charlie at the kitchen table.

"'Good morning, Charlie, how are you doing today? Have you had breakfast?" Natalie asked.

"No, I haven't," Charlie replied shortly.

"How about peanut butter on toast? Until I shop there isn't much else," she told him.

"Well, it's better than nothing," he said curtly.

While Natalie prepared the food, she chatted about this and that.

"It's a really great day out there—sunny and warm, and there's no wind. The Leafs lost last night to the Penguins, two to one. It looks like they won't make it into the playoffs again this year. I don't understand why anyone would be a fan of that team."

"The Leafs are just down on their luck," Charlie cut in. "You watch, they'll come back and show everybody."

"I wish I could believe you. It would be good for Toronto fans to have something to cheer about. Anyway, I'm glad you're up. I want to clean the bedroom today."

She gave Charlie his toast and coffee and headed for the bedroom. It smelled of unwashed clothes, so she opened the window.

Seeing clothes all over the floor, she called out, "Where do you keep your laundry hamper?"

"I don't have one," he called back.

"Do you have another set of sheets?"

"In the linen cupboard in the hall."

She found the laundry basket and a balled up mass which she took to be the clean sheets. She took the basket into the bedroom.

As she worked, she heard Charlie pop the tab of a drink can. She looked back to the kitchen and saw he was drinking a beer. Dear lord, and it wasn't even noon yet.

After changing the bed, picking up all the clothes, and dusting the dresser she started vacuuming the floor.

Charlie came to the door and shouted, "Miss, do you have to make that noise? It hurts my head."

"My name is Natalie, and it wouldn't hurt your head if you weren't hung-over. However, I'll close the door to protect your precious head!"

She banged the door shut and carried on with her work. Using the vacuum wand she hoovered under the bed. What a haul! She found four odd socks, a pair of Charlie's summer shorts, a grotty old T-shirt, and— my, oh, my!— a pair of ladies black bikini panties.

She was starting to feel hungry and was surprised to find it was already three-thirty. She found Charlie, comatose on the sofa. No point making him any food. He would just have to fend for himself. She used her remaining time to sort out the linen cupboard, which didn't take long because Charlie didn't have much in the way of linens.

She left, and went home to report to Paul.

"Natalie, what a great job you did on the kitchen!" Paul exclaimed. "I've never seen it looking so good. How did things go today?"

"A little better," she told him. "He wasn't as caustic as he has been. Did you speak to him about his attitude?"

"Yes, I did. He seems to think any show of kindness is just someone feeling sorry for him. I guess he's feeling sorry enough for himself right now. I hope he gets over that soon."

"Yes, that would be good," she agreed.

"Do you have everything you need?" Paul asked.

"Actually, there are a few things that Charlie needs. He needs a clothes hamper for his laundry, and food supplies that aren't just sandwich makings."

"I'll bring a hamper over on Saturday," Paul promised. "About the food—how do you feel about shopping for Charlie?"

"There's a grocery store close to the bus stop, so shopping would be simple enough," Natalie said.

"I'll get a prepaid charge card for you and leave it on top of the fridge on Saturday."

"Don't worry about charge cards. Just leave me cash. I'll keep the receipts and put them on the fridge for you."

"That sounds good to me. Your first week is half over, so how are you feeling about everything?"

"Well, I'm getting the place in shape. It isn't a very big apartment, so in a couple of weeks it should just be maintenance. Do you still want me to go every day?"

"Yes, I think having someone there for a few hours is good for Charlie," Paul said. "One of his problems is that he's alone too much, and he's refused to make contact with his friends. I don't think he's been outside since he left the hospital. He used to be out all the time. It's bound to be depressing for him."

"Yes, perhaps you're right. Soon the weather will be warmer and maybe he can be coaxed into venturing outside. Anyway, I'll continue what I'm doing and see if that makes any difference."

"Okay, give me a call tomorrow."

The next day Natalie got off the bus and stopped at the grocery store before going to Charlie's place. She let herself into the apartment and found Charlie still in bed. Good, she could clean up the living room before he got up. She found some empty bottles and beer cans along with the TV remote and Charlie's cell phone.

It didn't take long to clean, dust and tidy everything up because there wasn't much furniture and no bric-a-brac. There was a well-worn black leather sofa and a couple of arm chairs. One was a brownish fabric chair, and the other was a battered black leather one, which seemed to be Charlie's favourite. He also had a small table at each end of the sofa, a matching coffee table and an entertainment unit. The floor was parquet tiles with a faded blue patterned rug.

She got the vacuum out and began cleaning the floor. The noise woke Charlie and he groped his way out of the bedroom.

He stumbled into the living room. "Is that noise really necessary this early?" he growled.

"Yes, and it's already mid-afternoon," Natalie snapped, and then smiled, because Charlie was wearing his robe. Perhaps her presence was having some effect.

Relenting a little, she continued, "I shopped before coming here and picked up bacon, sausages, pancake mix and syrup. Would you like some breakfast?"

"Well, that would certainly make up for being jarred out of my sleep," he said, his tone softening a little, probably at the offer of a decent meal.

"What would you like?" Natalie asked.

"Pancakes and sausages would be perfect."

While Charlie showered, Natalie finished cleaning up in the living room. Then she went into the kitchen and started preparing breakfast. She looked up to see him coming into the kitchen. He was wearing jeans and a green and black striped sweater which showed his attractive physique to advantage.

Charlie sat at the table but didn't speak. It was obvious to Natalie he was hung over and not happy.

Hopefully breakfast would help his foul mood. She had noticed before that he tended to be more pleasant when food was offered.

"I'm making you a big breakfast with sausages, bacon and pancakes. The pancakes are the silver dollar size so I made a bunch. I hope you're hungry."

"I'm sure I won't have any trouble eating whatever you make," he blurted out, not too curtly.

Natalie smiled. Wow! He sounded almost sociable.

She set the table and asked, "Do you like salt and pepper on your pancakes?"

Charlie laughed. "That is really weird. I don't know anybody who puts salt and pepper on their pancakes."

Natalie liked the sound of Charlie's laughter. If she could only make him laugh more and brood less, she'd be happy.

"My dad used to. He said it made pancakes more of a meal to him that way." She served Charlie and was gratified to see him dig in heartily. "So tell me, what food do you like to eat?"

"Most of the time I eat at the pub—hamburgers, chicken wings, steak—that kind of thing, with French fries."

"What kind of vegetables do you like?"

"Vegetables? Yikes!" Charlie yelped with a wide grin.

"Yes, vegetables. Meat and potatoes are fine, but for vitamins, minerals and fibre you need vegetables," Natalie said.

"I like a salad sometimes, but as for other vegetables, I guess I'm out of practice."

"Well, if I'm going to be the one shopping and cooking, you'll have to reacquaint yourself with food, other than pub style."

When Charlie finished eating, he went into the living room and sat in his favourite chair. Natalie watched him and saw how tentatively he walked when he wasn't touching a wall or furniture. She turned on the TV where one of the afternoon game shows was on.

"Turn that thing off," Charlie snarled. "I can't stand daytime TV. It's for housewives and kids."

"Would you like me to read to you?" she asked. "I used to read to my parents when they were ill. It helped them to think of other things. Do you have any books I could read to you?"

"Books?" he scoffed. "I haven't read a book since college."

"Well, I have the newspaper I was reading on the bus. Would you like me to read that to you?"

"Well, since there's nothing else, might as well," he said.

"For the future I could get something from the library if you tell me what kind of stories you like."

"War or murder might be okay," he said. "But none of that 'feel good' crap."

Natalie got the newspaper and read from the sports page. It was all about the Blue Jays. Opening day was a few weeks away. The hockey scores were published, but as the Leafs were not in the playoffs, Charlie wasn't interested.

The afternoon passed quickly.

"I have to clean up the kitchen before I go home. What kind of sandwich would you like for your dinner? I'll shop on Monday so you can have a proper meal, but for now it's just sandwiches."

"Do you have to leave now?" Charlie asked.

Natalie was surprised to hear a wistful note in his voice. "Yes, it's already five-thirty."

As she walked to the door she felt the floor runner under her feet in the hall. That would provide a surface that Charlie could use to help him negotiate the space in his apartment. She dragged the runner over and laid it between the kitchen table and his favorite chair.

"What are you doing?" Charlie asked.

She explained her strategy and asked him to try it.

Grumbling, he got up and felt the rug under his feet. Following it, he reached the kitchen. Turning around he walked back to the chair.

"This works well," he marvelled. "I like it."

"I'm glad it is helpful. I've left a sandwich in the fridge for you," Natalie told him. Before she closed the door she saw Charlie pick up the whiskey bottle.

She sighed shaking her head.

At home Natalie dialled Paul's number.

"Just reporting in," she said.

"So, how did it go today?"

"It was a good day, I think. I bought a few groceries and left the receipt on top of the fridge. Charlie and I talked about what kind of food he likes. I'll shop on Monday. Tomorrow, I'll do the laundry. I've pretty much tidied and cleaned the apartment so there won't be much for me to do, so I'm going to get some books from the library and read to him."

"That sounds wonderful. Maybe it'll help Charlie forget alcohol for a while," Paul said approvingly. "I'll leave some cash for you on Saturday."

Friday morning Natalie arrived to find Charlie asleep on the sofa. He was still fully dressed so she guessed he hadn't gone to bed. Leaving him there she went into the bedroom and picked the clothes off the floor. She put them in the laundry basket and went down to the basement to start the wash.

When she returned, Charlie was awake and very grouchy.

"Good morning," she greeted him cheerfully.

"What's good about it?" Charlie snapped.

"Well, for starters, the sun is shining, the snow has melted, and spring is in the air. It's a perfect day to be alive!"

"For you to be alive," he snarled. "Not me."

She ignored his surly mood. "Would you like some breakfast?"

"No, I'm going to bed. My head hurts and my stomach is churning."

She watched him go and noticed that he was navigating his way around with a bit more confidence. In the living room she picked up the empty whiskey bottle and the remains of his sandwich and then went down to wait for the laundry.

After fluffing and folding everything she returned and found him still sleeping.

A couple of hours later he emerged. "Can I get that breakfast now, miss?"

She cringed at the word miss. "My name is Natalie. Please use it. What would you like me to make for you?"

"How about a bacon and egg sandwich with mayo, miss?" he replied, obviously ignoring her comment about her name.

Charlie went to shower and dress while Natalie prepared the food.

When he sat down to eat, she asked, "Do you mind if I organize your bedroom? You seem to have things all over the place."

"Yeah, sure. Whatever you want."

Natalie sensed by his dismissive tone that he just wanted her to be busy and not bother him. That was okay with her.

Sometime later she found Charlie in his chair in the living room and explained to him what she had done.

"Oh, and just so you know, I put your nighties in the bottom right hand drawer."

Charlie had the courtesy to blush, but offered no comment.

"I still have some time, so would you like me to continue reading the newspaper?" she offered.

"Sure. I'm out of touch these days so it would be good to catch up a bit."

Natalie found the newspaper from the previous day and continued reading where she had left off. There were two stories about shootings in the city. Natalie tried to engage Charlie by saying, "Don't you think that gun violence has escalated a lot over the past decade?"

"Sure, but it's just gangs that are doing it," he said.

"Perhaps, but innocent by-standers are also getting shot," Natalie pointed out. "The city doesn't seem so safe anymore."

"It happens mostly in the clubs. If people didn't go to those places, they wouldn't be in danger," Charlie insisted.

"What about the shooting at the food court in the Eaton Centre? Anybody could have been shot."

"Yeah, maybe you're right, but I don't want to talk about it."

"Well, let me try to find a happier story."

"If you're reading from the newspaper, don't be surprised if you can't find any."

"You're right, there is no good news. It's getting late,

so I better clean up the kitchen and get going. Would you like me to heat a TV dinner for you?"

"Do you have to go?" his voice almost sounded pleading. "The hours go so slowly when I'm by myself."

Natalie was touched by his words. It showed her presence was beginning to make a difference. "I'm sorry, but I really do have to go."

She finished her chores and said good night.

At home, she called Paul.

"How was Charlie today?" he asked.

"Better. I read to him and he seemed to be engaged. He's still drinking and depressed, but seems to be trying to be less surly, at least while I'm there. I think he needs more company to keep him occupied and not thinking about his situation."

"You're probably right. I'm going there tomorrow and I'll encourage him to reach out to his friends. I'll leave money for groceries and your wages while I'm there. Is there anything else you or Charlie need?"

"Don't forget the laundry hamper. Also, Charlie needs some way of telling time. He often sleeps half the day away and then has too many hours by himself. If he knew what time it was he might get his days and nights back on track."

"That's a very good point. I'll call the Canadian National Institute for the Blind and find out if they have anything that'll help."

"That would be good, and while you are doing that,

you could ask about a white cane and see if you could get one for Charlie. The weather is getting better and I might be able to coax him to go outside. And ask about any other tools they have. Anything that could help him cope."

"Sure. I'll look into it," said Paul.

After Paul hung up, Natalie thought about Charlie asking her to stay. Perhaps she was beginning to make a difference.

Saturday, Paul arrived with breakfast and the laundry hamper. "Hey Bro, come and sit down."

He noticed that Charlie was looking a little better. Healthier. "How is it going with Natalie?" he asked.

"Okay. It's nice to have someone to cook breakfast for me," Charlie admitted. "She's also been reading to me. I like listening to her voice. It has a pleasant, reassuring quality about it. It lets me know I'm not alone and that helps a lot."

"Why don't you call Tom?" Paul urged. "He calls me a couple of times a week to ask how you're doing."

"I can't call him. The last time I saw him, I called him an asshole."

"Yes, I know. But he understands that you were very angry and had to blame someone," Paul said. "You guys have been friends for nearly twenty years. One fight shouldn't destroy that."

"I'll think about it," Charlie said.

"I brought you another whiskey and some beer," Paul said. "And Natalie asked me to bring a laundry hamper. I'll put it in your bedroom. She said she would shop for groceries on Monday, so I'll leave some money for her."

"Thanks Paul," Charlie said. "How is Ilene doing?"

Wow! Charlie had to be feeling less depressed if he was thinking about Ilene. "She is doing very well. She seems to be over that morning sickness business and is now shopping for maternity outfits. We're both really excited about this baby. Why don't you come for dinner with us tomorrow, and see for yourself."

"Thanks Bro, but I don't think I'm up to that yet."

Paul put the hamper into the bedroom, and had a good look around the apartment. He was amazed at the improvement Natalie had made in just one week. He congratulated himself again on choosing her.

On Monday, Natalie arrived with groceries and found Charlie in the living room, half asleep. He looked like he was just getting over a hangover. He must have had a pretty rough weekend.

"Good morning, Charlie. Would you like some breakfast?" she asked.

Charlie looked pretty rough but answered politely enough, "Yes, but not a big one. How about just some toast and coffee."

As Natalie prepared the food, she chatted to Charlie.

"It looks like it's going to rain today. That'll be good. The ground is very dry because we didn't get much snow in March. I'm really looking forward to seeing some crocuses and tulips. Do you like flowers?"

"I never gave flowers much thought," he admitted. "I guess they're all right."

"I brought a couple of books from the library to read to you. One is a Tom Clancy spy novel, and the other one is a Steven Martini mystery. Which one would you like me to start?" she asked.

"Which one has the most blood and gore?"

"I really don't know. They're not authors I'm familiar with," she told him. "These were recommended by the librarian as popular with her male clients."

"I've heard of Tom Clancy, so why don't we start with him," Charlie suggested.

"Okay. I'll just clean up here and put the groceries away."

She joined him in the living room and began to read. Within half an hour, Charlie was sound asleep, sprawled in his favourite chair. Natalie busied herself around the apartment. She found the laundry hamper and picked up the dirty clothes, making a mental note to speak to Charlie about cleaning up after himself.

Charlie woke up late in the afternoon. Following the runner he lurched to the kitchen and grabbed himself a beer from the fridge. He gulped it down in three swallows, and then called out. "Miss, are you still here?"

"Yes, I'm still here," Natalie snapped. "And I want you to remember my name. It isn't miss, it isn't cow, and it isn't bitch. My name is Natalie. Please use it."

Charlie was taken aback by her sharp tone of voice, and was about to tell her where she could go, but decided against it. He realized that he liked his surroundings so much better since she had taken over. Hell, he even liked having her there. The endless hours went by so much more quickly and, while not exactly enjoyable, they at least were less dismal.

"A little touchy are we?" he growled.

"When you can't be bothered to remember my name, it shows that you don't respect me," she threw at him. "I won't be treated like some barmaid."

"Geez, I didn't think I was being offensive," he said, almost apologetically.

"That's your problem, you don't think. Anyway, now that you're awake I will make you dinner. Would you like pork chops or steak?"

"Is it that late already?" How the hell had he lost the entire afternoon?

"Yes, it is four-thirty. I've asked Paul to check with CNIB about what's available to assist you with telling time. Hopefully they have something, so you can get your days and nights re-oriented. In the meantime, pork chops or steak?"

He found her tone adversarial. "Steak, medium-rare, would be great," he replied, feeling chastened by her outburst.

While Charlie nursed his hurt feelings, he could hear Natalie in the kitchen preparing dinner. As the smell of the steak grilling assailed his nostrils, he began to lose his anger and realized how wonderful it was to have someone prepare a hot meal for him.

He heard Natalie setting the cutlery and a plate on the table.

"Would you like me to cut your steak for you?" she asked.

The thought appalled him. "God, no!" he yelped. That would be unbearable. His dependence was already too demeaning.

"Oops! Did I say something wrong?" Natalie asked.

"I'm not helpless," he replied tersely. "I can do some things for myself, so don't treat me like a baby."

"Sorry," she apologized. "I didn't mean to insult you."

"Just forget it." He cut into his steak and began to eat. "This is very good. I haven't had a proper meal for quite a while. Hell, I'm even liking the green beans." He laughed.

"I'm glad you're enjoying your dinner," she said. "As soon as you're finished, I'll clean up and be on my way."

All too soon he heard her cheery goodnight.

Shit! Now he had the whole evening ahead of him—

alone. Why had he slept the afternoon away? What was he going to do now?

Chapter Four

One morning, a few weeks later, Natalie arrived and found that the dinner she had prepared the night before was sitting, untouched, exactly where she had left it.

Her anger mounting, she waited until Charlie got up and came into the kitchen. "What was wrong with the dinner?" she hurled at him.

"I wasn't very hungry when you left, and then it got cold and totally unappetizing," he replied, his tone as angry as hers.

"Why didn't you put it in the oven to warm up?"

"Because I can't see the fucking dials, in case you hadn't noticed," he replied sarcastically. "Besides, I'm fed up with eating by myself all the time."

"Why don't you call some of your friends to come over sometime?"

"Because I don't want their pity."

"Is that why you don't answer the phone or take

your messages?" Natalie asked, continuing her tirade. "You think everybody pities you? You think your friends have nothing better to amuse themselves with than sitting around thinking about you? How arrogant you are! You think you're the only person who ever lost his sight? Why don't you stop living out of a bottle and take some responsibility for yourself?"

"You have no idea what it's like! How limiting it is! How depressing it is!" Charlie shouted.

"You're absolutely right. I don't know what it's like. But I do know that sitting around day after day, doing nothing but brooding isn't going to make things any better." Natalie took a deep breath and went on. "There are services out there that you can go to for help in coping with your blindness. And you haven't even tried to talk to a psychologist to see if they can help you."

"I don't want pity and I don't want charity," Charlie spat out.

"Then put up with it," Natalie said and stomped out of the room.

That night when she got home, she headed straight for the telephone.

"It's good to hear your voice, Natalie " Paul said. "Is everything all right with Charlie?"

"Everything with Charlie is the same. I wish I could say that it wasn't. Have you checked with the CNIB yet?"

"No, I'm sorry," he said. "I know I said I would, but things have been a little hectic so I keep putting it off."

She knew Paul worked and had his own life, but damn it all, Charlie was his brother and needed him, too. "I don't think he'll get much better, unless we do something. Could you go there on Saturday?"

"You're right. I've just been thinking of my own issues, and ignoring Charlie's problems. I'll definitely find time on Saturday morning to go," Paul promised.

"Could I come with you?"

"Yes, of course. I'll pick you up at the Tulip at eight-thirty."

"Great! I'll see you then." She hung up.

Together, Paul and Natalie went to the CNIB store to see what was available.

"Paul, here are some talking watches," Natalie said pointing to a display. "Which one do think Charlie would like?"

Paul chose a watch and took it to the desk to have it activated and the time set. While he was waiting, Natalie continued to browse for other aids. She noticed that a lot of the products were simple magnification tools and would not help Charlie at all. Then she found some clear plastic dots which could be used to provide a tactile surface.

"Look at this, Paul!" she said excitedly. "I can use these to help Charlie operate the stove and other appliances. That may help him become more independent, and start feeling better."

Natalie asked the clerk why so many of the tools were designed for people who could see.

"Only about ten percent of CNIB clients are totally without sight," the clerk told them. "Good magnification tools are all many people really need."

"Could you show us the white canes?" Paul asked.

"Yes, right over there," the clerk said and walked them over to the display.

"How do I know what size to get?" Paul asked.

"It's somewhat of a personal preference, but the cane should come to about the middle of the chest," the clerk told him. "How tall is the person you want it for?"

"He's about five ten or eleven," Natalie said.

"Then I recommend a cane about sixty inches long," the clerk said.

They chose a cane, and the clerk showed them how to fold it up for travelling. Paul paid for the purchases and they left.

"I'm going over to Charlie's now. Should I take this stuff to him?" Paul asked.

"Yes, take the watch and show him how to use it," Natalie suggested. "The sooner he can tell time, the sooner he'll get himself reoriented. I hope. Let me take the cane and the dots home with me. I'll practice with the cane, so I can help him use it."

Paul dropped Natalie off at the Tulip restaurant, picked up a couple of sandwiches, and headed to Charlie's.

"Hey, Bro," he called as he let himself in. "I've got us some lunch. Come and sit down."

Charlie was just emerging from the bedroom. "I'm glad you came. I was beginning to think you'd forgotten me. It is Saturday, isn't it?"

"Yes, it is. The reason I'm late is because I went to the CNIB store with Natalie. We got you a talking watch so you'll know what time it is. Eat your sandwich before the bacon gets totally cold, and then I'll show you how to use the watch."

"That's super! I didn't know such things existed," Charlie enthused. "You have no idea how long a day is until you can't even guess how much time has passed. Thanks, Bro."

"Don't thank me, thank Natalie. I'm sorry I've been so caught up in my own shit, I wasn't thinking about your issues," Paul apologized. "Natalie called and guilted me into doing what I said I would do three weeks ago."

Paul retrieved the watch from his jacket pocket and handed it to Charlie. "Feel the side of the watch. Do you feel the buttons sticking out?"

"Yes."

"Push the top one," Paul instructed.

Charlie did so. The watch chimed and a male voice

said, "The time is two-o-nine p.m."

Charlie was delighted, and continued to push the button several more times, laughing each time the watch spoke. He was happy as a kid with a new toy, and Paul felt an overwhelming sense of guilt for having waited so long to get him the watch.

"How is it going with Natalie?" Paul asked when Charlie finally stopped playing.

"Okay, I guess. Though she's very prickly," Charlie complained. "She took my head off the other day because I called her miss, instead of Natalie. I didn't think that was disrespectful, but she sure did."

"I can see her point. She's been coming every day for eight weeks. Why wouldn't you use her name?"

"Has it really been eight weeks?" Charlie asked, surprised. "What's the date today?"

"May fifteenth," Paul told him.

"May fifteenth?" Charlie gasped. "I thought it was March something. Oh, my God, that means that I've been wasted for four months. Why didn't you tell me what a jerk I was being?"

"Because you weren't interested. You needed time to come to terms with your situation. Have you finally decided to get back into life?" Paul asked hopefully.

"I don't know. I don't even know where to start. It's all so scary," Charlie murmured.

"You could start by going to a psychologist. If you talk it over with someone, it may not be so scary. Also, the CNIB provides services. You could find out how to use some of them. Would you like me to check on any of these things for you?"

"Not yet, I need to get my head around those ideas. I've always been able to take care of myself, so relying on other people is something I'm not used to," Charlie said.

"Don't wait too long. You've already lost four months," Paul warned him.

After Paul left, Charlie sat in the living room thinking about what Natalie had said. Nothing was ever going to get better if he didn't stop brooding and feeling sorry for himself. He was shocked to realize it was already May. That meant he had spent almost four months in a drunken stupor. How sick he was of hangovers and feeling cruddy and wasted all the time.

But he was scared. How could he face life when he couldn't see? He thought about the challenges he had faced in the past, like college, and dealing with the shock of his parents' death in that fatal head-on collision five years ago. But nothing came close to how he was feeling now. Never in his life had he been so afraid. He wished he could just die. He knew he should try to contact a therapist, but what if they couldn't help him? Then he wouldn't even have that slim hope to cling to that his condition was temporary. Oh God, what was he to do?

Monday morning Natalie came at ten as usual. To her surprise Charlie was up, showered and dressed.

"Hello Natalie." Charlie's greeting was very low key, almost beseeching. "I wonder if we could talk for a few minutes?"

Natalie, totally taken off guard, looked at him more closely and realized that he wasn't drunk, nor did he appear to have a hangover. What was on his mind? She had never heard him speak so tentatively before. Was this Charlie inside-out? She sure hoped so!

"Yeah sure, Charlie, let's sit down here in the kitchen. I'll make us some coffee and then you can tell me what's on your mind."

Natalie brought the coffee to the table and sat across from him. "Okay, I'm here now."

"First I want to apologize for being such a jerk these past months. Then, I want to start learning how to cope. Will you help me?" he asked.

"Oh Charlie, I'm so happy. Of course I'll help you." She reached over and gave Charlie's hand a squeeze. "Where do you want to start?"

"Well, I'd sure like to be able to use the microwave and the stove again," he suggested. "That would be a good beginning,"

"That's a perfect place to start," she agreed. "And then we could go for a walk. The day is glorious and too nice to be missed."

"Whoa! Hang on, I'm not ready to test my wings outside yet."

But Natalie couldn't curb her enthusiasm. She had watched this young man almost destroy himself, and now that he was showing clear signs of coming back to life, she didn't want to lose the momentum. This was the first day she had seen him sober and without a hangover, but she wasn't yet convinced that it would last.

She got out the purchases from the CNIB store. "Look, Charlie, Paul also got you a white cane, and these clear plastic dots. Feel them."

He ran his fingers over the package. "I give up. What are they for?"

"They're for attaching to flat surfaces to give them a tactile feel. For instance, your microwave oven panel is totally flat, but if I put one of these dots on the start button you'd be able to find it."

She took his hand and pulled him over to the stove. He had such nice hands with long slender fingers. She wanted to hold on longer but realized she really didn't know him all that well and she sure didn't want to stir up any feelings in him.

"Just run your hand over the rear panel of the stove. Feel the knobs for the burners on each side, and the indented square for the oven controls in the middle. Touching the knob, do you feel the notch on the dial?"

"Yes, but I get mixed up with which knob is for the

front and back burners."

"No problem. I'll place a dot on the knob for each of the front burners. Touch the knobs again."

"That's great! Now I'll always know which is which."

"Just make sure that the pot is securely set on the burner before you turn the stove on," Natalie warned. "Also, be sure you know what side of the stove it's on. It is very easy to put the pot on one side and turn on the burner on the other side."

"Really? Have you ever done that? I can't believe for a minute that anyone would actually do that."

"Yes, I have and I can see, so be careful," she warned and continued her instruction. "You know that the best cooking temperature is around the six or seven o'clock position of the knob."

"Yes, I think I can handle stove top cooking okay. It's the oven that I can't manage. There are no knobs that I can use for guidance."

"I'll fix that for you." After placing a plastic dot on each of the necessary functions, she took Charlie's hand and ran it over the control panel. "Do you feel the dots?"

"I feel four dots. And I like the feel of your hand on mine. It's somehow comforting," he said, surprising her.

Natalie blushed at the compliment, thinking of her own thoughts a moment before, but didn't respond. "Okay, extend your index finger and feel the outline of the control panel," she went on. "From the top right-hand corner, draw your finger down on a diagonal line, about half an inch. That dot is the start button. Now, draw your finger to the left about an inch, and down half an inch. That dot is the up-arrow button, and it starts the oven heating up."

As Natalie spoke, Charlie moved his finger and found the dot she was describing.

"The starting temperature is always 350 degrees. If you want a higher temperature you would push that button, once to start the heating process, and again for every five degrees you want to go up. The down arrow is the dot directly below the up arrow. And lastly, you have to turn the stove off when you are finished. The off button is directly below the on button, about two inches lower. Is any of this familiar?"

"Sort of, I was never much of a cook, and relied on the microwave a lot, but some things are better in the oven, so it's good to be able to use it."

"Okay, try turning the oven on and adjusting the temperature."

Charlie then went through the sequence and successfully turned on the oven and reduced the temperature to 300 degrees. He then turned the oven off.

"That's great, no more cold dinners," he said. "Could you do the same thing for the microwave?"

"What do you generally use the microwave for?" Natalie asked.

"Mostly for warming up food, or making popcorn."

She placed some dots on the keypad and explained what she had done.

"Okay, Charlie, feel the panel. The start button is the lower left, and the cancel button is the lower right."

Charlie touched the control panel and then showed Natalie he wouldn't have any trouble using the microwave.

"How about the telephone, or your cell phone," Natalie asked. "Or the TV remote? Do you want some dots on them?"

"It would be helpful if you could do something with the TV remote," Charlie suggested. "I need to be able to change the channel, and the volume on the TV."

Natalie went to get the remote. "This could be tricky, the buttons are very small. Which functions do you use?"

"Just put a dot on the channel and volume up arrows for now. If that doesn't work, I'll get you to put some on the numbers."

"What about the mute button?" she asked.

"I used to love that button when commercials came on, but now that I can't see when they end, I'll have to listen to them. Just one more inconvenience to get used to," he grumbled.

Natalie attached the dots, and handed the remote to Charlie. "The dots are much smaller, do they help at all?"

Charlie ran his finger over the remote. "Yes, it's better than without. Which is the volume and which is the channel button?"

Natalie explained. By now it was time for lunch and a good time to stop so Charlie could absorb what they had just set up.

"Think about what other things I can help you with," she said.

After lunch Natalie began her regular Monday chores.

"Natalie, what kind of music to you like?" Charlie asked.

Surprised by his interest, she responded, "I guess I like a variety of artists, from crooners and folk bands to country. I grew up listening to my parents' music and so I'm more familiar with older stuff."

"I like some of the older stuff myself," Charlie said. "I never got into the heavy metal and rap music like a lot of my friends. Would you like me to put something on?"

"Sure, put on whatever you like," she told him. "I have to go down to do the laundry now anyway."

When Natalie returned with the clean clothes, she heard music for the first time in Charlie's apartment. She didn't recognize the artist, but it was so good to see Charlie beginning to come to life.

"Who is that?" she called to him.

"Boz Scaggs. Do you like him?"

"I'm not familiar with him, but it sounds fine."

Natalie put the clean clothes away and began making dinner. "Tonight it's tuna casserole."

"Is it that time already?: Charlie marvelled. "This day has just flown by. Could you stay longer? Eating by myself all the time is such a drag."

Natalie heard the plea in his voice and understood. She also thought it would be a good time to get to know him better. "I'm not busy tonight so I'll stay and have dinner with you," she replied.

As they sat at the table, waiting for the dinner to cook, Charlie asked, "What do you usually do in the evening?"

"Mostly I go home and read, or watch TV and do my own chores," she told him. "A couple of times a week I volunteer at a retirement centre."

"Aren't those places depressing?" Charlie asked.

"Yes, the atmosphere can be little depressing," she admitted. "But the people, or at least those who still have their faculties, can be a lot of fun. Most of them are just lonely and want to talk or have some help writing letters. I often get a circle together and read. Before I came here, I occasionally went at dinner time to help the staff feed the residents who weren't able to feed themselves. It made me feel useful."

"What kind of things do you read to them?"

"I used to read books, but as the folks in the circle change all the time, it didn't work well. So I read the newspaper or articles from a romance magazine I like," she explained. "The romance stories are very popular and always have happy endings. I think they remind the old people of when they were young and courting."

Natalie got up and served their dinner, while Charlie continued to probe.

"Romance, eh? So you only read to the ladies?"

"Don't assume what you don't know," she said. "The men enjoy the romance stories as much as the women and everyone enjoys the personal ads, which I always read. They often stir up controversy among the folks, some believing that the writer was sincere and some, the more cynical ones, arguing that the writer was someone hired by the magazine."

"Probably was," Charlie said.

"Hey, eat up and enjoy your dinner while it's hot," she said. "Personally, I side with those who believe the ads are placed by real people, sincerely looking for love."

Charlie laughed. "You don't really believe that stuff do you?"

"Yes, I do. There are a lot of lost souls out there who are just looking for a little happiness, and so they put ads in magazines."

Charlie shook his head. "Natalie, I fear you're very naive."

"Perhaps," she replied. "But it's better than being cynical."

"By the way, this is very good," Charlie said through a mouthful of casserole. "Do you like cooking?"

"Eating is something you have to do every day, and so if you don't cook your diet is very limited. I don't love cooking, but I don't mind it either."

"But how did you learn to cook?" Charlie asked.

"When my mother was ill and could no longer cook, I took over for her. She taught me a lot, and I also started to read recipes. Between the two, I can now make okay meals." She helped herself to a dinner roll and buttered it. "But enough about me, what did you do before the accident?"

"I was an electrician on a new housing site north of the city. I made decent money and spent most of it enjoying life," he said with a hint of longing in his voice. "My best friend, Tom, and I went to the pub three or four times a week with the other guys. I very seldom cooked a meal for myself. It was the pub, or take out, or taking a girl out for dinner."

"Didn't you ever get tired of eating pub food?" she asked.

"I never gave it much thought. It was just what I did," he said.

They ate in silence for a while and then Charlie asked, "Are you a Blue Jays fan?"

"I'm not what you would call a fan, but I do like baseball. I used to watch it with my dad."

"Do you want to see if there is a game on tonight?"

"If there is a game, I'll stay and watch it with you," she said.

After dinner, Natalie cleaned up while Charlie went into the living room, found the remote and turned on the TV.

"Natalie, do you realize this is the first time in months I've put on the TV myself," he called.

He began flipping through the channels but couldn't find what he wanted.

Natalie came in. "Can I help?" she asked.

Charlie handed her the remote. She checked the TV Guide channel and read the listings. "Boston is playing the Texas Rangers. Do you want to watch that one? I don't see the Blue Jays anywhere."

"Sure, it's baseball so it'll be fun."

Natalie tuned in to the game. "It's the bottom of the third with no score yet. They must be playing in Boston because Boston is at bat. Who do you want to root for? I always find the games more exciting if I'm rooting for a team."

"You're right. It's good to have something to cheer for. I'll take Boston. Can you make us some popcorn?" he then asked. "Popcorn always makes it seem more like you're actually at the game."

"I never bought any. Do you have some?" Natalie asked.

"I keep it stored in the cupboard above the fridge."

"That's why I never saw it because I can't reach that

high."

"I'll go and check," said Charlie.

He went into the kitchen and reached up into the cupboard. "Oh, good, there's one package here." He handed it to Natalie.

She read the instructions and put the bag into the microwave. "Popcorn in two minutes. Would you like a coke to go with it?"

"I would prefer a beer but I'll settle for a coke," he replied.

She found a large bowl and took the popcorn and drinks into the living room. "I'll put the popcorn on the end of the coffee table so you can reach it."

"No, I'll sit on the sofa, and we can put the popcorn between us."

"Good plan," Natalie said.

By now it was the bottom of the fourth, with still no score.

Natalie brought Charlie up-to-date. "Boston has a runner on first with only one out."

The announcer started getting excited. "It's going over the wall!"

Charlie began to cheer. "Home run! Home run! Home run!"

"The Texas fielder's got it right at the stadium wall. Two out!" shouted Natalie.

"Shit," said Charlie. "Oh well, they still have a runner on first, don't they?"

"Yes, but not for long, I hope."

As they were both reaching for popcorn, their hands met in the popcorn bowl. Charlie took her hand up and said, "Caught you! You are now my prisoner."

She withdrew her hand, totally ignoring Charlie's innuendo. "Oh no," she groaned. "The stupid pitcher has walked the batter. You now have a runner in scoring position."

The next batter hit a pop-up fly, and the inning ended scoreless. "Phew," said Natalie. "I thought I was in trouble there."

"This is fun," he said. "I miss seeing the action, but between your commentary and the announcer's play-by-play I'm not missing much."

The evening flew by too quickly.

"I haven't enjoyed myself so much in a long time," Charlie said.

"I had a lot of fun too," Natalie agreed. "Tomorrow when I come, be prepared to go for a walk, if the weather's good."

The next morning Charlie heard the key at the door and Natalie's light footsteps down the hall.

"Good morning, Natalie," he called cheerily. "I've had breakfast, but could I ask a favour from you?"

"Of course."

"I like to wear my hair in a short ponytail but it's gotten too long. Would you be able to cut off a few inches?"

"Not a problem. I used to shave my dad and cut his hair after he had his stroke. Have you always had a beard?"

"No. I don't like beards much because they make my face too itchy. I just stopped caring and shaving at the same time, but now it's time to move on."

"I could shave that off for you, if you like," Natalie offered.

"I'm not sure about the shaving part, but I would be grateful if you cut my hair."

Charlie sat on a kitchen chair. His hair was still damp from the shower. Natalie found some scissors, and got his comb. She put a towel across his shoulders and began to run her fingers and the comb through his hair. Charlie closed his eyes and relaxed. It had been a while since anyone had touched him in an intimate fashion and he just wanted to lose himself in the moment.

All too soon he heard Natalie ask, "Check the length. Is that what you want?"

What he really wanted was for her to continue running her fingers through his hair, but decided she hadn't intended the experience to be sensual.

"Yes, this is good," he said, gathering his hair into a ponytail. "Thank you for doing that. I'll go and shave now."

"If I cut most of the hair off your face, it would be

much easier to shave," Natalie offered.

She proceeded to cut his beard while Charlie drank in the scent of her. She had a wonderful freshness about her. He just wanted to put his arms around her and lay his head on her breast. A strange, overwhelming desire to cry filled him. But he knew she wouldn't welcome any of this, so when she finished he went into the bathroom to shave.

"Are you ready?" Charlie called as he came out of the bathroom.

"Well, don't you clean up nice," Natalie exclaimed. "Without your beard I can see your resemblance to Paul."

"Who's the better looking?" Charlie asked, grinning.

"Why, you of course, my handsome prince," she replied in a teasing tone. "And now that your eyes are no longer bloodshot, I can see they're a beautiful, sparkling blue. They really must attract the ladies."

"Yeah sure, I fight them off with a stick all the time," he joked.

"Seriously, how do you feel without the beard?" she asked.

"Naked," replied Charlie.

"But how do you feel about going for a walk?" Natalie asked. "It's a beautiful sunny day, not really warm yet but still a good day to enjoy. It's time to take that new, white cane on its maiden voyage."

"I don't know. I haven't been out for months. I used

to jog around the park a few times a week before the accident, but there'll be no more jogging now."

"Well, we won't be jogging, but a little exercise won't do you any harm. So, would you like to go to the park?" she asked.

He knew he would have to get used to going out if he ever expected to have any kind of a life, but that didn't stop him from being apprehensive. He was glad Natalie would be with him. He had really begun to appreciate her help, and found himself looking forward to her arrival each day. How strange life was. It was only a few weeks ago he had resented her presence.

"This day is as good as any other to get started, I suppose," he admitted.

Natalie clapped her hands. "If you could see me, I'm doing cartwheels down the hall," she exclaimed.

She got the white cane and after handing it to Charlie, showed him how to take the elastic retainer off to let the cane spring to its full length.

He heard the cane clicking as it opened. "Wow! That's pretty neat the way it does that."

"Yes, I thought so, too. Its purpose is to help you to avoid obstacles on the ground and let people around you know you can't see them," she said in her instructor voice. "But you'll be with me, so you don't have to worry very much about obstacles."

They donned their coats and left the apartment.

"You might as well start here to get used to going

out," Natalie said. "Do you have your keys with you?"

"No, I guess I was relying on you."

"Okay, you can use my key today," she said.

Taking the key he felt around the side of the door for the lock. After locking up he started down the hall, holding the cane out in front of him.

"Stop!" Natalie cried. "You may as well start being aware of your surroundings. The lock and door knob are on the left side of the door. The elevator is on your right, so you have to turn right. Also, so you can find your own door when we come back, count the number of doors we pass on your left until we get to the elevator. You'll know when you are at the elevator area because the floor is tiled. Are you ready?"

"As ready as I'll ever be," Charlie said. "But I'm not bubbling over with confidence."

Chapter Five

Charlie started walking toward the elevators when
Natalie again stopped him. "If you put the tip of the
cane on the floor and sweep it from side to side, you
will detect any obstacles on the ground in front of you."

Charlie did as Natalie suggested. They were soon at
the elevator area. He put his hand out in front of him
and started forward, looking for the elevator buttons.

Once more Natalie stopped him. "Use the cane, not
your body, to find the buttons. Walk forward, with the
cane in front of you, to find the recessed metal door of
the elevator. Then run the cane along the door until
you feel the wall partition."

Charlie did as she instructed.

"Now walk forward and touch the wall until you find
the control panel. Locate the down button and stand
back to wait. You'll hear the elevator door open. Be
sure you have your cane in front of you as you approach. That way, if the door starts to close, it will

close on the cane and not on you."

The elevator arrived and they stepped in. "The control panel is on the left. The lobby button is the second from the bottom," Natalie continued. "You're on the third floor, and so your floor button is the fourth button up from the bottom. That's all you have to remember."

Charlie put his hand out to feel the control panel and was easily able to find the right button. When the elevator arrived at the lobby they came out and Charlie stopped.

"Describe the lobby to me," he said. "I've always driven and only came here occasionally to pick up my mail. I never paid much attention to the layout."

"It's an open space with a couch and chairs and the mail box area. So when you get off the elevator, turn left and walk straight forward. The seating area and mail boxes will be on your left and the front door is straight ahead."

Charlie turned and started walking and immediately bumped into one of the chairs. Natalie laughed and took his hand. "It's very hard to walk straight when you have no guidelines. Are you finding the cane helpful?"

"Well, I can't say that I like it very much, but it does a fine job communicating different textures to me, like the wall and the elevator door. I never thought about things like that before. I took so much for granted. I guess I'm going to have to learn a lot of new things from now on."

Still holding his hand, Natalie guided him out the front door. When they got outside, the sun washed over them. Charlie stopped and put his face up to feel the warmth on his skin and sighed. "I never knew I was missing the sun until now. I'm so glad you brought me out."

"So to the park, lead on MacDuff! Do you want to continue holding hands, or just walk by yourself?"

"For starters, I'd prefer to hold hands for a little guidance."

Hand-in-hand they set off for the park. When they came to the first cross street, Charlie's cane went down off the curb, and he stopped abruptly. Panic seized him. "If I were by myself, how would I know it was safe to cross the road?"

"You could speak out and ask anyone who is waiting for the light to tell you when it's safe to cross. Never be too proud to ask for, or accept help. The other thing you can do is listen to the traffic. You can tell which way the traffic is going. Don't step off the curb until you hear the cars beside you start moving in the direction you're going."

They crossed the road and continued for one more block to the park.

"It looks like they have a children's playground and wading pool, but it's not open yet. Do you want to walk around the park?"

"Yes, a few times. I haven't had any exercise for months and I'm really out of shape."

"It's lovely here. The trees all have their spring green leaves. I love that light green they have, before the sun turns them dark in the summer. Which do you prefer, spring or summer green?"

"I never noticed any colour changes. I guess I've never been much of a nature lover. It was just there. But now that you're talking about it, I'll certainly pay more attention—if I ever get my sight back."

"You'll get it back," Natalie said firmly.

Charlie hoped she was right.

"You must be getting hungry," she said. "I should have brought some sandwiches."

"Yes, I could eat something. There's a little corner store down the street, if I remember rightly. We could get some chips or something there."

"It's not a very healthy lunch, but it'll have to do. Do you want to come with me, or wait in the park?"

"I'll come with you."

Natalie easily found the store and they went in.

"Good to know this store is here," she said. "It's closer than the grocery store if I just want to pick up milk or bread."

Natalie told him about some of the available lunch options. "I've got a few packages of cheese and crackers," she said. "They'll be healthier than chips."

She paid for the food and they headed back to the park.

"Let's find a bench in the sun and have our picnic," she suggested.

They found a bench and Natalie made him the cheese and cracker sandwiches.

When they had finished eating, Charlie said, "I'm curious. Do you have any brothers or sisters?"

"No, I'm an only child and since my parents' deaths I've been quite alone."

"Don't you have any other relatives? No grandparents or cousins?" Charlie asked.

"Probably, but none that I know. My dad didn't get on with his father so he left home and cut all ties with his family. Somewhere in Nova Scotia there are Monroes I'm related to, but I have no idea where."

"Aren't you curious about them? Wouldn't you like to be part of a family? I know I'd feel very alone if I didn't have Paul."

"Yes, I'd love to be part of a family but it's too late for that now."

"What about your mother's people?"

"My mother was an only child. Her parents were very religious, and when she divorced her first husband, they disowned her."

"That seems very harsh," Charlie opined.

"Yes, I guess it was. The problem was that her parents had expected her to marry someone from the con-

gregation, but my mother had met a handsome, rogu-
ish fellow and fallen madly in love. Her parents warned
her not to marry him, but you can't tell a nineteen-
year-old girl who's in love, that she's making a mis-
take." Natalie paused for a drink of water. "The
marriage was a disaster. As long as things were going
well he was great, but let something go wrong and he
would fly into a rage and take it out on my mother.
After her second miscarriage, she was determined to
be free of him. She returned to her parents, but they
told her she must go back and make the marriage
work. Instead she got a divorce and so the parents
turned their backs on her."

"People can be so misguided. How old was your
mother when that happened?"

"She was twenty-three or four. The good thing was
that she had a job and was able to find a small apartment she could afford. Once she got used to being by
herself, she was glad she no longer had to be part of
her parents' stifling religion. She actually started to
enjoy life for the first time."

"So, it's not a totally unhappy story," he said.

"No, I guess not. My mother told me she got a lot of
satisfaction from her job and had no desire to marry
again. But then a friend introduced her to my father.
He was a very calm, controlled individual. My mother
was drawn to him and they got married. By now my
mother was forty-one and my dad was fifty and they

never expected to have children, but fate had other plans. My mother gave up her job after I was born and never worked again. She was a gentle person who had a lot of love to give. She was always my best friend and I miss her still."

As Natalie told her story, Charlie thought how lonely it must have been for her with no brother or sister to play with, and it didn't sound like she had many friends either. No wonder she seemed as if she didn't need other people in her life.

The sun had moved and it was starting to feel chilly. "We should head back," Natalie said.

"Yes, I guess we must," he said. "It was a wonderful afternoon and I hate for it to end."

"There will be lots more," she assured him. "Now the weather is getting better."

In the lobby of the apartment Natalie told him to find his way to the elevator. Remembering what she had told him about using the cane to find the elevator and the control panel, Charlie proceeded. He went off track a couple of times and bumped into the lobby furniture before he found the elevator door. He pushed the up button and when the door opened, he stepped in and reached out to the left for the control panel. Counting up four buttons from the bottom, he pushed the one for the third floor.

Standing beside him, Natalie said, "That was excellent. You're beginning to get the hang of the cane."

When they reached the third floor, Charlie stepped off the elevator and, using the cane, found the carpeted hallway. He stepped to the right and put his arm out to touch the wall. Walking down the hall, he counted the doors and when he got to the fifth one he proudly announced, "We're home!"

Natalie opened the door and let them in. "Charlie," she said, "that was well done. You'll soon be able to go solo."

A grin spread across his face. "I don't know about going solo, but it was good to feel a little independent again. I'm going to need a lot more practice going out and finding my way home again. Tomorrow can we look for landmarks that'll tell me when I've reached the apartment building?"

"Of course, I should have thought of that today," Natalie said as she began making dinner.

"Can you stay for dinner tonight?" Charlie asked hopefully.

"No, I'm sorry, but I'm committed to my volunteer job," Natalie said and smiled at his crest-fallen look.

That evening he turned on the TV, but found it very frustrating. Damn. He couldn't tell if it was a commercial or a program. He finally switched the TV off and put on some music. Again, it was damned annoying, trying to find a particular CD, but at least he knew the albums he had and could recognize which one he had loaded as soon as it began to play. He was going to have to figure out some way to store them so he could find what he wanted a little easier. Maybe Natalie would have some ideas.

As he listened to his David Bowie album, he thought about Tom and the concerts they had gone to when they were in college, about all the girls they had dated, the hockey and baseball games they had attended together, and all the fun times at the pub. Charlie wanted to call him, but was too embarrassed when he thought of their last meeting. Why had he called him an asshole? Paul had said that Tom called regularly to ask about him. Maybe Tom wasn't as mad as he thought. Oh shit, he just didn't know what to do.

The next day when Charlie heard Natalie's key in the lock he came to the hall to greet her.

"What's it like out?" he asked. "Will we be able to go to the park again?"

"It's not as warm as yesterday, but if we bundle up a bit, and stay in the sun, it should be alright. I have to do some grocery shopping today. Would you like to come with me?"

"I'd probably just get in your way."

"What I was thinking was that we could go to the park for an hour or so, and then head over to the grocery store. That way we can spend a bit more time in the park. But if you'd rather not go to the store, that's okay."

"Oh, no, that makes sense. I'll go with you."

"Today I'll make us a picnic lunch. Don't forget to put a heavy sweater on under your jacket, and bring your keys."

This time he took the lead and walked confidently down the hall to the elevator. Outside, he reminded her to check for landmarks.

Taking his hand they walked a little way along the street and stopped. "Let's turn around now and pretend we're coming back from the park. Concentrate on your right side. We're approaching two mail boxes placed at the curb."

Charlie's cane contacted the boxes.

"Touch them so you can recognize them. Now continue walking. The next obstacle will be a lamp post."

Soon his cane touched that.

"Stop. This lamp post is directly opposite the door of your building. Turn ninety degrees and walk forward about seven steps and you'll come to the door." He did as instructed and reached the apartment door.

"Well, that seems simple enough," he said with a little more confidence than he actually felt.

They set out for the park. Charlie took Natalie's hand, and when she didn't object, he continued to hold it. As on the previous day, they walked around the park a few times and then found the same bench in the sun.

Natalie handed a sandwich to Charlie, and asked,

"So now you are no longer drinking, what do you do at night to amuse yourself?"

"That's a bit of a problem. TV is very frustrating when I don't know what's on. I've tried a couple of times but it's hopeless, so instead I've listened to music. Which reminds me, I need to find a system for storing my CDs so I can find what I want a little easier. Perhaps you could think about that."

"Yes, I'll give it some thought. But why don't you call your friends?"

"Yeah, I've been thinking about that, but I was such a jerk when they came over after the accident, I'm too embarrassed," he admitted. "Besides, it's been months since I spoke to anyone other than you or Paul. How can I explain why I didn't call or don't pick up the phone when they call me."

Charlie could smell the orange as Natalie peeled it. She handed it to him saying, "I brought clementines instead of sodas."

"Mmm, these are good," Charlie said.

Natalie continued the conversation. "You might be surprised. If they were true friends, they'll understand. Anyway, what do you have to lose? Right now you don't have any friends, so if you apologize and they turn their backs on you, you won't be any worse off. It's that simple."

"You make a lot of sense," he said, finishing his orange. "How did you become so wise?"

"I'm not so wise, that's just common sense" she said. "So is Paul your only relative?"

Before Charlie could answer, Natalie laughed. "There are two squirrels fighting over a chestnut one of them found. Can you hear them chitter?"

"Yeah, and they do sound funny," Charlie agreed. "I have an aunt and uncle in Florida," he said in answer to her question. "And some cousins in Alberta I don't keep in touch with, because they're a lot older than me. We haven't much in common. My aunt and uncle are retired. I went to visit them seven or eight years ago but it was kind of a blah time, so I never repeated the experience."

"Are you and Paul close?"

"Not really, but since the accident, he's been a real prince. Without him, I would've gone completely over the edge. He's taken care of everything for me. I don't know how I can ever repay him."

"I suspect he doesn't want any repayment. He just wants to see you happy, or at least that's the impression he gives me. Your parents are both dead?"

Charlie finished off his sandwich before answering. "Yes, five years ago they were killed in a head-on car crash, when a drunk driver crossed the median," he answered in a bitter tone. "I saw their car afterward and it was easy to see why they didn't survive. The front end was totally smashed in."

"Maybe that's why you reacted so forcefully to your

own accident," she said. "Headlights coming straight at you must have triggered an overwhelming response. The terror you must have felt at that moment may have sent your brain scurrying for cover. The brain is an amazing thing and does strange things to protect us."

"Yeah, you could be right. That's the most rational explanation for it, anyway."

"Do you miss your parents?" she asked.

"Yes, they were so much fun. Dad was such a joker, and Mom was a perfect foil for him. I hope when I get married I'll have as good a relationship as my parents had," he said dreamily. "When Paul and I were kids, Dad spent all day Saturday with us doing all kinds of things like fishing, skiing, bike riding or going to an amusement park. When we got home, Mom would have a fun dinner like chili, pizza or spaghetti ready and we'd spend the evening telling her all about what we had done. Sometimes we picnicked with Mom and Dad in the country. They were good days but not as much fun as with Dad alone, because Mom was always too concerned about falls and accidents."

"It sounds like you had a wonderful childhood."

"Yes, I did. Didn't you?" he asked.

"Most definitely not," was Natalie's emphatic response.

Charlie wondered at her vehemence. "So, you didn't enjoy your childhood?"

"Not much. Most of the time I was with my mother. My dad worked a lot and when he was home I was expected to be quiet and well behaved. He liked watching sports, hockey, baseball and some football and would have liked a son to share it with. When I was old enough to understand the games, we watched them together. I enjoyed that because it gave me some time with him when he wasn't criticizing me. He was a Bankruptcy Trustee so a lot of his time was spent listening to other people's misfortunes which was depressing for him. I think my parents were just too old to do all the things that kids like to do. But it's getting late and I still have to shop. We better go."

They stood up and Natalie guided Charlie out of the park. At the store Natalie grabbed a shopping cart.

"You'll have to hold onto my shoulder and stay behind me because the aisles are full of bins and other obstacles."

As Natalie moved through the store, picking up the items on her list, she chatted to him about what they were passing, and commented on people who left their carts higgledy-piggledy all over the place. Charlie enjoyed her sometimes acerbic comments.

"Buy enough meat and vegetables so you can stay for dinner sometimes," he suggested.

"That is a good idea. It must be difficult to entertain yourself for so many hours alone. I'll definitely plan on staying for dinner a few nights," she assured him. "I believe it'll help with your recovery if you have more company. Which is another good reason to call your friends."

Natalie paid for the groceries and they carried the bags in their joined hands. When they got to the final block, Charlie immediately moved to the right, searching for the mail boxes. He found them and proceeded to walk slowly until he came to the light standard. He made a ninety degree turn toward the apartment door. Walking forward, he counted his steps until his cane contacted the building. He then reached out with his left hand, found the door handle and let them into the lobby. Carrying the groceries, Natalie followed him in.

Again, Natalie congratulated Charlie on how well he had negotiated the path home. "You are doing very well. I'm proud of you."

She put the groceries away and then asked him about his CDs. "How do you usually store them?"

"I don't own that many so I never bothered to organize them. I have a carousel and each side holds about twenty-five CD's, but it isn't full. I used to just put them in anywhere."

"Okay, I'll look at them tomorrow. Rain is in the forecast so we won't be able to go to the park," she said. "I can stay for dinner tonight, if you like."

"Wonderful!" Charlie whooped.

Natalie laughed, and began preparing their meal. "Dinner will be about forty minutes. Do you want to watch TV?"

"No, I'll just sit here and talk to you. Tell me what you do for fun."

"I read my magazines, and mystery novels," Natalie said, peeling a potato. "While I watch TV I also do cross-stitch projects. I volunteer a few times a week at a seniors centre and in good weather I take long walks."

Charlie was curious. "What's a cross-stitch project?"

"It's a form of embroidery. You create a picture using coloured threads. I like it because it's challenging, and rewarding as the picture emerges."

"Don't you ever go to the movies, or to a pub with friends?"

"When there's a movie I particularly want to see I'll go by myself. But mostly I spend my evenings at home."

Charlie could hear the pork chops sizzling, which reminded him how hungry he was. Continuing the conversation he asked, "Don't you spend any time with friends?"

"No, I lost touch with everyone when I was taking care of my parents," Natalie said. "I haven't tried to make any new friends, and now I'm quite used to my own company. When I go back to school in September I won't have much time to socialize anyway."

Natalie handed the cutlery to Charlie and he began setting the table for dinner.

"What about a boyfriend?"

"Definitely not!" was her emphatic answer.

He was surprised at her vehement response and wondered why she was so down on men. It must have been something to do with her childhood. Pity she saw male relationships in such a negative light. And yet, she seemed like such an upbeat, positive kind of person.

As Natalie served their meal she told Charlie she had asparagus and small red potatoes, dressed with butter and sour cream, to go with the pork chops.

As they ate, Charlie changed his line of questioning. "What are you going to study when you go back to school?" he asked.

"I dropped out of school after grade eleven, so I need to get the credits required for my high school diploma. And then I'm going to apply to a university to take a nursing degree."

"That's going to take a few years. Don't you want to get married and have children?"

"I don't think marriage and children are in the cards for me," she said. "I enjoyed taking care of my parents and a nursing career would allow me to feel useful. There's a lot of pain and suffering out there and I think I can help."

"I'm sure you'll be able to," Charlie replied. "After all it's mostly due to you that I was able to start facing my situation and take responsibility for my actions. It's your optimism that helps me to try."

"I'm glad I've been able to help you," she said and Charlie could hear the pleasure in her voice.

They finished eating and Natalie cleared the table. As she started washing the dishes, Charlie found a tea towel and began drying.

"This is a pleasant surprise, " Natalie said.

"Well, I enjoy your company and this gives me a reason to stay in the kitchen. Do you know if the Blue Jays are playing tonight?"

"No, but I'll look when we finish."

In the living room Natalie sat on the sofa, and checked out the TV listings. "No baseball," she reported. "How about watching Jeopardy? I don't get many of the answers correct, but it's fun to try."

"Yeah," Charlie agreed. "I always hope there'll be a few sports questions, so I'll have half a chance."

They tuned into Jeopardy. They both called out answers but got most of them wrong.

"Boy, this is a tough one tonight. I usually get at least one right," Natalie said, chuckling.

After Jeopardy, she asked, "How about this crime drama?"

"Yeah, that's usually pretty good," Charlie enthused.

The story was about the suspicious death of a midshipman.

Charlie said, "I bet it's the wife or her boyfriend who

did it."

"No, the mid-shipman wasn't a nice man, so I bet it was one of his ship mates who killed him. Men always suspect the wife, but it's usually someone else."

"We'll see," Charlie snorted.

It turned out they were both wrong. The mid-shipman was involved in a drug smuggling ring, and it was one of his partners who killed him because he was holding back money.

"You see," said Natalie. "He wasn't a nice man, and that's what got him killed. But, now I have to go home. It always takes longer after rush hour, and I don't like getting home too late."

"You could always stay here," he suggested.

"No, I don't think that's an option. I'll see you tomorrow."

After Natalie left, Charlie turned off the TV. He wanted to listen to his Boz Scaggs album but it was such a struggle finding it. For sure tomorrow he would ask Natalie to organize his CDs.

Chapter Six

When Natalie arrived the next day Charlie called out, "I can hear the rain lashing at the windows, it must be pretty awful out there."

"Yes, it's the most miserable day you could imagine," she said. "Today will be a good day to organize your CDs, if you like."

"Oh, hooray! Last night, after you left, I tried to find my Boz Scaggs album. It took me four tries. Not that I had anything else to do, but it was frustrating, nevertheless."

"I understand. Let's get started. Do you know how you want them organized?"

"Not really. I'm not much of an organizer, as you probably know by now."

"Okay, let's see what you have to work with."

She gathered all the CDs from the carousel. Sitting on the floor she sorted them into several piles.

"It looks like you have four main categories of

music, like groups or bands, male and female vocal, and then some miscellaneous ones like Christmas music, a classical album and a few other odd things. Would that work for you?"

"Yes, sounds logical to me."

As Natalie began sorting the CDs she asked, "Can we listen to Frank Sinatra while we do this? He was my mother's favourite singer, after Johnnie Mathis. But you don't have any Johnnie Mathis albums."

Sinatra was Charlie's seduction tape. It was all love songs, and with the lights turned low and Frank singing softly, most girls relaxed. He hesitated, but didn't want Natalie to know what he was thinking, so he said, "Oh, sure, that would be fine."

"I've sorted the CDs into the four groups. I'll use a different side of your CD holder for each group and use the plastic dots to differentiate the categories. Groups and bands is the largest pile so I won't put any dots on those CDs. The next largest category is male vocal so I'll put one dot on the spine of each of those cases, two dots on the female vocal and three on the miscellaneous. I'll put the corresponding number of dots on the top of the carousel so you always know where to put the case back. Makes sense?"

"Yeah, that's perfectly clear. How will you arrange them in the carousel?"

"I thought alphabetically, unless you have a different idea."

"No, alphabetically will also be best for those who can see."

Natalie read the titles of the CDs in each category to Charlie, to confirm that she had placed them where they made the most sense to him.

"Spike Jones is pretty zany, so put that with the miscellaneous CDs. Otherwise the rest of them are where they should be."

As Natalie worked, Charlie relaxed in his chair and thought about the girls in his life. There was Brenda, the girl he had dated a couple of times before the accident. She was cute and liked hockey, but had probably moved on by now. There was Janet, or was it Jane, who was a lot of fun, but her loud, braying laugh was just too irritating. And Carol, who was wonderful in bed, but just too anxious to get married and have kids for his liking. And then there was Amy, wonderful Amy, whom he had almost married. How different his life would be if they had.

He was clearly missing female company, and wondered if any of his old girlfriends would be interested in him now. Maybe he was wrong but he didn't think any of them would. Damn, he was going to have to stop feeling like a cripple. He was still Charlie, wasn't he? So, why did he think girls wouldn't want him now? Oh hell! This line of thinking was just too depressing.

"Okay, Charlie, I've finished," Natalie said. "Come and see what you think."

Charlie stood up and walked beside the coffee table to the CD unit. Natalie took his hand just as the Sinatra album finished. Still holding her hand, Charlie leaned over and started the album again. He shoved the coffee table out of the way and drew Natalie against him.

"Let's dance," he murmured.

Natalie pulled away. "I don't dance," she said sounding slightly panicked.

Charlie held on and drew her in again. "Just relax," he said soothingly.

"No, really Charlie—"

"Hush, don't talk. Just listen to the music," he crooned, as he put his other arm about her waist.

He moved his feet but Natalie stood still, stiff as a board. Then, slowly she began to move her feet and let Charlie pull her closer into him. She put her arm around his back, laid her head on his shoulder and moved, ever so slowly, with the music.

Being held by him was comforting and she felt less alone for the first time since her father's death.

"This is nice," Charlie murmured. "And the scent of your hair reminds me of a fresh spring morning."

He had stopped dancing and was now just swaying to the music. Natalie suddenly felt his male hardness. She stiffened and jumped back as if she had been scalded.

"Let go of me," she shouted in alarm.

"I'm sorry!" he whispered hoarsely. He let go of her and quickly made his way into the bathroom.

Natalie was totally embarrassed by her own reaction. Hadn't she been fantasizing about Charlie when she had lain in bed? He was a decent guy and she really liked him. She wished she hadn't acted like a little schoolgirl. But although she wanted to experience sex, the prospect still frightened her.

When he emerged some time later, he called out, "Natalie, where are you?"

The Eagles had replaced Sinatra.

"I'm in the kitchen, getting lunch ready."

He came into the kitchen. "I'm so sorry Natalie," he apologized. "That wasn't supposed to happen. I just wanted to dance."

"Forget it," she said. "Would you like scrambled eggs and brown beans?"

"Sure, that would be fine."

They remained silent, as Natalie prepared the food.

She told Charlie to come to the table, but he apologized again. "Natalie, believe me, I didn't want that to happen. I just lost myself in the moment. I realize it must have been a surprise to you, but I don't understand your almost hysterical reaction."

"Yes, I over reacted," she admitted. "It just brought back some ugly memories."

"What kind of ugly memories?" he asked.

She placed his lunch plate on the table. "I really

don't want to talk about it."

He sat down to eat. "But if you never do, the memory will haunt the rest of your life," he said. "Is that what you want?"

"No, of course not, but I still feel ashamed even after all these years."

"Is it something to do with your father?"

"Oh, Lord no!" Natalie exclaimed. "Put that idea out of your head."

"Well, what?" he persisted.

Natalie sighed. "Obviously you'll make up your own story, if I don't tell you. But first you must understand that I am not pretty, and I didn't have any friends at school. So when I was fifteen, one of the popular boys asked me to go to a movie with him. I was surprised, but very proud to think he had chosen me. We went to the movie and afterward he drove us out to Lovers' Lane. I thought it would just be a little kissing, but he had an entirely different agenda." Natalie's voice quavered as she continued her story. "He told me that as he had taken me to the movies, I now had to 'put out'. Why else would he, a popular guy, take an ugly thing like me out. I refused and tried to get out of the car. He was much stronger than me and forced me down. He ripped off my underwear, and drove himself into me. I was a virgin and it was very painful. I was so ashamed that I had let that happen to me." Natalie took a deep breath to calm herself. "I never told anyone about it," she whispered.

"I'm so sorry," Charlie said quietly. "It certainly explains why you feel as you do about men."

"Yes, but that wasn't the worst of it. After that, all his friends asked me out, but now I knew why and so I refused them all. All except one. Nick didn't ask me out right away. He would just come and sit with me and we would talk about school. We even shared notes for a short time. He often walked me home and even carried my books. I thought he was a true friend. How wrong I was." Tears of shame and betrayal rolled down her cheeks and she wiped them away. "After a few months, he asked me to a movie," she continued. "I accepted, but after the movie, he turned out to be as big an animal as his friends. All the attention had been for that moment, and nothing else. I cursed myself for being such a fool. Since then I've never dated."

"Oh, Natalie, guys can be such jerks where women are concerned," Charlie said. "But I've never met anyone who's been a real victim. Please believe me when I tell you I'll never knowingly hurt you. I promise I'll never do anything that you don't want me to do."

They had finished eating while Natalie had been telling her story, and now Charlie reached for her hand. "Come, show me what you've done with my CDs," he said and walked with her to the living room.

Happy to leave the uncomfortable revelations behind, Natalie took a CD out of the unit and handed it to Charlie. "Feel the spine. Can you feel the dots?"

Charlie did as he was asked, and felt two raised dots. "So this would be a female vocal, correct?"

"Yes, that's your Tina Turner album. To put it back into the unit, you can feel the two dots on the top, then run your hand down to the first empty slot. Of course, if you have several out at the same time, it'll be pure guesswork putting them back. Will it help you if I read each side from the top?"

"No, I'd probably forget anyway. Just having some way to identify the major categories is a big help."

"I should get some laundry done today. Do you want me to put the TV on?"

"No, I didn't sleep well last night, so I'll just stretch out on the couch and have a nap."

Natalie got on with her chores. The afternoon sped by and it was soon time to make dinner. While she was preparing the meal, she noticed that Charlie was experimenting with the new organization of the CDs.

"This is working really well," he said. "I find what I want much quicker. Thanks for doing that for me, Natalie. Will you be able to stay tonight?"

"No, I'm sorry, but I have my volunteer night tonight," she said. "But tomorrow, as a treat for both of us, I'm going to take us out for dinner. The place I'm thinking of is almost downtown, so I may drive. Where's the visitor parking?"

"At the back of the building," he said. "There are

quite a few spaces, so in the morning there shouldn't be any problem getting one. What restaurant are you thinking of?"

"It's an Italian place at River and King streets. They have great pasta, but they also do a mean steak or burger, and there's usually at least one special."

"That sounds great. I haven't been out for dinner since the accident. I'll dream about it tonight."

"Good, so we have a date."

Friday was a lovely, sunny day. Natalie parked her car in the visitor parking area and went upstairs. She had decided to make the whole day a special one.

She found Charlie sprawled in his chair, sound asleep, still wearing the same clothes as the day before. Her heart sank. Oh please, let him not be drunk! She reached down and touched him lightly on the shoulder.

"Wake up, Charlie," she said.

Charlie started. "Natalie, is that you?"

"Yes, why are you sleeping in your chair?"

He ran a hand through his tousled hair. "I was trying to sort things out in my mind and I guess I fell asleep."

"Well, get yourself up and showered. Today is going to be a holiday!" Natalie announced happily, relieved that Charlie was sober. "Think of something you'd like to do. I have my car here so we can go anywhere you want."

Charlie got up and headed for the bedroom. Natalie made coffee and waited for him to emerge. He was soon ready, dressed in jeans and a bright blue sweatshirt.

"So, have you decided where you'd like to go on this holiday?" Natalie chirped.

"Yes, I'd love to go to the ocean and walk along the beach looking for shells and smooth stones," Charlie replied light-heartedly. "When I was in college, a bunch of us went to Florida during Reading Week. I loved walking on the beach and smelling the salty sea air."

Natalie laughed. "I don't know about going to the ocean, but we can certainly go down to the lake and walk along the beach or the boardwalk. It's not quite the same, but you can still smell the water and feel the hot sand under your toes."

"That sounds great."

Natalie gave him some toast and coffee. "We'll have brunch at the beach. Take your jacket in case it's cooler by the water. We'll park at the foot of Coxwell Avenue. Do you have an old blanket we can take for our picnic lunch?"

"I don't have an old blanket, but I do have a couple of beach towels that should work."

Natalie found the towels and they left the apartment, heading for the elevator. She noticed Charlie was now more confident in his stride and in using the white cane. They reached the lobby and she took Charlie's hand, leading him to her car. She helped him, handed him the seat belt, and closed the door.

"Everything okay?" she asked as she settled herself beside him.

"Yes, it just feels strange to be sitting in the passenger seat," Charlie said. "I'm used to always doing the driving."

The beach was not far away and they soon pulled into the parking area.

"Oh look," Natalie cried. "A chip truck. How about a hot dog and the best fries in the world for brunch?"

Charlie laughed and matched her joyful mood. "That sounds like a terrific brunch to me."

At the chip truck they gave their orders.

When their food was ready, Charlie held Natalie's shoulder and she steered them to a vacant picnic table. It didn't take them long to eat.

Natalie wiped some mustard off Charlie's nose and stood up. "I'm just going to put the garbage in the bin. I'll be right back."

She returned and pulled Charlie to his feet. "So, sand or the boardwalk?"

"Let's walk in the water," Charlie suggested.

"Good idea, I'll just run back to the car and get the towels. Wait here."

When she returned with the towels, they took off their shoes and socks and headed for the beach.

"I love to feel the sand between my toes," Natalie said. But as they stepped into the water, she let out a yelp. "Yikes! It hasn't warmed up at all!"

Charlie went in and splashed the water with his feet. "Don't be such a wuss," he said, laughing. "This'll help build your character."

"I already have plenty of character, thank you very much," Natalie snapped, but laughed with him.

They held hands and carrying their shoes, they walked through the water for a few minutes.

"Your feet must be pretty cold by now. Why don't we just walk in the warm sand," Charlie said.

"Now who is the wuss?" Natalie crowed.

"No, no, I'm fine. I was just thinking of you," he said playfully.

As they walked on the hot sand, Charlie began to reminisce. "When Paul and I were kids, my parents rented a cabin on Georgian Bay. The water was pretty icy, until high summer. Every year Paul would dare me to swim in the deepest part where it never seemed to warm up and I, like an idiot, did. When I was thoroughly chilled I'd have to run back in and put on pants and a sweater. Then he'd tease me and call me a sissy."

They slipped and slid in the soft sand, while Charlie continued. "One day my mother asked me why I played his silly game every year, and why didn't I just ignore him and swim where it was warmer. Hadn't I noticed that Paul never swam in the really cold parts of the bay himself? From that day on I ignored Paul's taunts and eventually he left me alone."

"It must have been fun to have a brother," Natalie said wistfully.

"I guess it was, most of the time, but there was a lot of rivalry between us until we were older and not forced to be in each other's company so much. What was it like to be an only child?"

"It was okay. I learned how to amuse myself, and my mother was always there when I needed to talk. She watched the kids' shows with me, and taught me how to appreciate books and stories." Natalie sighed. "My father wasn't very interested in me until I had a long enough attention span to watch an entire period of hockey. He taught me about the rules and strategies of baseball and hockey, his two favourite games. So, although I didn't play much with other kids, between them my parents kept me amused. I only missed other kids when my mother took me to the park. But now that my parents are dead, I wish I'd had a brother or sister."

Natalie steered Charlie to a bench beside the board-walk and used a towel to brush the sand off their feet. As they donned their socks and shoes, they continued their conversation.

"Last night I was thinking about my future," Charlie said. "Up till now I guess I've just drifted along, having fun with the fellows, dating women and not considering the future at all. When I finished college, I was engaged to Amy, who was a couple of years older than me. She was beautiful, funny, smart and everybody loved her. We were going to be married as soon as I finished my apprenticeship. What I didn't know was that she'd been engaged to another man who didn't want to get married, so she had broken it off. She was still in love with him, and when he came back, hat in hand, she took off without a backward glance. The experience left me a little gun-shy, and I haven't had a serious relationship since then."

"She must have really hurt you," Natalie sympathized.

"Yes, I was pretty broken up at the time," he admitted. "But Tom and Paul got me through it. Now I've decided that if I get my vision back, I'll be more serious in my relationships. I'm thirty-two years old, and if I don't start a family soon I'll be too old to enjoy my kids. I guess I needed this wake up call to make me think about the future."

"Yes, we often need a kick in the pants to make us think about things," Natalie agreed. "After my dad died I drifted along not knowing what I wanted to do. Then I tried to get a job, and realized that my education didn't qualify me for much. I knew I had to go back to school. That's when I decided that I wanted to work with people in some useful capacity, and so my decision was to become a nurse. It's going to take a few years, but I'm sure I can do it."

"Well, we both seem to have come to some conclusions about the future. I hope we both get what we want."

"But enough of this heavy talk," Natalie exclaimed. "This is supposed to be a holiday. Let's walk on the boardwalk for awhile."

As they strolled along, Natalie provided Charlie with a running commentary on the other beach-goers. She described body and face piercings, odd-looking hats, strange-looking people, and anything else that caught her attention. And when there wasn't much to comment on, she made up something for Charlie's amusement.

"You paint very realistic pictures," Charlie said. "I can almost see the strange and odd things you describe which helps me feel like I'm part of the scene."

"I'm glad to hear that," Natalie replied.

After an hour or so had passed, Natalie looked at her watch and was surprised to see it was already four-thirty. "We should head back. Our dinner reservation is for six o'clock."

They walked back to the car, and headed for Charlie's apartment.

"I brought a dress with me for our date," Natalie told him. "So, if you don't mind, I'm going to have a shower and get ready."

While Natalie was getting dressed, Charlie thought about the day, and realized that he hadn't had so much fun for a very long time. He found himself drawn to Natalie and her natural, easy ways. He couldn't believe he had ever thought her prickly. He knew she would make a good nurse because she had so much to give.

"Your turn," Natalie called.

Charlie, for the hundredth time, wished he could see her. He went into the bathroom for a shower and emerged wearing chinos and a bright Hawaiian shirt. "Is this okay?" he asked.

"Charlie, you look good enough to eat," Natalie replied happily. "So, let's get going."

They went out the back door to Natalie's car. As she held the door open for him, he noted her perfume—a very light, flowery scent.

"You smell good. Your perfume reminds me of my mother. It's funny, I never thought of her scent at all, until just now."

"Oh dear," Natalie said. "I certainly don't wish to remind you of sad times."

"Don't worry," Charlie said. "It brings back good memories of happy times with my family."

Traffic was light heading toward the downtown area, and they soon arrived at the restaurant. Natalie held Charlie's hand as they strolled along the sidewalk.

"There are a few steps up to the restaurant and if

you hold your cane straight, you can touch each stair as you ascend," she said. "That way you'll know when you've reached the top."

The aroma of good Italian cooking assailed his nostrils as they entered.

Charlie breathed in deeply and said, "There is nothing like the smell of garlic to awaken your taste buds. Suddenly I am starving."

The hostess seated them at a table for two, gave them menus, described the specials of the day and asked if they would like anything to drink.

"I'll have a cranberry juice. Would you like a beer or a glass of wine?" Natalie asked.

"I'd love a beer," Charlie said and named his favourite brand.

When the hostess returned with their drinks she clinked Charlie's glass. "To a perfect day," she said.

"Yes, to a perfect day," Charlie agreed, smiling.

She opened the menu and began to read the main course selections.

"Don't bother reading everything," Charlie interrupted her. "I feel like having a steak."

"Would you like to share an escargot appetizer?" Natalie asked.

"I'd love to. What are you going to have?"

"I'm going to have the penne in a rosé sauce with shrimps and scallops," she replied. "How's your beer?"

"Excellent!" he said exhaling with satisfaction. "After

a week of not drinking, it really tastes good."

The escargots were delivered.

"I've put some French bread on your small plate for dipping. If you need more, let me know. Be careful, the serving plate is very hot. Perhaps you should use your little fork rather than your fingers. There are six snails so you get three. I'll be watching, so don't try to sneak any of mine."

It didn't take long to eat the escargots and then Charlie, to tease Natalie, started to range around the serving dish for pockets of garlic butter.

"Hey, back off! I thought you were supposed to be blind. You're certainly doing a fine job of finding my garlic butter."

Charlie laughed. "Gotcha!"

Soon their dinners arrived.

"Your steak is at six o'clock, your baked potato is from three to twelve, and on the other side from twelve to eight you have mushrooms and a roasted red pepper," Natalie explained. "There's also a small container of Béarnaise sauce for your steak. I'll put that beside your plate at three o'clock. Would you like any salt or pepper?"

"I'll have salt on my potato. Does it have butter and sour cream?" Charlie asked.

"Yes, it's all dressed."

They ate with sighs of contentment.

"How is your steak?" Natalie asked.

"It's great. How is your pasta?"

"Perfect, as it usually is here," she said. "It's been a while since I had scallops. They're so good. Do you like scallops?"

"Yes, but I'm really more of a meat guy," he said.

They ate in silence for a time. The restaurant was filling up and getting much noisier.

"This has been a very special day for me," Natalie said. "Sunday is my birthday. I usually celebrate it by myself but it was so nice to be able to share this day. On Sunday I'm going to go shopping and buy myself a whole new outfit. Summer will be here soon and it'll be fun to try on summer clothes. I have dark brown curly hair and hazel eyes. What color do you think would look good on me?"

"With hazel eyes, I'd say some shade of green," Charlie said and then laughed.

"What's so funny?" she asked.

"Nothing really. It just amuses me that you would ask for a man's opinion, particularly, a blind man's."

"Well, I guess you're right. It does sound a little strange. But it's as good as relying on a sales girl. Most of them would say anything to make the sale."

"So, Sunday is your birthday? How old will you be?"

"Charlie, you know it's not polite to ask a woman her age, but I'll tell you anyway. I'll be twenty-eight."

"Ah, twenty-eight—a very good year. When I was twenty-eight I went on a Caribbean cruise, started working for Harry, and generally enjoyed life. I hope your year is as good as mine was."

"I guess mine will be a little different, going back to school and all," Natalie said. "But, nevertheless, I am looking forward to the challenge."

The hostess came to clear the table and asked if she could get them anything else.

"Yes. It's this young lady's birthday," Charlie said. "And she should have the biggest piece of chocolate cake you can find."

"I'd rather have tiramisu if you'll have some of it," Natalie spoke up

The hostess returned in a few minutes, carrying a large portion of tiramisu with a birthday candle. "Enjoy, and happy birthday!" she said, placing two forks on the table.

"I've never had this before. I had no idea how good it is. Do you know how to make it?" Charlie asked.

"No. I don't make desserts. If I did, I'd eat them and get fat," Natalie quipped. "So it's better if I never learn how to make them."

When they had finished, she asked the hostess for the bill. Charlie reached for his wallet.

"No, Charlie, this is on me," Natalie said. "It was my idea and my day. Some other time you can plan it and it'll be your turn."

"But it's your birthday, so I should treat," he insisted.

"No, but thank you for the thought."

"It's still early, is there anywhere else you'd like to go?" Natalie asked when they had left the restaurant.

"Yes, I'd like to buy you a present for your birthday and to thank you for this wonderful day," Charlie said.

"That would be nice. But nothing expensive," she said.

"What kind of stores are there around here?"

"There isn't much around here," Natalie said. "But we can drive over to the mall where there are lots of stores."

Chapter Seven

Natalie drove to Shuter Street and managed to park in a rather tight spot.

"Wow!" she crowed. "You would've been impressed at that neat bit of manoeuvring I did to get us into this spot. I just hope I can get us out again."

She took Charlie's hand and guided him to the mall. "Do you know what store you want to go to?" she asked.

"Yes, I want to buy you a CD," he said. "So start thinking about what you'd like."

"There's a music store on the lower level. Do you think you can manage the escalator downstairs?"

"Hmm, that could be tricky," he admitted.

When they got close to the escalators, Natalie assessed the situation. She knew that just holding his hand would not be enough to prevent Charlie from falling if he lost his balance.

"Perhaps we should try and find an elevator," she

said.

"No, I'll be okay if I just hold on to the hand rail. Guide me to it, please."

Natalie, with great trepidation, placed his hand on the end of the moving hand rail that took him forward to the escalator steps. Charlie stepped onto the escalator but his foot landed between two steps. As the steps separated, Charlie was thrown off balance, but since he was holding on to the hand rail, he was able to step down to a full stair and managed to stay upright.

Natalie quickly stepped onto the escalator and caught up to Charlie. "I'm impressed. That was very well done. Now put your cane on the step below, so you can feel when we get to the bottom."

Charlie did so, and was able to step off without difficulty.

"Well, that was interesting," he said.

Natalie once again took his hand and they headed for the music store.

"So, have you decided what CD you want for your birthday?" he asked.

"Yes, I'd like to get a Billy Joel album. While we're here, is there anything you want for yourself?"

"Yes, you intrigued me with your Johnnie Mathis talk, so I'd like to get one of his CDs."

At the store Natalie found Johnnie Mathis and chose a CD with many of his greatest hits, and all her favourites on it. She then quickly found the Billy Joel CDs and made her selection.

After Charlie had paid for the CDs, they headed back to the car.

"I'll walk you in," Natalie said back at the apartment. "Then I must be on my way. Thank you for a wonderful day, and for my birthday present."

"Do you have to go?" Charlie asked. "The night is still young. We could go upstairs and listen to our new CDs."

"I'm sorry, but I have to be up early tomorrow and have to get going."

"Why do you have to get up early on a Saturday?" Charlie grumbled.

"I have a dentist appointment," she told him.

At Charlie's door Natalie was about to say good-night, when Charlie stopped her. "Just a good-night kiss to end this perfect day?" he asked.

"Okay," she said and stretched up to kiss him on the cheek.

But Charlie took her face between his hands and kissed her gently on the lips. Natalie had been expecting this and did not resist. He pulled her closer and kissed her properly. He ran his tongue around her lips, probing gently until she opened her mouth. He deepened the kiss and Natalie soon began kissing him back.

Breaking away, Charlie said huskily, "Come inside."

"Not tonight, Charlie," Natalie responded, a little breathless. "I really do have to go."

Charlie sighed and reached for her again but Natalie backed away and turned to go. "Good-night Charlie," she called over her shoulder. "I'll see you on Monday."

As she walked down the hall she relived their kiss and the sensations it had aroused in her. She had no idea that she could feel this way. She thought of the stories in her romance magazines and wondered if they were true after all.

In the car she sat for a few minutes to calm down and sort out her emotions. Charlie was clearly a very different person when he was sober. She was very attracted to him and had even dreamed about him. What exactly did she want?

As she drove out of the parking area, she realized she wanted exactly what Charlie seemed to want. And why not? Wasn't he the perfect candidate? He was blind and couldn't see that horrid purple birthmark, so he wouldn't judge her on her looks. How she hated that ugly thing that had robbed her of her confidence! With Charlie she could be natural. Yes, she decided, it must be him. But how to do it?

Realizing she had almost gone through a red light, she concentrated on her driving once more. But soon her thoughts drifted back to Charlie. Although she had over-reacted and been such a fool the day they were dancing, yet he still showed every sign of desiring her.

But what about when she would have to leave him? Was it fair to start a relationship? Well, if she kept their affair very light, what was the harm? Wasn't he used to casual affairs? But what about Paul? How would he react? Well, Paul must never find out.

Natalie looked up and was relieved to see she had arrived home safely. She would go to bed now and think about all this tomorrow.

Paul arrived early the next day. "Hey Bro," he called. "I have the usual breakfast. Come and sit at the table."

As soon as Charlie entered the kitchen, Paul noticed the change in him.

"Charlie, you've had your hair cut and you've shaved off your beard. You even have some sun tan on your cheeks and nose. What's been happening?"

"Natalie cut my hair," Charlie said. "We've been going to the park for exercise and I'm getting used to the white cane. Yesterday we went to the beach, and then out for dinner. It was wonderful to get out into the sunshine. Natalie is a good teacher and a super guide."

"So I see you're getting more confident in dealing with your situation," Paul observed. "That's good, because your employment sick benefit has ended, and you are now paying everything from your savings, which won't last long. The only way for you to save money is to let Natalie go."

"There's always the money from Mom and Dad's estate," Charlie reminded him.

"I thought you wanted that money to buy a house in the next couple of years," Paul said.

"That was the plan, but nobody could've foreseen the last few months. So, if I have to use it for something else, that's the way it is. Besides, I need Natalie. It's not just a question of being able to do everything myself, I just can't go back to being alone, day and night."

"So, why don't you call Tom, and rekindle your friendship?" Paul asked. "He still calls me to ask about you."

"Actually, I was planning to call him today," Charlie said.

"Good, make sure you do. I must say you're looking a lot better and I'm pleased to see you aren't even hung over. Do you want me to buy anything at the liquor store?"

"No, I'm done with that," Charlie said firmly. "I'm ready to get on with my life now. I don't like it much, but I realize it's not the end of the world. If I don't get my vision back in the next six months or so, I'll try to find a career I can pursue as a blind man. By the way, how's Ilene?"

"Ilene is just great! She's wearing maternity clothes now, and is so proud of her baby bump. Why don't I pick you up tomorrow and you'll have dinner with us?"

"I'd like that," Charlie said.

"Super! Ilene will be happy to see you."

The brothers talked for a few more minutes, then Paul had to go.

"Don't forget to call Tom," he reminded Charlie as he left.

Charlie went back into the living room to think about what he was going to say to Tom. It was still too early to call because Tom liked to sleep in on weekends. And Charlie hoped no lady friend had stayed over.

His mind drifted to Natalie. She was a lot of fun to be with. She always had something amusing to say about her surroundings. He wondered what she looked like. From the two times he'd held her, he knew she was quite petite, and she had a nice low voice, which was easy to listen to. Sexy even. She was also very competent and self-assured. She would make a very good nurse and she would probably make a very good wife, as well.

He wondered again why she thought marriage wasn't for her. It sounded like her parents had been happy enough. Then he realized he was thinking of her as his own wife. She was already doing most of the things a wife would do. Well, except for the bedroom part. But that might come, if he was patient.

He remembered her parting words last night, "Not tonight, Charlie." He savored the implied promise and found himself becoming aroused. But what did he really want besides the physical sex? Was he really thinking of marriage? Natalie had her own dreams and a husband wasn't one of them. What on earth was he thinking? Why was he so domestic, all of a sudden? Time to call Tom.

Charlie found his cell phone and dialed Tom's number.

"Hi, Tom, this is Charlie.," he said hesitantly.

"Charlie? Charlie who? Do I know a Charlie?" Tom sounded sarcastic. "Oh just a minute, it's coming back to me. Are you the Charlie that used to be my best friend? Are you the Charlie who called me an asshole, and wouldn't talk to me? Are you the Charlie whose life I saved? Are you the Charlie—"

"Yeah," Charlie broke in. "I'm all of those Charlies. I'm calling to apologize for being such a jerk, and for not letting you be the friend I know you are. I was totally wrong, and I know how much I hurt you."

"Do you?" Tom demanded. "Do you really know how much you hurt me?"

"No, you're right, I don't. I was too caught up in my own misery to give much thought to anyone else. I'm truly sorry for that. Can you forgive me?"

"Yes, of course. I've missed you, you crazy bastard. Nothing was the same without you. Are you better now?"

"I've come to my senses, if that's what you mean.

But no, I'm not better. I'm still blind, but I'm learning how to cope," Charlie told him. " But if you don't have anything going on tonight, why don't you come over here and we can watch the Blue Jays, if they're playing."

"I'm not doing anything special," Tom said. "Should I ask the guys if they want to come?"

"No, let's just make it the two of us tonight. Another night I'll come to the pub with you and apologize to them all."

"All right, that sounds like a plan."

"I'll have to ask you to pick up some beer, or whatever you want to drink. I've nothing in the place to offer you."

"That's okay. You know I wouldn't come empty handed in any case."

"Yeah, I know. So, come whenever you want and we'll order a pizza."

After he hung up, Charlie breathed a deep sigh of relief. It had gone better than he had any right to hope. Tom was such a good guy, and Charlie truly was sorry he had treated him so badly. He really owed Tom a lot.

That night, just before seven o'clock, Charlie heard a knock on the door. He walked down the hall, using the wall as a guide, and let his friend in.

"Hi Tom," he said. "It's so good of you to come."

"You're my brother, so how could I not come?" Tom said. "I would've been here before, if you'd let me, you know."

"I know. And again I apologize for being such an ass. Let's sit down and catch up. Are you hungry? Shall we order pizza?"

"Sure, pizza would be good." He took the six-pack of beer into the kitchen and put it into the fridge. "Hey man, you've got real food in this thing. What's going on?"

Charlie heard cupboard doors banging and drawers being opened. "Are you looking for something?" he called out.

"No, do you want a cold one?"

"Yes, I'll join you."

Tom opened a couple of beers and returned to the living room. "What's going on, Charlie? I've never seen real food in your fridge before, and your kitchen is so neat and clean."

"That's Natalie's doing," Charlie told him.

Tom whistled. "Who's Natalie? How did you meet her?"

"She's the housekeeper Paul found for me when he realized I wasn't coping on my own. She does my laundry, cooks my dinner, shops for me, and keeps the apartment clean."

"Judging by what I'm seeing, she's doing an excellent job. You should hang on to her."

"Yes, she's been very helpful. As a matter of fact, she's partly the reason I came to my senses." Charlie took a gulp of beer and continued. "She's also helping me to learn how to cope with the blindness. She's been showing me how to use the white cane and how to find landmarks to help me know where I am when we're outside. I never realized just how much I took for granted. It's been a real eye-opener for me, pardon the pun. Anyway, I'm adjusting slowly, and beginning to feel more confident again. It isn't much fun being afraid all the time. But enough about me. What have you been up to?"

"Let's order the pizza and I'll bring you up to date."

Charlie found his cell phone and ordered a large meat-lovers with double cheese.

"Okay, so what's been happening?" he asked.

"Well, first off, Jonesy's getting married," Tom announced.

"Married? When did this happen? Who is she? How long has he known her? When's the wedding?" Charlie was full of questions.

"The wedding isn't until next year. Her name is Katherine, and apparently she was Jonesy's high school sweetheart, but they both went to different colleges and so lost touch of each other." Tom paused to take another gulp of beer. "He met her again at a dance club, just before Christmas. They started dating and realized they still cared deeply for each other, and so decided to get married. I've met her and she's perfect for Jonesy."

"I'm happy for him," Charlie said. "What about Vic, any changes there?"

"Yes, he's starting a new job. His old boss retired, and Vic applied for the job, but they hired an outsider instead. So Vic thinks that he doesn't have a chance there and found another job. He lucked out and was able to get a better job, for a higher salary."

"Is it still in the computer business?"

"Yes. He's going to be a supervisor in the IT department of one of the banks. I don't remember which one."

"Wow, nothing happens for a couple of years, and then, just when I'm out of commission, everybody decides to do something spectacular. What about you, Tom, are you going to tell me something amazing, as well?"

"Not really," Tom said sounding evasive. "Harry has just started building a whole new subdivision and has enough work for the next five years. Good news for us, as long as we want to work for him. He keeps asking me when you'll be back."

"Soon, I hope, but we'll just have to see. But anything happening on the personal front?" Charlie asked.

"Yes, I saved the best for last," Tom said. "I finally met a girl I really like. She's really smart—well not so smart if she picked me. But she's beautiful, sexy, a good cook, and totally easy to be with. And you'll never guess—she's an electrician as well. Isn't that something?"

"Hey man, that's really great!" Charlie whooped. "What's her name? How did you meet her?"

"Her name's Sara. She is a building inspector. She goes to new housing sites and inspects the plumbing and electrical installations to make sure everything's up to code. She came to our site in March. Harry was busy and couldn't show her around, so he asked me to do it. We spent about three hours going through all the houses. I liked her and so when she finished, I asked for her phone number. The rest, as they say, is history."

Just then the pizza arrived. Charlie paid, and then got dishes from the kitchen. "Put on the ball game, Tom," he called.

The men ate pizza and watched the game, whooping whenever the Jays had a hit.

"That was great," Tom said when the game was over. "But if you don't mind, I'll go now. I'm really beat. Sara and I had a late night. Nudge, nudge, wink, wink. But what night do you want to go to the pub? The guys still go on Tuesdays for the wing special. Would that work for you?"

"Tuesday would be good. It'll be great to go to the pub again. Will you pick me up?"

"Sure, not a problem. I'll come at six-thirty."

"That'll be great, something to look forward to," Charlie said.

At the door, Charlie felt himself being grabbed in a big bear hug.

"I'm so glad you called," Tom said gruffly. "Nothing seemed right without you. See you Tuesday."

Charlie closed the door after Tom, and found he had tears in his eyes.

Natalie arrived on Monday to find Charlie just getting dressed. She called out to him, "Hey, lazy bones, I'm here. What do you want for breakfast?"

Charlie came to the kitchen freshly shaved and smelling clean and soapy. "Since I'm not making my own breakfast today, how about the works—eggs, bacon, toast and coffee?" he asked.

"Okay, and then you can tell me all about Tom's visit."

"How did you know Tom was here?"

Natalie laughed. "Easy. I just guessed from the pizza box and the empty beer cans."

"Well, you're right. He came Saturday night. We watched the Blue Jays and he told me what's been happening with the guys."

"So, you and Tom made up?" she asked.

"Yes," Charlie said and smiled. "Tom is such a good friend. I don't know how I couldn't have realized that. I've been such an ass. I'm lucky to have such good friends."

"You certainly are," she agreed. "True friends should

be treasured. I envy you. So has anything interesting been happening with the guys?"

Charlie told her Tom's news. "Maybe it was good that I wasn't around for a while because it may have made Tom think about his life and what he wants," he said. "Lord knows, it certainly has made me think more about my own future."

"I am so glad you made up with Tom," Natalie said. "Congratulations!"

"I also went to Paul's for dinner on Sunday. It was good to see Ilene," Charlie continued. "She's six months pregnant and so happy. She and Paul can hardly wait for this baby to be born. It's practically all they talked about. And Ilene's roast beef and Yorkshire pudding were just as good as I remember."

"Well, you certainly had a busy weekend," she said. "Good for you."

"How was your weekend? What did you do for your birthday?"

"I had a nice weekend as well. On Sunday I treated myself to a new outfit. The spring colours are so pretty and happy, I just couldn't resist."

She also thought about the new sexy panties she'd purchased because she knew the women Charlie had dated wore this kind of underwear. And, she had to admit, they did feel nice and silky.

"So what's your new outfit like?" he asked.

"It's a pale pink mini skirt, and a short-sleeved

blouse with lots of tiny, bright coloured flowers on a pink background. They look really good together, if I do say so myself," Natalie bragged. "I wore them today so I could start getting some sun on my legs. They're so white after the winter. Today we'll have a picnic in the park and sit in the sun."

"I like that idea," he said. "I'll help you clean up."

Together they did the dishes. After Natalie made sandwiches they set off. She noted that Charlie wasn't having much trouble walking in a straight line. That would be very helpful when he would venture out on his own.

Out on the street, Charlie reached for her hand. They walked to the corner and Natalie said, "I want you to tell me when it is safe to cross."

"Oh, wow, that's pretty scary," he admitted.

"Well, if you ever expect to go out by yourself, you'll have to learn how to cross roads," she said. "While I'm with you, you won't come to any harm, so it is a good time to practice. Just take your time and concentrate. There's no need to hurry."

"What you say makes perfect sense. Okay, let me listen."

Natalie stood patiently while Charlie listened for the traffic flow. When the cars beside them started to move, he said, "We can cross now."

When they reached the park, Natalie said, "Let's take a few laps around the perimeter."

"Yeah, that'll help me work off some of the food I stuffed myself with on the weekend."

They walked around the park three times and then found their favourite bench.

"Wow, doesn't that sun feel good?" Natalie said, stretching out her legs. "You sure notice the difference in temperature when you walk in the shade."

"You're right, but it won't be long before we'll be wanting it the other way round," he reminded her.

"Have you listened to the Johnnie Mathis album yet?" Natalie asked.

"No, not yet," Charlie said. "I wanted to wait until you were there, and share it with you."

"We could do that tonight. I don't have to be any-where special today, so I could stay later, if you like," Natalie said, knowing he would like that.

"That's great. The fewer hours I spend by myself, the better I feel."

"So, when are you going to see Tom again?" Natalie asked.

"Tom's picking me up to go to the pub with him on Tuesday night. It's wing night and the guys usually show up. I can then apologize to them for being such a jerk. Lord knows it's past time for apologies," he said ruefully. "It'll also feel good to do normal things again. I have you to thank for showing me I could be some-what independent."

Looking around the park, Natalie saw people with

their kids playing on the jungle gyms and swings. "When I was just a little kid, my mother would take me to the playground where I could run and shout and use up my energy. When my dad was home I had to be quiet and well-behaved. He never wanted children, and definitely not a girl." Natalie sighed.

Taking Charlie's hand she continued, "But when I was old enough to participate in the things he liked, like sports, and walking on nature trails, he mellowed. Then when he had his stroke, life became a burden for him, and he had too many hours to think. He regretted that he had missed so much of my childhood. In the end, he told me he loved me, and that he was glad I was a girl. So why am I telling you all this? Because I see that father in the playground with his little girl, and they're having so much fun. It makes me sad for what my dad and I missed. You were fortunate that your dad spent a lot of time with you."

"Yeah, Paul and I were very lucky. I wonder what kind of a father Paul will be. He was always a bit bossy where I was concerned. As the eldest he considered it his job. But my mother, when she noticed, would always come to my rescue and either make him stop, or give me good advice on how to deal with him. My mother was a wise woman," Charlie said nostalgically.

"Yes, it's funny how different parents approach the responsibility of raising children. I guess that's what makes us all so different. What kind of parent do you think you'll be?" Natalie asked.

"I don't know since I haven't had much experience with kids at all," he said. "I would hope that I could be like my dad and enjoy my family. I guess I'll just have to wait and see."

"Maybe you could get some practice when Ilene's baby comes. But hey, are you hungry yet? I had a smaller breakfast than you, and much earlier, so I'm hungry now," she said.

"I could eat now too," he agreed.

Natalie unwrapped the sandwiches and gave one to Charlie. "I brought some water instead of soda. There's too much sugar in soda."

They finished their lunch and she took the sandwich papers into a nearby garbage receptacle. "Let's walk a little more. I'm used to doing a lot of walking—something I did with my dad."

"I never walked much," Charlie admitted. "Having a vehicle makes you lazy. But with you, I enjoy walking."

After one more lap around the park Natalie said, "We should head back now. I have some work to do in the apartment and I need to make a shopping list for tomorrow. Think about what you'd like to eat this week."

Chapter Eight

The afternoon sped by as Natalie busied herself cleaning and tidying the apartment and making dinner. Charlie helped where he could.

"Where's the Johnnie Mathis album?" she asked. "I need to put a dot on it so you can find it."

"I think I left it in my coat pocket."

Natalie found the album and proceeded to code it. "Do you want to listen to it now?"

"No, let's listen to it when we're finished dinner."

Charlie went to the CD carousel and selected an album. Soon the apartment filled with the music of Blood, Sweat and Tears.

"That's a good one," Natalie said. "Now come and have dinner. I have your plate set up. Your meat loaf is at six, the asparagus is at nine and the potatoes are at three. Do you want butter on your asparagus?" she asked.

"Yes, thank you.

Natalie couldn't believe her ears. Charlie had never directly thanked her before for anything. Progress was definitely being made!

While they ate, they listened to the music and chatted about the day. When they had finished, Charlie helped with the clean up.

"It's still really early. Let's watch Jeopardy," Natalie suggested, switching on the TV.

They called out answers to the questions and Natalie was surprised at some of the answers that Charlie knew. When the show ended, she suggested they watch Bones.

"That's one of my favourite shows," Charlie said. "I love all the arcane information that Jack Hodges has at his finger tips about insects and their life cycles. Don't you find that fascinating?"

"Yes, I find it quite amazing that anyone would want to learn all that stuff about little tiny insects."

As they watched, Natalie filled Charlie in when the dialogue didn't properly explain what was happening.

"It is so nice to have someone keep me in the loop," Charlie said. "We certainly live in a visual world."

"Yes, that's something we sighted people take for granted."

Soon the show was over and Natalie turned off the TV. "Now it's time for Johnnie," she said.

She put the CD on and the room filled with the strains of violins and the wonderful voice of Johnnie

Mathis singing, "Chances Are".

"This is one of my favorites, come and dance with me," she invited, hoping he wouldn't refuse because of her previous histrionics.

Natalie pushed the coffee table aside and took his hand. She put her arm about his waist and was relieved that Charlie wasted no time in pulling her close, showing that her fears had been groundless. He began moving to the music and Natalie laid her head on his chest.

"You feel so good in my arms," Charlie whispered.

"You feel pretty good yourself," she murmured.

Charlie reached to find Natalie's face. He stroked her cheek and then raised her chin. Leaning down he kissed her, slowly at first, exploring her lips with his tongue. As Natalie relaxed, she could feel his urgency growing and returned his kiss. He stopped moving and embraced her entire body, running his hands over her back and cupping her buttocks.

Natalie felt her panic rising but pushed it down, forced herself to remain calm. It was now or never, and she dearly wanted to experience sex the way her romance magazine promised it could be.

"Come, let's sit down," Charlie invited, holding her hand. He sat on the sofa and drew her to him. She perched tentatively on his knee, feeling strange and shy and very exposed, as her mini-skirt was too short to allow much fabric under her buttocks.

"This is kind of awkward," Charlie murmured. "If you straddle me it'll be more comfortable for both of us."

When she hesitated, Charlie whispered urgently, "Please, Natalie."

Hearing the longing in his voice, she gave in and straddled him.

His hands went around her and then slid up to the back of her head. Pulling her face to him, he kissed her passionately. As she relaxed and kissed him back, he began to explore her body. He stroked her face and neck and finally her breasts. He ran his thumb over her nipples and they hardened, thrusting against the fabric of her blouse.

"Oh Charlie, that feels so wonderful," she moaned.

He unbuttoned her top and again Natalie felt her panic rising, but she forced herself to remain calm. He slipped the blouse down over her shoulders and dropped it to the floor. He then reached for the hooks at the back of her bra, but they weren't there. Instead he lifted the cups of the bra up and over her breasts and the front fastener flew open.

"Wow! That's real magic!" he cried.

Natalie giggled.

Charlie cupped her small, firm breasts in his hands, stroking the nipples with his thumbs.

"Please, don't stop," she moaned. She had never felt such exquisite pleasure before. She was surprised to feel herself getting wet between her legs.

"Let's go into the bedroom," Charlie urged.

Natalie got up and took his hand to lead him. When they reached the side of the bed, he began taking off his clothes. Natalie, following his example, also stripped naked.

He threw back the sheet and comforter, grasped her around her waist and sank down onto the bed. Leaning back and stretching out, he pulled her to him until their naked bodies were touching everywhere. Natalie felt his male hardness pushing against her groin and wanted to run away. It felt so big and brought back such painful memories.

But as Charlie stroked her all over and ran his hand up her inner thigh, she soon lost her fear. Drawing circles, ever so lightly with his finger tips he slowly moved his hand to her sex. Gently he parted her legs and rubbed her clitoris. Wrapping her legs around his hand Natalie moaned.

Charlie reached into the nightstand drawer for a condom. Tearing the package open he slipped it on and slowly entered her.

She stiffened.

"Are you okay?" he asked, with evident concern.

"Yes, I'm fine, it was just a surprise, that's all," she replied.

Charlie stroked her thigh and kissed her breasts. Soon she relaxed and he move inside her, slowly at first and then with more urgency. He moved faster, thrusting in and out, holding Natalie's buttocks, not allowing her to move. She was ready to scream, but then Charlie shuddered and went limp. It was over. A moment later he got up, mumbling something about the bathroom as he stumbled away.

Natalie felt distressed. That certainly wasn't what she had expected. Disappointment filled her. From her romance magazines she had come to expect a more romantic experience. She didn't know what to do. Perhaps she should just get dressed and go home. She reached down and pulled up the sheet to cover herself. The kissing and stroking had been wonderful. When Charlie had brought her body to life, never had she known such delicious sensations. But then he seemed to forget everything but his own need and the ending had been a complete disappointment.

While she was trying to decide what to do, Charlie returned.

He climbed back into bed and took her hand. "Natalie, I am so sorry. It shouldn't have happened like that. I'm totally embarrassed. I didn't consider you at all. It was only about me. My only excuse is that it's been such a long time since I've been with a woman. I promise you, the next time will be better. Do you forgive me?"

"I guess I don't have much choice," she replied, wondering if she even wanted a next time.

He kissed her gently on her nose and lips, and gathered her in his arms. "You're so wonderful to me. I think I might be falling in love with you."

"Hush, Charlie, let's not talk about that," she said.

They lay quietly in each other's arms and Natalie dozed off wondering if this was as good as it would ever be.

A while later Natalie awakened and went to the kitchen for a glass of orange juice.

"Natalie, are you still here?" she heard Charlie call.

"Yes, I'm in the kitchen," she called back.

Charlie joined her, and she poured him a glass of juice, feeling self-conscious about her nudity. Idiot! Charlie couldn't see her. However, this was her opportunity to check him out, and she liked what she saw.

"Are you hungry?" she asked.

"Only for you," he said, smiling broadly. "It must be pretty late. I hope you aren't planning on going home tonight."

"You're right. It's after midnight. I won't go home this late by myself."

"Then let's go back to bed and I'll try to fulfill my promise."

To her surprise she felt a stirring in her groin at the thought of Charlie's caresses.

They climbed into bed and Charlie gathered her in his arms. He kissed the top of her head, then moved down to her eyes, nose and mouth, where he lingered.

"The juice tastes much better from your lips," he murmured.

Natalie kissed him back, but he pulled away and moved down to her neck. He licked the hollow below her chin and continued to move his lips down to her breasts. There he lingered, caressing them with his tongue and fingers.

Enjoying all the sensations he was arousing in her body, she gave herself over to the moment. She was his and she would follow him wherever he wanted to lead her.

Charlie continued to kiss and nibble his way down her body. When he reached her groin, he moved over and knelt between her legs. He slipped his hands under her buttocks and lifted her up. Natalie put her legs over his shoulders and surrendered herself to him.

He spread her apart with his thumbs and probed her with his tongue. When he found her most erotic place he stopped exploring and concentrated all his attention there.

Natalie went wild with pleasure and arched into him. "Charlie, oh Charlie, you're wonderful," she kept repeating.

When she was totally aroused, he moved away and lay back on the mattress.

"Come on top of me," he murmured. Handing her a condom he said, "You do the honours."

"Gladly," she replied.

Rising up she straddled him and guided him into her. She was surprised to find that in this position, he entered her more deeply. She leaned over and kissed him.

Charlie reached up and stroked her breasts and began moving inside her. Natalie moved with him. He then rolled her over onto her side, and together they became a surging, pulsing, grinding entity. Taking and giving pleasure, sighing, moaning and calling each other's names, they reached a crescendo together.

Natalie breathed a huge sigh of contentment. This time she was not disappointed. She felt whole and desirable for the first time in her life.

As they lay in each other's arms, Charlie reached down and pulled up the sheet to cover them. "Let's just stay here like this forever," he said in a languorous tone.

"Thank you, Charlie. I think I love you," Natalie whispered.

But to her relief Charlie was asleep and did not hear her. She snuggled into him and drifted off to sleep.

When Natalie awoke it was light outside. She checked her watch and was surprised to see that it was already eight o'clock. She got up and headed for the shower.

When she returned to the bedroom, Charlie was still

luxuriating in bed. He stretched. "Life is good," he sighed, grinning.

She dressed in the jeans and T-shirt she had left there on Friday when they went out for dinner.

"Okay lazy-bones, time to get up," she commanded. "We don't have any eggs, and I feel like a large breakfast, so we're going out."

While Charlie was in the shower, Natalie put the coffee table back in place and turned off the CD player. She tidied the kitchen and sat down to wait for Charlie.

He emerged dressed in jeans and a black polo shirt.

"Black really suits you," Natalie noted. "I don't know this neighbourhood very well. Where can we get a decent breakfast?"

"There's a little mom and pop cafe about four blocks down the street, the opposite direction from the park," Charlie said. "They make a good breakfast and are really good at cooking things the way you ask. Let's go there."

They walked to the cafe in the early morning sunshine.

"I just feel so good today," Charlie exclaimed. "It's the happiest I've felt since the accident. I almost feel like singing!"

Natalie laughed. "Sure, sing if you like. I don't mind!"

In the restaurant there were lots of empty tables

and Natalie guided Charlie to a booth in the corner. "I don't see any wait staff," Natalie observed. "I guess we have to place our order at the counter."

"Yes, they bring the food to the table, but you have to go tell them what you want."

"So, do you know what you want?" she asked.

"Yes, they have a breakfast special. That's what I always have here. It's a large meal so I generally don't eat anything else until dinner. I like the bacon and sausages well done, the eggs sunny side up and rye toast."

Natalie went to the counter, placed their order and returned to the table.

"Charlie, about last night, she began hesitantly. "It was very special for me. But I have to ask you to promise not to tell anyone, particularly Paul or Tom, about us. Do I have your promise?"

"Why don't you want anyone to know?" Charlie asked, puzzled.

"It's just that I was hired to be your housekeeper, and they may think I'm taking advantage of the situation, so it is better they don't know. Do I have your promise?" she insisted.

"Yes, you have my promise, although I don't see the need for it."

The woman bringing their breakfasts to the table exclaimed, "It's good to see you again, Charlie. You haven't been here for a long time." She laughed. "And who is the pretty girl you have with you this time?"

Charlie grimaced. "Oh Hannah, you just gave me away with your chatter about pretty girls. How have you been keeping?"

"Fine, Charlie, just fine. Eat your breakfast before it gets cold," Hannah said and left.

"So, do you bring all your over-night guests here for breakfast?" Natalie asked, surprised that Hannah's words had caused her a twinge of sadness. She took a bite of her toast.

Charlie laughed. "Are you jealous?"

"No," Natalie said. "I'm just curious."

"Oh, really? Just curious?" Charlie teased her. "Well, mostly I meet Tom here, but I have brought a couple of different girls here for breakfast. I'm sure Hannah thinks I'm a real Romeo."

"And are you?" she asked, much too quickly.

"Not more than your average bear," was his light-hearted response.

As they ate, Natalie commented on some of the folks coming in. As usual, she was trying to make Charlie feel like a part of the scene.

"I have to shop and do some laundry today," she said. "What will you do?"

"Well, for starters, I'm going to listen to the Johnnie Mathis album that we didn't pay attention to last night," he said with a huge grin on his face. "It really is a very romantic CD. I can understand why your mother liked it. But to more pressing matters, would you like some help with the groceries? I could come with you."

"Sure, your company will be welcome."

They left the restaurant and walked along, holding hands, thoroughly enjoying the beautiful June day. As they passed the park, Natalie commented that there were a lot more nannies and mothers out with their charges, enjoying the playground.

"By the way, Charlie, have you thought about going to the CNIB to see what kinds of services they could offer you?" she asked.

"Yes, I have, but I've decided to wait until Thanksgiving to see if my vision comes back."

"Why are you waiting so long?"

"Well, even though the accident happened in January, it's really only been a few weeks since I accepted my situation. I want to give myself six months, and then if nothing happens, I'll seek professional help. In the meantime, you're helping me so much. You make me feel alive and confident again and I want to build on that," Charlie said.

"I guess that's as good a plan as any, but don't leave it too long," Natalie said. "You do recall I'm leaving in September?"

She noticed Charlie frowning, but as they had reached the grocery store, he didn't respond.

Natalie again advised him to hold onto her shoulder,

so they could navigate the crowded aisles. She was quickly able to get what they needed and they were soon on their way home.

"It's nice to have help carrying the bags," Natalie said. "They can get quite heavy by the time I get to your place."

While she put the groceries away Charlie went into the living room and put on the Johnnie Mathis album. Soon Natalie joined him on the couch and they sat and listened without speaking.

Charlie was remembering the previous night, and how wonderful Natalie had felt in his arms. He marveled at how responsive she had been to his touch, and how well he fit inside her. Just remembering that was giving him an erection. He wondered if Natalie was also becoming aroused, and if she would like to make love again.

He put his arm about her shoulders and pulled her close. "Oh, Natalie," he whispered. He held her tight, stroking her hair, and Natalie snuggled into him. She put her head on his shoulder and he was acutely aware of her body close to his.

"You make me feel like I belong," Natalie murmured. "Thank you." She raised her face up to him and kissed him softly on the mouth. Charlie caressed the back of her head and began kissing her in earnest. She pushed her body into him and there was no stopping him now.

"Let's go to bed" Charlie whispered.

In the bedroom, they stripped naked and slipped under the sheets.

They kissed and touched each other everywhere. She explored his body and then slid down the bed and took him into her mouth.

"Oh Natalie, that feels so wonderful, Charlie moaned. "But come up here so I can taste you as well."

Charlie found her sweet spot, and soon had her gasping.

"I can't wait, I want you inside me," Natalie urged. She found a condom and rolled it down on his erect penis.

Charlie mounted her and began slowly moving in and out, teasing her. Natalie relaxed and joined in his rhythm.

Their need for each other was all-consuming. Charlie bruised Natalie's lips in his hunger, and she raked her nails over his back, as they slammed into each other. When they had climaxed, they fell back onto the mattress, spent.

"Natalie, you are becoming very dear to me," he said, stroking her softly.

She reached up and put a finger on his lips. "Don't say it, Charlie. We're good together, but don't expect more from me than I can give."

Charlie shook his head. He didn't want to hear this. He wanted to believe that she would be here forever.

"Truly Charlie, I wish I could be your wonderful Amy, but I'm not, and never will be. Please, let's just enjoy what we have without making promises."

"Don't say that," he growled. "Amy was a lifetime ago. You're so much more than she ever was!"

Ignoring his words, she continued. "I don't mean to hurt you, but believe me, it's better this way." She got out of bed, dressed and picked up the laundry basket. "Right now I have to do the laundry," she said and left the apartment.

Sitting there alone, Charlie thought about how wonderful their lovemaking had been. How passionate and playful Natalie was. How willing she was to follow his lead. He rehashed her words. He knew he was falling in love with her—no, not falling, had already fallen. He was pretty sure she loved him too, so what was her problem? They were perfect together. Why didn't she see that? He was sure in time he could change her mind. After all, they'd only been lovers for such a short time. That would be his mission.

Natalie returned with the clean laundry, and was ready to leave. "What time is Tom picking you up?" she asked.

"About six-thirty," he replied. "Will you come back here after your visit to the seniors' residence? I would really like you to."

"No, Charlie," Natalie said. "I do have my own place to take care of, too. Maybe on Wednesday I'll stay."

Chapter Nine

As Charlie waited for Tom, he wondered what kind of reception he would get from Victor and Jonesy. It had been so long since that evening in January when he'd been such an idiot. Well, he wouldn't have to wait long to find out.

Tom knocked on the door and when Charlie opened it, he was grabbed in a big bear hug.

"Hey, Charlie, it's good to see you back!" Tom exclaimed laughing. "Vic and Jonesy are great guys, but they can't replace you. If you're ready, we best go before those pigs eat all the wings."

It felt great to be part of the group again. "Where are you parked?" he asked.

"I'm out the back," Tom said.

When they reached the lobby, Charlie turned to the hall leading to the visitor's parking.

They got to the back door, and Charlie said, "You'll have to guide me to your truck."

Tom took Charlie's arm and led him to the truck. "I was watching you negotiate the halls and elevator," he marvelled. "You're doing so well, it's almost as if you could see."

"It's all thanks to Natalie," Charlie said as they headed for the pub.

"Again, what's with this Natalie? Who is she?" Tom asked.

"I told you, she's the housekeeper Paul hired."

"Housekeeper sounds like an old lady. Is she old?"

"No, she's twenty-eight," Charlie replied. "I think Paul hired her because she'd nursed her father after he'd had a stroke. Paul figured if she could nurse an invalid, she would be perfect for taking care of me. I wasn't looking after myself very well at that time. Not at all, really."

"And now?" Tom asked.

"Now with her help I'm learning to cope. She's quite resourceful and helps me figure things out," Charlie said. "She's also very funny. Where ever we go she amuses me with her commentary. I really enjoy being with her."

"So, is there a romance in the offing?" Tom asked.

"For me, yes, for her, no," Charlie confided.

"Why? Does she have a boyfriend?" Tom continued his inquisition.

"Not one that she admits to," Charlie replied

They arrived at the pub, Tom parked the truck and

guided Charlie inside. As soon as they entered, Charlie stopped dead in his tracks.

"What's wrong?" Tom shouted over the noise.

"The noise, it hits you like a wall! I forgot how loud this place is. I've been living in a monastic environment for the past six months, but, hey, it's good to be back."

"I see the guys at the back," Tom said taking Charlie's arm. "It looks like Jonesy has brought Katherine with him. You'll like her, she's a lot like him."

Vic and Jonesy greeted Charlie with hugs, and welcoming words.

"Hey you guys, I want to apologize for being such a jerk and ignoring you for so long," Charlie blurted as soon as he had a chance to speak. "You're such good friends and I've missed you."

"Apology accepted," Vic and Jonesy said in unison.

"It's so good to see you, man. You look very healthy. What have you been doing?" Vic then asked.

Jonesy jumped in with, "Come and sit down. I want you to meet Katherine, the most wonderful girl in the world."

Charlie sat down and a soft, female voice said, "Hello Charlie, I've heard a lot of good things about you."

Charlie laughed. "Well, you can't believe everything you hear. What're you doing with an old reprobate like Jonesy?"

"Reprobate he may be, but old he isn't," Katherine replied. "And besides, how else would I get to meet such a good bunch of guys like you?"

Everyone fired questions at Charlie which he did his best to answer.

"Enough about me," he finally said. "Where's the wings and beer?"

Tom poured Charlie a glass of draft from the jug on the table. "Wings coming right up."

After everyone had caught up on the news, the conversation turned to the Blue Jays and their chances of winning that year, while the wings and fries quickly disappeared.

The time passed too quickly for Charlie who was bursting with good spirits. It was wonderful being back with old friends. He'd had three beers and was feeling a bit light headed.

"I hate to break up a good party," Tom said, "But I have to be up early tomorrow. Charlie, are you on for next week?"

"You bet! I wouldn't miss it," Charlie answered.

Tom took Charlie's arm and guided him to his truck. On the way home, he asked, "What did you think of Katherine?"

"Not being able to see her makes it difficult to form an opinion," Charlie said. "However, her conversation certainly blended well with the guys. She seems to know a lot about baseball and Jonesy certainly sounds very happy."

"Yes," Tom agreed. "Let's hope it works out for him."

"How are you and Sara doing?" Charlie asked.

"We're good," Tom said. "We see each other a couple of times a week, but it's still early days. How about you, are you looking to pick up with Brenda again? I've seen her at the pub a couple of times, and she's always been by herself."

"No. Until I get my sight back, I'll remain celibate," Charlie fibbed.

"Are you sure about that? It could take longer than you think, and I'm sure there are girls who'd be interested in you."

"I'm not so sure, and I don't want any pity dates."

They arrived back at Charlie's apartment building. "Do you want me to come up with you?" Tom asked.

"No, I'll be fine. Are we at the front or back door?"

"We're at the front door. Is that okay?"

"That's fine, I'll be okay from here," Charlie said with confidence.

He got out of the truck and began walking along the street keeping his white cane close to the curb, feeling for the light standard.

"Hey, bro, where are you going?" Tom called.

"I'm searching for the lamp post. That's the guide I use to find the apartment door," Charlie explained.

"Oh," Tom said. "It's the other way."

"Thanks, Tom," Charlie replied. "Good thing you're

watching me!"

He turned around and began walking in the oppo-site direction. Soon he came to the lamp post, turned ninety degrees, and walked forward to the door.

"Well done," Tom shouted. "You amaze me."

"Good night, Tom, and thanks for taking me to the pub," Charlie called.

He let himself into the empty apartment and checked his watch.

"The time is ten nineteen p.m.," the watch said.

In the kitchen he drank a large glass of water and headed for bed. When he stretched out between the sheets, he noted Natalie's scent, and suddenly felt very lonely. He wished she was there. Just holding her in his arms made his world a better, more hopeful place. He grabbed Natalie's pillow and hugged it to himself and fell asleep thinking of her.

Natalie arrived next morning with a cheery greeting. "Good morning! How was your night with the guys?"

"It was great! Being back in the pub almost felt like old times. Funny, I forgot how noisy that place is, but I soon got used to it," he told her. "I met Katherine, Jonesy's fiancée. She fits in well with the guys and Jonesy's so happy. Vic seems to like his new job. We'll see how long that lasts. Vic tends to always start off on a high note, but then something happens to piss him off and then all you get is complaints. Oh well, maybe this time it'll be different. I had a really good time, but I wish you'd been there with me. How was your visit with the seniors?"

"It was fine," Natalie said. "Mae, my favourite grandma, has a cold and was feeling kind of low. I think my visit and the romance story cheered her up. I'm glad I went. Today I brought my car so we could take a picnic to the conservation area and do the trail."

"A good long walk is a great idea," Charlie replied. "I miss my workouts at the gym, so some exercise would be welcome."

"Couldn't you get Tom or Paul to go with you to the gym?" Natalie asked.

"I thought of that, but the exercises take a few hours," Charlie replied. "I don't know about Tom, but I know Paul always seems to have plenty to do. I think Ilene keeps him hopping."

After Natalie had prepared some lunch for them, they set off.

"Hiking in this park was my favourite time with my father," she told him as they drove along. "He was relaxed and I was not on the hot seat to remember the name of the second baseman, or the goalie of the Buffalo Sabers. I could just be myself."

Charlie chatted about his own childhood. "We always lived in the same house, and on the street there were a lot of families with kids my age. We played all kinds of games and annoyed the neighbours, especially those who didn't have children, and generally had a good time in the summer. In the winter, Paul and I were allowed to bring our friends home and we played board games in the basement. My mother would bring us Cool Aid, but I think it was just her way of checking on us without appearing to do so. I don't think she ever guessed that we'd figured that out."

"You had such a happy childhood," Natalie said. "I was so isolated. I didn't know it at the time, but looking back I realize that I rarely played with other kids. My mother was very protective. I envy you."

"Well, maybe you didn't have my kind of childhood," Charlie said. "But you certainly seem to be very self-assured and confident. You know what you want, and how you're going to get there. That's more than I do."

"You're partially right. I did grow up being self-reliant, but knowing what I want to do is a recent thing," she said. "I only decided a few months ago."

They reached the conservation area and Natalie parked the car.

"There aren't many cars in the parking lot," she observed. "Probably because it's only June and the kids are still in school. We'll do the walk first and have our lunch when we get back."

They joined hands and walked down the trail. The leaf canopy overhead made the path cool and comfortably shaded. Natalie made the trail come alive with descriptions of the surroundings, birds, chipmunks, squirrels and even the occasional rabbit. She also talked about the different kinds of flowers and plants.

"Wow, Natalie, your descriptions are really making this walk enjoyable for me," said Charlie.

"Let's stop here and let the sun warm us up," Natalie suggested when they entered a clearing.

"Good idea," he agreed and drew Natalie to him, kissing her warmly on the mouth.

She willingly responded to his embrace and they stood, locked together for some time.

"I want you," Charlie said huskily.

"Not here, we're not alone."

To prove her right, just then another couple came walking down the trail.

"Good afternoon," the woman said. "Doesn't the sun feel good after the shady trail?"

"Yes, it certainly does," Natalie responded, blushing a little, afraid they had been caught in their embrace.

The couple continued their walk and Natalie and Charlie laughed. She took his hand and they continued on. Forty minutes later, they came back to the parking lot, not having encountered any other walkers.

"Lunch time," Natalie announced.

They sat at a picnic table in the sun and enjoyed their lunch after the exercise.

Back at the apartment Natalie said, "I should do some cleaning."

"Forget the cleaning," Charlie said, reaching for her. "Come and amuse me."

She protested weakly, but Charlie scooped her up in his arms and carried her into the bedroom, almost banging her head on the door frame.

"Hey, watch it!" she yelped. "You almost killed me."

"Sorry," he replied. "But that's what you get for trusting a blind man."

When he bumped into the bed, he set her down on it and cupped her breasts in his hands. He drew his thumbs across her nipples and they responded to his touch.

"Are you certain, you want to clean house?" he teased, as he began unbuttoning her blouse.

"Charlie, you are insatiable, and incorrigible," Natalie scolded him, laughing.

"Isn't that what you love about me?" he teased.

She sighed. "Oh, Charlie, I love everything about you."

Soon they were both naked, exploring each other hungrily with hands and lips. Never had she expected to feel so alive and happy. None of her romance stories had prepared her for the reality that was Charlie. She didn't know how she was ever going to be able to leave him. She just knew one day she would have to. Again she cursed that ugly purple birthmark that had defined her whole life.

Charlie fell back onto the bed and brought Natalie down on top of him. His hands roamed over her body, awakening wonderful sensations in her. She had never imagined there were so many sensitive, sexy places on her body.

"Oh, Charlie," she whispered. "I'm so happy I found you. Being with you like this is a prelude to heaven!"

She stroked his face, slowly moving down his body until she reached his groin. There she kissed and nuzzled and squeezed his penis until Charlie groaned.

"Natalie, stop, before I lose my mind," he gasped.

She only laughed and continued until Charlie picked her up, threw her back onto the mattress and straddled her. He sheathed himself and proceeded to tease her. Stroking, kissing, sucking and nuzzling her, just as she had done.

Before long she was begging him to finish. "Please Charlie, I can't wait, come inside me."

He laughed with joy at her capitulation. Entering her, they moved together as one.

Afterwards they lay, exhausted, momentarily sated, and altogether at peace. The late afternoon sun stole into the bedroom and kissed Natalie's shoulder. Realizing how late it was she got up and dressed.

"Don't go," Charlie wheedled. "Let's just stay here for the rest of our lives."

"That's a grand notion, but soon you'd get tired of

living on love and then what would we do?"

Reluctantly Charlie got up and dressed. "Are you staying tonight?" he asked.

"Yes, that was my plan," Natalie said. "If you have no objections."

"Objections? Let me see now . . ." he said, laughing. "You know damn well I don't. As a matter of fact I'd love you to move in with me."

"No, Charlie," she said. "I have my own place and there's a lot I want to do before I could possibly consider any serious relationship."

"I knew you'd say something like that," he grumbled.

"Don't pout, it doesn't suit you," she riposted. "I've never told you anything different. Soon you'll get your sight back and pick up your old life. I don't fit into that lifestyle. You need someone like Amy who understood and knew how to live your way. We're very different, you and I."

"Stop throwing Amy in my face," he cried angrily. "Amy was a lifetime ago. And as far as my kind of life goes, you don't know anything about it, so don't tell me you wouldn't fit in. But you're convinced we're incompatible despite how well we get on together, so let's just leave it there. I don't want to fight with you."

Natalie went over to Charlie and kissed him softly on the cheek. "I don't want to fight either, so let's not talk about it anymore."

She set about getting dinner ready. "Tonight we're having scalloped potatoes, roast lamb, baby beets and asparagus. The potatoes take a long time, so I have to get them in the oven soon."

"I love scalloped potatoes," Charlie said. "Can I help you with anything?"

"Sure, you can peel the potatoes," Natalie said. "But first, go and put some music on. Maybe one of your female vocals?"

Soon she heard Bette Midler singing "Wind Beneath My Wings". "Good choice," she called. "I love that song."

She busied herself getting the dinner ready. She would have to be careful, because obviously she was giving him the wrong signals. In a couple of months she'd be leaving him to go to school and she didn't want him to get depressed and start drinking again. Hopefully he would get his vision back soon, and then he wouldn't need her.

"Dinner in about twenty minutes," she announced.

"It certainly smells good," Charlie said. "I didn't think I was all that hungry, but smelling the potatoes and the lamb has me salivating."

In the kitchen she set the table. "Would you like a glass of white wine?" she called.

"That would be wonderful, as long as you join me," he replied.

"Yes, I'm not driving, so a glass of wine will be very

nice."

She served Charlie and told him where everything was on his plate.

"This is just like Sunday dinner when I was a kid," he said. "Without the wine, of course."

"Our Sunday dinner was generally roast chicken," Natalie said. "Next day my mother would make my dad's favourite lunch, chicken sandwiches. I got kind of tired of chicken, so I rarely cook it now."

"We mostly had beef in our house. I don't know who didn't like chicken, but we hardly ever had it. What I really enjoyed most was when my dad barbequed. Then we had hot dogs, hamburgers and ribs. But that was only in the summer. In the winter my mother did all the cooking and she never made those things. Her big thing was soups and casseroles."

"I thought perhaps after dinner we could go to the park for a while," Natalie suggested. "It's still early and the air is still warm. It'll be fun to watch the kids playing."

"Sure beats sitting around watching TV," Charlie agreed.

When the dishes were put away, they headed for the park. She let him take the lead and was happy to see that his movements were so confident. It was almost as if he could see. She knew he would do fine on his own.

On the street, Charlie reached for her hand and

they walked slowly along, enjoying the evening breeze.

"I've never walked so much in the past few years. Having a vehicle makes you lazy," he said. "Having someone to walk with of course helps. You told me that you do a lot of walking. Do you walk by yourself?"

"Pretty much," she answered. "I often see the same people walking and occasionally I walk with some of them. But the problem is that you have to walk at their pace instead of your own. There was one lady who often walked at the same time I did, and she was a great talker. But all she did was complain about her kids or her husband. It depressed me, so I changed my route to avoid her. Now I mostly keep to myself."

They soon reached the park, and could hear the kids shrieking and laughing. The wading pool was open and many kids were splashing and running through the water. Natalie described the scene to Charlie.

"So, do you want to sit near the kids, or should we find a quieter spot?" she asked.

"Let's sit near the kids. It reminds me of my summers growing up. I never realized it till now, but I'm looking forward to being an uncle and taking Paul's kid skating and to ball games and other fun stuff."

Natalie laughed, "It'll be a few years before any of those things can happen. Are you planning on babysitting and changing diapers?"

Charlie laughed. "Sure, why not? How bad can it

be? Of course, Ilene may not trust me alone with her baby."

"Why wouldn't she trust you?" she asked.

"No special reason. I just think she sees me as being a bit irresponsible because every time I see her, I have a different girlfriend. And of course, I go to the pub with the guys, at least once a week. I'm very different from Paul. He's always been more serious and focused on the future. That's what Ilene likes, but hasn't seen it in me."

"But you're younger than Paul, and have no ties, so why wouldn't you be more carefree?"

"Oh, she doesn't have a problem with my lifestyle. I just don't think she would trust me with her baby."

The air cooled as the sun sank in the western sky. The noise of the children's playing diminished as the parents began to take their charges home.

"How about three times around the park, and then home?" Charlie suggested.

"Good plan," Natalie said. "I'm starting to get cold."

They walked briskly around the perimeter. On their third circuit, Natalie noticed that several of the benches were occupied by men stretched out with raggedy old blankets over them.

"I didn't realize there were street people in this neighbourhood," she said.

"What street people?" Charlie asked. "Why do you say that?"

She told him about the men lying on the benches.

"I didn't know that. I never come here at night and when I used to run in the morning, I never saw anyone sleeping on the benches. It must be a very hard life, particularly in the winter."

"Yes," she agreed. "It makes you feel very fortunate to have a roof over your head and a comfortable bed."

They headed back to the apartment with Charlie taking the lead and deciding when it was safe to cross the road.

"You're doing so well, you really don't need me anymore," Natalie commented."

"I need you to keep me sane," Charlie said "I just can't go back to being by myself all the time."

"There are lots of programs available for folks with disabilities," she said. "And people to help them out."

"You sound just like Paul. He keeps telling me that I should fly solo. But you're leaving in a couple of months anyway, so if I don't have my vision by then, I'll look into all those things. But for now, I just want to continue with you as my guide. Is that a problem for you?

"Not at all. I enjoy our times together, and you're right, it is only a couple more months."

Natalie was happy that Charlie seemed to be accepting the idea that she would be moving on. That would make it so much easier when she left—even though what she really wanted was to stay.

It was too early to go to bed, so she suggested she could read to him some of the personal ads in her romance magazine. She knew Charlie found them amusing and they generally sparked a good debate between them.

"There's still some wine left. Would you like a glass?" Natalie asked. "I'm having some."

"I'd prefer a beer," he said.

She got the drinks and then began reading the personal columns in the magazine. Soon she and Charlie were in a heated discussion about the sincerity of one of the writers. He claimed the ad was so sappy it had to have been written by a computer, while she argued that the writer was probably a very sad person looking for love.

"Okay," said Natalie. "Here's what we're going to do. We're each going to compose an ad, as if we wanted to attract someone for a serious relationship."

"Right," Charlie said. "You go first."

"Here's what I would say. 'A serious minded, young woman, seeking a quiet male partner, non-smoker, who enjoys long walks, reading, baseball and 'slow-hand sex', just like the song says. Preferred age between twenty-five and thirty-five. Objective: matrimony.' Your turn."

"I think you're wasting your money with that one. You need more pizzazz to attract a hot-blooded young male. Now, if you wanted an old man, that would be the perfect ad."

"Oh, come on," Natalie said. "If you're so good at this, what would your ad say?"

"'Wanted, attractive female, twenty-eight years old, who likes long walks, reading, baseball and is a good cook. No previous sexual experience necessary, will teach. Objective: fun.'"

"You're not being serious," Natalie rebuked him. "Try again."

"Okay, I was just teasing you," Charlie admitted. "Here's what my ad would say. 'Good-looking young male desires a relationship with a witty, sports-loving, beer-drinking woman who enjoys sex. Preferred age: between twenty-five and thirty-five. Objective: fun.' Is that better?"

Natalie sighed. "Well, I guess that might attract some women. If we were hoping to meet each other this way, we never would. We're obviously very different."

Charlie frowned. "You keep saying that but I'm not so sure. We seem to be doing just fine."

"Perhaps, but what about when you get your vision back? Then you'll not be so happy with long walks and a quiet life."

"You don't know that for sure," he said. "If I had the right person to stay home with, I might find it more satisfying. Besides, you've never tried my kind of life, so don't knock it until you do."

"You're right," she said. "I've never spent any time

in social situations. Maybe I'd like it more than I imagine I would."

"Come with me next Tuesday and meet the guys," Charlie urged. "I'm sure you'd enjoy yourself."

"Tuesday is one of my senior nights. I don't like to miss them because the folks look forward to my visits so much."

"We could go some other night," Charlie persisted. "I'm sure Tom and the guys would love to meet you."

"No, Charlie, that isn't going to happen."

"I wish I understood you. I have only known you for a little time and you seem to be a very caring, well-adjusted, happy person, but for reasons I don't understand you're afraid of people."

"I'm not afraid of people, but as I told you before, I don't fit in, so it's easier to not put myself in situations where people may reject me."

"I think you're paranoid. For some reason I don't know, you avoided other kids at school and then you quit to take care of your parents, further avoiding people. I think you're selling yourself short. It's time to get over whatever it was with the other kids, and give people a chance to get to know you."

"Charlie, I don't want to fight. I just want to enjoy what we have," Natalie said and patted his knee. "It's getting late, do you want to watch TV?"

"No, I'd rather go to bed and explore other options."

Natalie smiled and headed for the bathroom. "I'll meet you there as soon as I brush my teeth."

Chapter Ten

They spent another glorious night together, learning each other's touch and movements, what excited and what did not. They whispered and giggled as they tried different positions and postures. It was early morning before they fell asleep, entwined around each other.

Natalie awoke first, moved her cramped body and burrowed more deeply into Charlie.

This awakened him and he leaned down and kissed her gently on the mouth. "Good morning, my little Aphrodite," he murmured. "How are you feeling this morning?"

"I'm feeling like a very contented kitten. But it's not morning, it's already afternoon. I don't know about you, but I'm starving. What would you like to eat?"

"Are you sure breakfast is all you're hungry for?

"Yes, you sex maniac! I'm heading for the shower and then I'll see what's there for us to eat.

After her shower, Natalie opened the fridge and viewed the available options. As she hadn't shopped for a few days, there wasn't much that appealed to her. She went to the bathroom door and told Charlie that they would be going out to eat.

Charlie emerged from the bedroom, dressed in jeans and a light blue polo shirt. As always, Natalie found him looking good enough to eat.

"Shall we go to the mom and pop place that you like?" she asked.

"Sure, they do a good meal. But before we go, I have to ask you a favour." Blushing to the roots of his hair, he explained. "I need to replace my stock of condoms, and since you wouldn't want me to ask Tom or Paul, you are the only one I can ask."

Natalie laughed. "You don't have to be embarrassed. I have no problem purchasing something like that. I used to be a cashier and I can promise you they don't pay any attention to what people buy."

"There's a drug store half a block from the café so we can get them after we eat."

The sun was already high in the sky, the day was bright and warm, and the world was a happy place.

When they arrived at the café, Natalie found an empty booth, got Charlie seated, and placed their order.

When Hannah delivered their meals she said, "So Charlie, I see you have brought your pretty girlfriend again." She turned to Natalie. "You better watch out for this one. He's a real Casanova."

Natalie laughed and responded, "I rather suspected that."

Charlie broke in. "I hope you two are finished maligning my character."

Hannah laughed. "Enjoy your meals," she said and left.

"So, what would you like to do today?" Natalie asked, taking a sip of her coffee.

"It seems like such a nice day," he said. "Let's go to the beach."

"I don't have my car here, but I guess we could take the bus."

"We could take my car. It's been parked in the basement since the accident. It would be good to take it for a spin and get the cobwebs out."

"Are you sure it's okay? It wasn't damaged in the accident, was it?"

"No. Paul drove it back from the police impound lot and said everything was working fine."

They finished their breakfast and Natalie paid the bill.

After purchasing the condoms at the drug store they returned to the apartment.

Gathering the beach towels and some drinks, Natalie asked, "Where are your car keys?"

"They should be in the night table drawer," Charlie

told her.

She went to look and came back with a large ring of keys. "Are they part of this mess?" she asked.

"Yes, it's the one with the fob attached."

In the parking area Charlie said, "My car is halfway down on the right. It's a black GMC and the licence is 'WIRED 1'."

"'WIRED 1'? What's that about?"

"Tom and I got those licence plates when we became electricians. Tom's is 'WIRED'."

"That's cute!" Natalie exclaimed.

She opened the car door for Charlie. He got in and commented that the air was pretty stale.

"As soon as we get outside I'll open the windows," she said.

She turned on the engine and surveyed the dashboard. "First thing we have to do is get gas. Your gas gauge is almost on empty. Is there anything about the car I should know?"

"No, I keep it tuned up and in good repair. The steering and brakes are fine and everything else is monitored on the car's computer."

"Okay. How do we get out?"

"Back the way we came, past the elevator and up the ramp. You have to stop at the top to give the garage door time to open."

Natalie followed his instructions and they were soon outside. She opened all the windows and let the fresh breeze blow around them.

After filling up the gas tank they headed for the beach. There she parked the car and they walked toward the water.

"Let's wade in the water, like last time," Natalie suggested.

"Sure, that was fun," Charlie said. "The water must be a few degrees warmer by now."

They removed their shoes and rolled up their pant legs. She took his hand and walked him into the lake.

"It doesn't feel much warmer to me," Natalie observed.

"You're right. I think the lake probably doesn't really warm up until mid-July."

They strolled along, hand-in-hand, enjoying the sun and cool water on their feet. Natalie chatted about the other people on the beach.

"I'm always amazed at how many people are around on week day afternoons," she observed. "I have it in my head that the rest of the world works during the day, but obviously not everyone does."

When her feet started to feel cold, Natalie drew Charlie to a bench in the sun and gave him a towel.

"Why are all those people shouting and laughing?" he asked.

"It's a beach volleyball game," she explained. "Did you ever play?"

"Not on the beach, only in high school. I had a

pretty mean serve, but always hit the ball too hard when I was on the court. Consequently I was always one of the last to be chosen for a team," Charlie replied, chuckling.

"What were you good at?" Natalie asked.

"I was pretty good at basketball and field hockey. And I was captain of the school baseball team in my final year of high school. The team did pretty good and we made it to the semi-finals, the best showing for the school of all their teams that year. I liked sports but wasn't great at the more intellectual stuff, like the debating team and the chess club. I guess I'm not much of a thinker."

Natalie laughed and patted his shoulder. "Oh, Charlie, you're doing okay," she said. "I wouldn't worry about it."

They spent a pleasant afternoon soaking up the sun, strolling on the boardwalk and enjoying being together. All too soon it was time to go.

"I'll stop on the way back and pick up some fish for dinner," Natalie said.

"Are you staying tonight?" Charlie asked, hope in his voice.

"No, it's seniors' night so I have to get going. I'm already running late."

Natalie ran into the store for the fish and was soon back in the car.

"Wow! That didn't take long at all," Charlie said.

"What fish are we having for dinner?"

"Salmon," Natalie replied. "With salad and chard."

She discovered that parking in the cramped underground space was a real challenge, but she didn't want Charlie to know that, so she kept up a constant chatter.

"That was excellently done," Charlie complimented her. "I usually have to take a few passes at it myself."

"Beginners luck!" she said and laughed.

After dinner Natalie had to run. "Don't forget I'm shopping in the morning, so I'll be a bit late," she said and kissed him goodnight.

The next day Natalie arrived, carrying bags of groceries. She was surprised to find the kitchen counter full of empty beer cans and the remains of chips and pretzels. Charlie was nowhere to be seen. She put the bags down and went to the bedroom. Sure enough, Charlie was stretched out on the bed, snoring.

What on earth had gone on here after she left? She prayed that Charlie had not had a relapse into depression. While she put the groceries away and cleaned up the kitchen all she could think about was Charlie and how easily he could sink back into the alcoholic he had been when she first met him. Her mind was in turmoil. She had been hoping that he was over his dependence on alcohol but now she wasn't so sure. Perhaps he had more of a drinking problem than she had supposed. It wasn't good to jump to conclusions, but the evidence was hard to ignore. Damn! What had gone on here last night? She wanted to wake Charlie to find out but wasn't sure she was ready for the answer.

After scouring the bathroom she moved to the living room. It was obvious there had been a party. Who had been here? How many people? And had there been girls here?

She was surprised to find she was jealous. What right did she have for jealousy? Hadn't she made it clear she wouldn't be around much longer, so if he had contacted an old girlfriend how could she complain? Very easily! Were they not lovers? Couldn't he at least have waited until she was out of the picture?

She was working herself up into a self-righteous rage, and thinking of all the things she would say when he woke up. Soon her anger turned to self-pity and tears filled her eyes. Part of her didn't believe any of the things she was telling herself, and part of her hoped it was true, because that would make it easier for her to leave him. Lord, what a mess!

Stop it! She had to stop thinking about all these things. She was just driving herself crazy. She had to wait until Charlie woke up and told her exactly what had happened. It was probably something very innocent. Probably just Tom and the boys. At least that was what she wanted to believe with all her heart.

She got the vacuum out and began in the hallway.

As she had hoped, the noise woke Charlie.

He stumbled out of the bedroom. "Good morning Natalie," he shouted over the noise.

"Good afternoon, Charlie," she responded angrily.

"I'm sorry for the mess we left," he said. "I intended to clean it up before you got here today, but I guess I didn't."

"I guess you didn't. Get yourself cleaned up. I'll make you some breakfast and you can tell me all about it," she said in a more reasonable tone.

While Charlie showered, Natalie prepared bacon, eggs, toast and coffee.

Soon Charlie joined her in the kitchen. "Thanks for making breakfast," he said. "I'm starving."

Natalie gave him time to eat before asking, "So who came over last night?"

"After you left, Tom called and wanted to bring Sara over so I could meet her. They arrived with a case of beer and some snacks. Sara was driving so she only had one beer, but Tom and I split the rest. That's why I didn't get around to cleaning up. I had six beers and it knocked me on my ass."

Relief flooded through her. It was what her rational mind told her had happened. What an idiot she was!

"So what's Sara like?" she asked.

"She's great! I think I told you she's an electrician like Tom and me, only she went further and did the management courses at college. She's very smart. I know Tom's in love with her and I hope she feels the same way about him. We had a lot of fun comparing war stories and generally shooting the shit. They didn't leave till three or four this morning. Tom and Sara must be taking the day off, for sure, because Tom won't be in any shape to work."

"You must have a hangover, too," Natalie said.

"Surprisingly, I don't. I took a couple of aspirins last night and maybe that's why."

"Let me finish vacuuming and then we can go to the park," she said.

When they were still half a block away they could hear the shrieks and laughter of the children.

"It sounds like there are a lot of kids out today," Charlie observed.

"It's because it's almost four o'clock and a lot of school kids are there."

"Oh wow! I didn't realize it was that late."

"So, a few brisk laps around the perimeter?" Natalie suggested.

"Sounds good to me."

While they were walking, Natalie said, "When I arrived today and saw all the empty beer cans, I was afraid you had relapsed into depression."

"For goodness sakes, have some faith in me!" Charlie admonished her. "I told you I was over that. Whatever happens now, I'll be able to deal with it. With your help I've regained my pride and my desire to live."

Natalie was pleased to hear the confidence in his voice. She was also happy to know she had played a part in his recovery. "It's good you're so strong now. I was an idiot to have doubted you."

"Let's sit on our favourite bench, if it's not in use," Charlie suggested.

At that distance they could still hear the kids in the playground, but the noise was not intrusive.

Charlie started telling her about Tom and Sara, and Jonesy and Katherine. "It is so good to see the guys with girls they really like, are proud of, and want to spend the rest of their lives with. I envy them their confidence that their girls are totally committed to them. I feel like that about you, but you won't let me have that assurance. I wish I could make you change your mind."

"Oh Charlie, Charlie. What can I say? I wish it were possible for life to be the way you want it, but believe me, it's better this way."

Natalie wanted to scream. Every time they had this conversation it was harder for her to keep up the facade. She loved Charlie and wanted to spend the rest of her life with him, but she knew he would hate her when he saw how ugly she was. Just like the other boys had. She felt horrible hurting him because that was the last thing she wanted to do. Maybe she should end it now. Why wait?

"Let's not talk about it anymore," she said. "Tomorrow is Saturday and you'll see Paul. Will you go there for dinner on Sunday?"

"If he invites me, I'll go, if not I'll make my own dinner, I guess. What are you doing on the weekend?"

"Nothing too exciting. I haven't spent much time on my place for a while, so I'll put some effort into cleaning it. Also, there's going to be a birthday party at the seniors' residence and I promised Mae I'd go."

"You spend a lot of time at that place," Charlie grumbled.

"Not that much, really. But since my parents died I get a lot of enjoyment from talking to some of the people there. There's a lot of sad cases which are hard to accept, but that's life. They are my surrogate grandparents, the ones I never had growing up. When you get your vision back, maybe you could visit there. You never had grandparents either, so you may enjoy it."

"I'll keep that in mind," Charlie said.

"As you had such a big breakfast a couple of hours ago, you won't be wanting dinner for a while. I'll stay and make you dinner a bit later when you're hungry."

"Will you stay the night?" he asked.

"No, not on a Friday. You know that. But I don't have to rush off at five o'clock either."

They sat in silence for a while and then Natalie spoke. "Losing your sight has been a very traumatic experience for you. Do you think it has changed you or what you want for the future?"

"I don't know. It has certainly made me more un- derstanding of people's limitations. I never thought much about the kinds of problems disabled people face daily, but now I know how much courage it takes to get up every day when you believe there's nothing much to get up for. That's what I learned when I stopped drinking. But I was lucky because I had you to help me. A lot of people don't have anybody. It also made me realize that life doesn't always move in a straight line. There are many curves and sometimes there's no line at all, but we're here and must adapt. If we don't, there is only the abyss."

"That's pretty philosophical," Natalie remarked. "I've not seen that side of you before."

"I don't know about philosophy," Charlie said. "I just know that's what I've learned."

"It's too bad it sometimes takes a major event to give us these insights. But it's starting to get cool," she said, shivering. "Let's go back to your apartment."

As they walked, Natalie chatted easily, happy to be talking about anything except their relationship. "Next week will be the summer solstice, a big night for witches and druids," she said. "Feel like dancing under the moon?"

Charlie chuckled. "Sounds like fun to me!"

Before Natalie had closed the door of the apartment, Charlie whisked her up into his arms and said, "You be the witch and I'll be the druid."

He carried her into the bedroom, dropped her on the bed and began stripping off his clothes.

Natalie watched him. "Aren't you afraid I'll cast a spell on you, Mister Druid?" she asked.

"You already have, you saucy witch!"

Just as Charlie reached for her, she rolled to the other side of the bed. "If you want to bed this witch, you're going to have to catch her."

"Hey, it's not nice to take advantage of a blind guy," he grumbled.

Natalie slipped quietly out of the bedroom, leaving Charlie groping for her on the bed. She went into the living room and found his Sinatra album. She put it on and then slipped into the kitchen.

Charlie came out of the bedroom, rushed into the living room and barked his shin on the coffee table. "Damn! You'll pay for this when I catch you."

"That's what I'm hoping," Natalie said, giggling. "But first you have to catch me."

As Charlie headed to the kitchen, Natalie snuck by him and went back into the bedroom. There she removed her clothes. "I'm waiting for my punishment," she called.

Charlie went back into the bedroom, holding his arms out so she couldn't sneak past him again. "Okay you giggling little witch, here I come."

"So, Mister Druid, what is my punishment?"

"Just this," he said, and sat on the edge of the bed.

He reached for her and was surprised at her nudity. "Ah, my little witch, you're naked already! You have beaten me to the punch."

He joined her in bed and she immediately began to devour him with her mouth. She kissed his eyes, his ears, his face and finally his lips. She drew his tongue into her mouth and Charlie lay back, succumbing totally to her caresses. She stroked his torso, slowly moving her hand down to his groin. There she teased and tickled him, grasping his erect penis and stroking it with her thumb.

Charlie moaned and writhed, moving with her strokes. Just when he thought he would explode he gasped, "Natalie! I'm going to—"

Natalie rolled a condom down his shaft and straddled him, joining in his passion.

"You truly have bewitched me," he said. "Being with you makes me believe anything is possible."

"Hush. Let's just enjoy the moment. But I do have to say, Mister Druid, that was a strange kind of punishment."

"Next time, look out," Charlie warned.

Natalie laughed. "I'm already quaking in my boots. But to give you back your energy, I'll make us some dinner now."

Charlie got dressed and joined her in the kitchen. "What are we having?"

"Tonight it's simple—tortellini with an oil and garlic

sauce."

After dinner, Natalie said, "I have to go now. Have fun with Paul tomorrow. Give one of the guys a call and do something on Saturday. If Tom and Jonesy are busy with their ladies, maybe Vic could go with you to the pub, or something."

"Good idea. But I'm already looking forward to Monday."

Charlie closed the door slowly after her, thinking how good Natalie made him feel. He loved her so much! Why couldn't she just tell him she loved him? Because she did, he was convinced of that. He was sure she wasn't faking when they were making love. She was much too ardent and willing a partner. Was it something about him? Wasn't he good enough for her? No, he never sensed even the slightest sign of anything like that. It was clearly something about herself that was the problem. Those rapes so many years ago—could that be it? No, she definitely seemed to be over that hurdle. He wished he could talk it over with Paul, who at least had met her. Maybe his brother could shed light on her problem. Well, for sure he wouldn't be able to figure it out on his own.

He went into the living room and put on his Boz Scaggs album. Collapsing into his easy chair, he gave himself over to the music.

Saturday morning, as always, Paul arrived with

breakfast. "How goes it, brother?" he asked.

"Just great! Everyday I feel more positive and convinced that I'll get my sight back. Natalie's been so helpful. She never lets me feel sorry for myself. Speaking of Natalie, what's your opinion of her?"

"I haven't talked to her for quite a while now," Paul said. "But she always seemed like a capable, compassionate person. Why do you ask? Is there a problem?"

"Not really," Charlie mused. "It's just that we spend so much time together it's natural to wonder about her. You know, is she pretty? Is she sexy? Those kinds of things."

"Oh, I see. Well, I guess I'd say she's cute, rather than pretty, and although she's not my type, I'd say she's sexy. Is that what you wanted to know?"

"Yeah, I guess so. But how's Ilene, now that it's so close to the due date?"

"Ilene's fine, although she finds it annoying to have to go to the washroom so often. She's still working, but the added weight makes her more tired than usual. The baby is very active sometimes, and although it's hard to believe, that kid can pack a pretty good wallop. You can actually see Ilene's stomach move!"

"Why don't I take you guys out for dinner on Sunday?" Charlie suggested.

"Thanks for the offer, bro, but Sunday is Father's Day and Ilene has invited her parents for a barbeque. Why don't you join us? I'll pick you up about four o'-

clock."

"I'd rather not intrude on a family gathering," Charlie said.

"Nonsense, if you're not family, I don't know who is. It's settled, I'll pick you up on Sunday."

The brothers began reminiscing about past Father's Days when their own father had been alive. They laughed when Charlie mentioned how Mom had insisted on cooking every Father's Day, and so the steaks were always overdone. The breakfasts they had made when they were little kids—what a mess some of them had been! But Mom and Dad had bravely eaten everything, and had complimented them on their effort.

"I really miss Dad now that I am about to become a dad myself," Paul said.

"Yeah, I miss them both and the great times we had as a family, even though you were such a prig at times."

"I wasn't a prig. I was just trying to keep you from being an idiot."

Charlie laughed. "Have it your way. I still say prig."

Paul laughed too. "I have to get going. Ilene and I are going to St. Jacob's Market to get the stuff for the barbeque tomorrow. I'll pick you up at four."

Chapter Eleven

After Paul left, Charlie thought he would enjoy some time in the park. It would be good to get some fresh air. But could he do it on his own? Well, only one way to find out. He grabbed his keys and white cane and, locking the door behind him, he went out.

Outside, he walked forward from the apartment door, until he touched the lamp post with his cane. Oops! Too far. He needed to slow down and concentrate. Going a little slower than usual he made it to the intersection. As Natalie had instructed, he stopped to listen for the traffic sounds. When he heard the cars moving forward on his left he tentatively stepped off the curb and walked forward. Not hearing brakes squeal or horns blast, he knew he was okay. If Natalie could see him now she would be so proud of him.

He soon reached the park. There were lots of kids about, he could tell by the noise level. He cautiously tapped his cane until he found the path to the other side of the park. There he used his cane until he felt the bench.

"Anybody here?" he spoke out.

Getting no response he turned and sat down.

His thoughts turned to Natalie. He was on cloud nine and didn't want to come down. If only he could pull Natalie up there with him life would be perfect. But she was determined to leave. How would he fill the hole in his heart where she had taken up residence?

Damn! He wished he'd never met her. No, that wasn't true. She was wonderful and had helped him so much. He was just going to have to convince her to stay. He still had a couple of months and felt confident he could do that. After all, no girl had ever ended a relationship with him.

He considered what Paul had said about her. There was nothing there that gave him any clues to the mystery that was Natalie. If he understood it, he could try to fight it. If only she hadn't made him promise to keep their relationship secret, he could ask Paul more direct questions.

He sighed.

As he continued to relax in the sun and listen to the children's voices, his mind turned toward the future. If he got his sight back, his life would be more or less normal again. But if his vision didn't come back, what then? How would he earn a living? How would he take care of himself? Without Natalie, how would he shop, cook, do laundry, find his way around, and amuse himself? It didn't bear thinking about. He had to convince her to stay!

Time to head home and see if anyone was going to the pub tonight.

Charlie got up and found the path to the street. He followed it to the corner where he could hear children talking with their father. When he sensed that they were crossing the road, he stepped out and crossed with them.

Good. That was the first hurdle. He walked the block to the major intersection and listened for the traffic sounds. While he was getting his bearings, a man's voice beside him asked if he needed help.

"Yes, that's very kind of you," Charlie replied. "If you could just tell me when it is safe to cross, that would be great."

Charlie made his way home, using the mail box and lamp post as guides to find his front door. He congratulated himself on his first solo excursion.

He called Tom and found out that he and Jonesy had tickets for a Blue Jays game but Vic wasn't going with them.

"Enjoy the game," Charlie said. "I'll give Vic a call and see what he's up to tonight."

He dialled Vic's number. "Hello, Vic. I just wondered if you were wanting any company tonight."

"As a matter of fact, I'm at loose ends tonight," Vic

told him. Why don't I come over, or would you rather go to the pub?"

"It would be really great to get out. I spend far too much time in this place."

"Okay, I'll pick you up about seven."

On the way to the pub Charlie heard all about Vic's new job. Charlie was surprised to hear that so far, Vic was still enjoying the work, and still not complaining about his boss. Charlie filled Vic in on his daily routines, not giving any details about Natalie except that she was helpful and was getting him out and teaching him how to cope. Vic, unlike Tom, wasn't suspicious about Charlie's relationship with Natalie.

Charlie was on his third beer when Vic said, "Don't look now but here comes Brenda."

A strong smell of perfume invaded Charlie's nostrils.

"Well, look what the cat dragged in!" Brenda shrieked, sitting down beside Charlie. "Where have you been hiding out? I thought you had died or something. I tried calling you a few times, but you never called back. What the hell happened?

"Brenda, I'm sorry, but I've been out of commission," he said. "I'm just beginning to get back to normal. I'm sorry I broke our date and didn't call you. I just wasn't able to."

"Why couldn't you? I know we'd only had a couple of dates, but we seemed to be getting along so well. I felt so let down," Brenda said, pouting. "I didn't know what I had done wrong."

"It wasn't you," Charlie protested. "You didn't do anything wrong."

"So why did you leave me hanging?" Brenda sounded hurt. "I'm a big girl, so if you didn't want to see me, you could have just told me. You didn't have to hide out."

"No, it's not like that," he said. "I was in a car accident and it left me stressed out. I didn't see anyone or talk to anyone for months. It was nothing personal against you."

"So, if it wasn't me, and you're getting back to normal, how about dinner on Friday night?" Brenda proposed.

Charlie groaned inwardly. He didn't need this complication right now. "I can't!" he exclaimed.

"You really are a piece of work, Charlie Weaver!" Brenda spat out, got up and left.

"Well, that went well, don't you think?" Charlie commented wryly.

"Yeah, she's one angry lady," Vic said with a chuckle. "I hope for your sake she isn't one of those crazy broads that play revenge games."

"Me too. Anyway, that puts the capper on the evening for me. Let's get out of here, if you don't mind."

"No, I'm good," Vic agreed.

Charlie stood up and Vic guided him through the tables toward the exit. Suddenly Charlie felt his hand being grabbed. It was Brenda.

"Oh, Charlie!" she cried. "I didn't know you were blind. Please forgive me for not understanding. Can I help you with anything?"

Charlie patted her hand. "No need to apologize. You couldn't possibly have known I was blind. Thank you for your offer, but I have all the help I need."

When they got into Vic's car, Charlie said, "Maybe she won't be so angry now."

"Yeah, I hope so, for your sake," Vic said.

Weeks flew by. Natalie stayed over a couple of nights every week. Charlie went to the pub on Tuesdays with the guys and saw Paul on Saturdays. He loved the carefree, easy days and the wonderful nights of love, companionship, and learning about Natalie. He wished life could go on like that forever—but with his vision intact, of course.

One morning Charlie woke up and checked the time on his talking watch. "The time is eight ten a.m." He rolled over and got out of bed. Wondering what kind of day it was, he looked toward the window and was surprised that it seemed lighter than the rest of the room. He shook his head, rubbed his eyes and looked again. Definitely it was a little lighter at the window. He walked out to the living room and looked toward the picture window. It, too, seemed lighter than the rest of the room.

He went into the bathroom, not bothering to turn on the light, but then, thinking about the windows, he changed his mind. He flipped the switch and was astonished to realize that the room was brighter! He went into the kitchen and turned on the light. Yes, indeed, it was brighter, too! His world was not totally dark grey anymore. There were patches of lighter grey!

Oh God! Was he getting his sight back? He was so excited, he went around the apartment turning on lights just to see his world become a little brighter. He went to the window and looked out. He still couldn't see anything, but the world was definitely brighter than before. His heart was pounding! He wanted to shout out to the whole world that he could see light. He wanted to sing and dance and most of all he wanted to tell Natalie. Oh, what a glorious day!

Quickly he got ready for the day. In his excitement he cut himself shaving. He swore softly and slowed down, finishing his ablutions without further incident.

What time was it? How long before Natalie would arrive? He checked his watch again. "The time is nine forty-eight a.m." He sat down in the kitchen to wait.

Natalie arrived five minutes later. "Hey Charlie, what's going on? Why are all the lights on?"

"My vision is coming back!" Charlie whooped from the kitchen. "I can see light."

Natalie ran to him and threw her arms around him. "Oh Charlie," she carolled. "That's the best news I've ever had. I'm so happy for you! We must celebrate. What would you like to do today?"

"I don't know," Charlie said. "I still can't see anything but it must be a good sign, don't you think?"

"Of course it's a good sign. Have you told Paul?" Natalie asked. "I know he'll be as happy for you as I am."

"No, I wanted you to be the first," he said, groping for her hand. "I'll give Paul a call after breakfast. Have you eaten yet?"

Natalie squeezed his hand. "I just had some orange juice, so I could eat something. Do you want to go to your favourite café?"

Charlie laughed. "That would be great and then Hannah can tell you again what a Casanova I am."

"Well, if you're ready, let's go, and you can think about what you would like to do to celebrate."

On the way to the café Charlie turned his head this way and that, testing his new-found light-vision.

"I feel like a tourist. I'm like a kid with a new toy," he crowed. "I can't help looking around to make sure the light I see doesn't go away. Pretty stupid, huh?"

"Stupid? Not at all," Natalie said. "For months you've seen only darkness so why wouldn't you want to check out the light, now that you can see it. You'll get used to it soon. And I'm sure it'll keep improving."

At the café Hannah greeted them with a welcoming smile. Natalie guided Charlie to a table and then went to place their orders.

"It's not very busy right now, so breakfast should be here soon," she told him.

"Good," he said, "although I think I'm too excited to eat."

"I'm sure you'll manage. Did your doctor give you any idea about what to expect with your situation?" Natalie asked.

"No, at least nothing I remember. But then again, I was so angry and scared, I didn't really pay much attention to what he was saying."

"Maybe you should go to an ophthalmologist to get a prognosis, given this new development," she suggested.

Just then Hannah delivered their food. "Well Charlie, this must be some kind of record," she exclaimed. "You've never brought the same lady for breakfast so many times before. Do I hear wedding bells?"

Charlie laughed. "Don't be giving this young lady any ideas," he said. "You know I'm a confirmed bachelor, unless of course, you become available."

"Oh Charlie, you're such a tease," Hannah said, blushing. She turned to Natalie. "Didn't I tell you he was a rogue?"

"Yes, Hannah, you did," Natalie said, smiling. "I believed you then and now I see the proof of it. I'll be very careful."

When Hannah left, Natalie turned to Charlie. "So, what do you think you'd like to do to celebrate? And don't say sex, because we'll do that anyway," she added, chuckling. "How about something really exciting like parasailing or zip-lining or parachute jumping?"

"Wow! I never thought of anything like those activities. I think parachute jumping is out, because you can't see when you'll hit the ground. But do you know where could we go for those other things?"

"I saw an ad in the paper for a place in Wasaga Beach that has parasailing. And I bet they have zip-lining too."

"Yeah, parasailing particularly appeals to me. It would be better, of course, if I could see, but I think it would be wonderful to feel like you were flying. Could we really do that?"

"I don't see why not. I'll get a map and see how to get there. I don't think we have enough time today, but we could plan to do it Friday."

"That's way cool. Friday it is."

When Hannah brought their food, the aroma told Charlie he was hungrier than he had thought.

"So for today we'll just go out for a celebratory dinner," Natalie announced.

"Sure, that's good for me. Are you staying tonight?"

"Yes, I am. Where do you want to go for dinner?"

"There's a great steak house on King Street, near Church, called Cyrano's, do you know it?"

"No, I've never heard of it, but if that's where you

want to go, then that's where we'll go," she said. "But I'll have to go home and get some dressier clothes. Everything I have at the apartment is very casual. If I drive your car it won't take me very long. While I'm doing that, you could call Paul and tell him the great news."

"Yeah, I'll do that. But hey, why don't you bring that mini skirt you bought for your birthday," he growled sexily.

Natalie giggled. "Okay, but how do you remember that?"

"That's easy, you were wearing that the first time we made love. I'll never forget it."

"Charlie, you are a romantic," she exclaimed. "I would never have thought that of you."

"There are lots of things about me you don't know. Just hang around for the next forty years and you'll find out."

"On that note I think it's time to leave. I'll just pay the bill.

Back at the apartment Natalie grabbed the car keys. "See you in an hour or so."

Charlie went to the telephone and dialed Paul's number at work. "Paul, it's me, Charlie," he said.

"Charlie?" Paul asked in alarm. "Has anything happened? Are you okay?"

"Relax, it's okay. And yes, something has happened. I woke up this morning and found I could see light!"

Charlie crowed. "Isn't that wonderful? Paul, I'm getting my sight back!"

"That is fantastic news!" Paul whooped. "We have to celebrate. On Sunday I'm picking you up and we're going to spend the day together. What would you like to do?"

"How about a day fishing? I still can't see yet but I'd love to go fishing like we used to do. Ilene is welcome to come if she wants."

"Ilene would be so uncomfortable sitting in a boat in the hot sun. No, it'll be just us," Paul assured him. "We could go to the lake where we fished with Dad. I'm sure the marina still rents boats and fishing gear. It'll be fun. I'll pack us a lunch and pick you up about six so we can get an early start."

"Six? Yikes!" Charlie yelped. "I'm afraid, brother, I've gotten lazy in the past months and don't usually get up till about eight. You'll have to phone me when you wake up so I can be ready for you at six."

"Okay, no problem. Anything else happening?"

"Yes, Natalie's taking me parasailing at Wasaga Beach on Friday to celebrate. Isn't that cool?"

"Yeah. You seem to be getting on very well together. Is there anything to it?"

Charlie blushed and was glad that it was a tele-phone conversation because he was about to lie to Paul, and knew his brother would see it if they were face to face.

"No, there's nothing going on," he lied. "She still plans on going back to school in September. For that reason she hopes my sight is back by then. She just believes that if I'm happy, whatever happened in January will lose its power over me and I'll regain my vision. Who knows, maybe she's right."

"Let's hope she is," Paul replied. "I have to go now, but have fun on Friday, and don't break any bones."

"Don't intend to do that," Charlie said. "And don't forget to wake me up."

Charlie wished he could call Tom and tell him the good news, but he knew his boss discouraged personal calls. And Tom probably wouldn't have his cell phone with him. He'd have to make that call later today. Feeling drowsy he stretched out on the couch and fell asleep.

"Wake up sleepy head," Natalie said kissing him lightly on the lips.

Charlie reached for her, but she stepped quickly back and all he got was an armful of air.

"What time is it?" he asked.

"It's almost three o'clock. Time enough to go to the park before dinner."

Hand in hand they walked along the street, with Charlie still looking around him in all directions.

Natalie laughed. "You're going to wear your neck out if you keep that up."

The park was full of kids. Charlie could hear them from half a block away. Summer holidays were in full swing.

"Do you remember when summer holidays were that much fun?" he asked.

"I guess I never played like that. On the few occasions my mother took me to the park, I always played by myself. I was envious of the kids who had lots of friends, and I watched them. I bet you had lots of friends."

"I guess I had my share. We lived on a cul-de-sac with a lot of other families. There was very little traffic so we played on the road. Our neighbour, Mr. Watts, would turn his sprinkler on and we'd run through it. When I think of how cold the water was, I'm amazed we enjoyed it so much. Ah, the sweet, happy, carefree days of youth."

"If you could go back to your childhood, would you?" Natalie asked.

"In a heartbeat," he said. "To have my mom and dad alive and not have any worries would be wonderful. How about you?"

"Not for one minute," she replied emphatically. "As much as I would love to have my parents alive again, I have no desire to relive my childhood."

Charlie knew her childhood had not been very happy and he wondered if he would ever learn why. The amazing thing was, she was such a fun-loving, cheerful person. He sighed.

"That was a big sigh," Natalie commented. "What are you thinking about?"

"I guess I was just wondering why some kids have such a hard time."

"Lots of different reasons," she said, but her response gave nothing away.

After their usual three times around the perimeter, they sat on their favourite bench and stretched out their legs to the sun. They listened to the shrieks and laughter and even the occasional bout of tears. Charlie found it pleasant to be so close to Natalie and not have to talk.

The sun made him drowsy and he dozed off. He imagined how wonderful it would be to take her places, expand her world, show her how great life could be. He wanted to crack open that shell she lived in.

Natalie was thinking that with Charlie she could have a normal life and not be afraid of rejection. But the only way that could happen was if he never regained his sight. That she could never wish for him! The next few weeks were all they would have. She wanted them to be perfect for Charlie, because she loved him so much. Oh Lord! If only they hadn't fallen in love! Breaking up would kill them both. Why, why, why did life have to be like this?

Gradually the sound of kids' voices died down. Natalie looked at her watch and discovered that it was almost five-thirty. "I guess we should be getting home," she told Charlie.

They walked back to the apartment and Natalie noted that this time he didn't look in all directions. He was obviously getting used to seeing the light.

"Time to get ready," Natalie announced as soon as they were in. "I'll put your blue shirt on the bed—that's my favourite—along with your khakis. The blue matches your eyes, and the khakis look really great on you."

"Okay, and you're going to wear what I asked you to?"

"Yes, that's what I brought."

When they were ready, Natalie checked them out in the mirror and decided that they were a very handsome couple. They left the apartment via the back door and climbed into Charlie's car.

"So, to King and Church?" she asked.

"Yes, it is just east of the King Edward Hotel."

After Natalie had parked the car they walked to the restaurant, and were seated in a cozy alcove at the back of the main dining room. Natalie looked around and was impressed with the décor and the very formal demeanour of the waiter.

"This is a pretty posh place," she commented.

"Yes, it's a typical sixties steak house," Charlie said. "My dad loved this place and always brought us here for my mother's birthday. Since then I only come for very special occasions, like this one. I think the last time I was here was about seven or eight years ago."

"Well, thank you for sharing it with me," she said. "I'm honoured."

She perused the menu and was surprised at the prices. Her frugal upbringing made her wince. "Do you know what you want, or shall I read the menu to you?"

"You know I like steak, but tonight I'm going to celebrate with surf and turf. It's a very special day after all."

The waiter approached and took their drink orders.

"I'm driving so I won't have alcohol," Natalie said.

"Then in that case, I'll just have a glass of Merlot and the lady will have a virgin Caesar."

"What's a virgin Caesar?" Natalie asked after the waiter left.

"It's a drink made with clamato juice and vodka, with celery salt around the rim and Tabasco and horseradish sauces stirred in. But the virgin variety leaves out the vodka. I am sure you'll like it."

When the waiter returned with their drinks, Natalie ordered their dinners. "A sirloin steak, medium rare, with a grilled lobster tail for the gentleman, and I'll have the grilled salmon."

"My goodness," she exclaimed. "This drink is a whole meal in a glass. There is a stalk of celery, a shrimp and cherry tomato on a pick and what looks like a green bean in the glass. Is that how they're always served?"

"Pretty much," Charlie answered. "Every pub and restaurant has their own little twist, but usually there's lots of stuff in it. Do you like the taste?"

Natalie sipped the drink tentatively, not knowing what to expect, but found that the combination of the celery salt on the rim of the glass, with the spicy Clamato juice was both exotic and yummy. "This is excellent," she said. "I think it'll become my favourite drink."

The restaurant was not crowded. There were only three other couples. Natalie filled Charlie in on the rest of the patrons, commenting in her amusing way about each of them.

"I always enjoy your comments," Charlie said. "They're funny without being catty or nasty."

Their food arrived.

"So tell me what Paul said when you called," Natalie asked, cutting her salmon.

"He was very happy and suggested we spend Sunday together. We're going fishing at the lake where we went with my dad. I'm really looking forward to it," he told her. "He's not coming on Saturday, so you could stay over on Friday night. It might be late when we get back from Wasaga Beach."

"Yes, I like the sound of that," she said. "How are the steak and lobster?"

"They're excellent. Have you ever had lobster?"

"No, is it really worth the money they charge?"

"See for yourself," he said, offering her his fork with a chunk of lobster on it.

As she bit into the succulent meat, her eyes opened wide. "Oh. my goodness," she exclaimed. "That is so good. I've never tasted anything like that before."

She reached into her drink, pulled out the green bean and took a bite. "Whoa! That is one hot bean," she cried, reaching for her water glass. "I wasn't expecting that at all. Did you know it would be hot?"

"Not really, but I'm not surprised. Most things in a Caesar are spicy. How is your salmon?"

"It's excellent, just like everything else. Would you like some of it? It's really too big for me."

"Yes, I'd like to try it."

Placing a large portion with a bit of sauce on his plate she said, "It's at nine o'clock."

"Mm, this is really tasty," Charlie said "That sauce is excellent."

After they had finished their dinner, the waiter brought the dessert menus. Natalie liked desserts but usually skipped them to avoid the unnecessary calories.

"For old times' sake, I'd like the Black Forest cake," Charlie said.

Natalie perused the menu. "What is crème caramel?"

"It's a baked custard with a burnt sugar sauce but

that description doesn't do it justice. It's very light and tasty. It was my mother's favourite," he said. "If you're just looking for taste without bulk, it's perfect. You should try it."

"Yes, I think I will."

The waiter returned and took their orders.

Soon the desserts were delivered and Charlie dug right in. "This is exactly the way I remember it. It brings back such wonderful memories for me."

Natalie looked at her crème caramel and wasn't very impressed. But after taking a small bite, she changed her mind and quickly consumed it.

"Charlie, that was absolutely the perfect choice! I think it may become my all-time favourite dessert."

Natalie signaled the waiter for the bill.

Charlie took his credit card out of his wallet. "When we went to Fusili's it was your treat, tonight this is mine."

"Thank you, Charlie," she said. She reached across the table and squeezed his hand. "This was a night of firsts for me. I'll always cherish this memory."

If only she could be sure that Charlie wouldn't loathe her after his vision returned, it wouldn't have to be just a memory. They could have such a wonderful life together. Why couldn't she trust him? Because no boy had ever accepted that ugly purple birthmark.

No, a memory it must remain.

"Oh no," Charlie said as they were driving home. "I

forgot to call Tom and now it's too late. Remind me to-morrow to call him."

"No problem," she assured him.

"This has been a magical day," Charlie exclaimed. "I would never have thought anything could make me feel this happy. Life is full of surprises!"

"Well, getting some vision back certainly was a wonderful surprise," Natalie agreed.

Chapter Twelve

When they got back to the apartment, Natalie managed to park the car without difficulties.

"Nicely done," Charlie complimented her.

She glanced at her watch. "It's only ten o'clock. Would you like to go for a moon light stroll in the park?"

"It's probably not a good idea," he cautioned. "Remember the other day we found a homeless person sleeping on the bench. If there are many of them, it won't be a very pleasant walk."

"Yes, I guess you're right. That's too bad because it is such a nice night to be outside."

"There's a place a few blocks from here that has a patio. We could go there and have a nightcap," Charlie suggested.

Holding hands they soon arrived at the patio. Natalie chose a table outside so they could enjoy the soft warm breezes.

Charlie ordered a draft beer and Natalie ordered a Caesar.

"So, you really liked the Caesar?" he asked.

"Yes, but this time I'm also having the vodka. Tonight is a night for love and starlight and long walks by the ocean," Natalie said dreamily. "Have you ever been to the Caribbean?"

"Yes, I went with Amy, but that was long ago. Yes, tonight feels very much like some of the nights in the tropics."

She was glad that he could speak of his past so casually. A clear sign that the affair with Amy was behind him.

Their drinks arrived. "Oh, that's too bad," Natalie said, disappointed. "There's nothing except the celery in this drink."

Charlie laughed. "Already you're spoiled. Celery is the traditional accompaniment, but more expensive places try to impress their patrons by dressing it up. Does it taste okay, though?"

She tried the drink and found, to her delight, that it was just as good as the one she'd had earlier. "It's just as delicious."

"That's good. It really is about the taste, not the decorations," he said.

The couple at the table beside them were quarrelling. It was impossible not to hear them. The woman's voice was very strident, and the man was trying to calm her down.

"She sounds like a right witch," Charlie observed quietly.

"Perhaps she does, but have you been listening to what she's saying? It seems that he was hitting on her best friend at a party. I guess she has a right to get a little angry, wouldn't you say?"

"I suppose so," Charlie mused. "What's his excuse?"

"He claims the girl came onto him."

"That could certainly be true," Charlie said. "I know from personal experience that women are no better than men when it comes to relationships. Some people have no loyalty whatsoever, so don't just assume that the guy is the bad one."

"Yes, I know that from my romance magazines," Natalie agreed. "It's just so inconceivable to me that anyone would try to steal her friend's boyfriend. Perhaps I'm being too naive."

"Yes, about some things I believe you are," he agreed. "You have very high moral standards and expect the rest of us to be the same. Your sense of loyalty would never allow you to stoop to such tricks. That's why I want you on my side for the rest of my life."

At that moment the couple got up and left.

"I'm glad they're gone," Natalie said, ignoring Charlie's words. "Their unhappiness with each other was spoiling my mood. I want to be beautiful and warm and sexy just like the night."

"And that's exactly how you are to me," Charlie whispered.

They sat quietly, sipping their drinks. Natalie was sad she couldn't respond to the love reflecting in his words for she knew she loved Charlie with every fibre of her being. She anticipated the future with trepidation and knew her life would never be the same after having known him. He would always be her lover and she was sure she would never have another. She would have to hang on to the memory of their time together for the rest of her life. A silent tear ran down her cheek and she brushed it away with the back of her hand. With these dreary thoughts the magic of the day evaporated like snow in summer.

The waitress came by to see if they wanted another drink.

"Not for me," Natalie said.

"No, I'm fine, thanks," Charlie replied.

The disappointment in his voice almost broke her heart. How she wished she could have responded to his words and told him what was really in her heart.

"Let's go home," he said, getting up.

The soft night breeze wafted in through the open apartment window, and brought back the earlier magic with it. Natalie took Charlie's hand and led him to the bedroom. She ran her hands up under his shirt, over his torso. Pulling his head down to her. She gave him a long, sweet kiss. They quickly undressed and tumbled naked onto the bed.

There was no rush. They began stroking each other, knowing what would tantalize, what would arouse insatiable desires, what would please the most. They had the whole night ahead of them and Natalie knew it would be a night like no other.

Charlie kissed Natalie from her toes, lingering over her inner thighs, while stroking her breasts.

She pushed him away. "Charlie Weaver, you are not to be trusted. You want me to beg for mercy? Well, now it's my turn."

Natalie kissed him all over his face, biting his ears and shoulders and stroking his penis. He tried to stroke her, also, but she pushed his hand away.

"Not until you're as aroused as I am," she told him. "Just let me kiss you all over first and then I am yours to command."

Natalie continued down Charlie's body, kissing, licking, biting and stroking. Charlie relaxed, moaning, obviously enjoying all the sensations she aroused in him. She reached his groin and took him into her mouth. She nipped him, she nuzzled him, she fondled him, and through it all Charlie groaned and spoke her name over and over. Nothing existed except the two of them and this time and place.

When Charlie was fully aroused, she straddled him but did not take him inside her. Instead she rubbed against him, bringing her body to full arousal.

"Now my Adonis, I am yours," she whispered.

He slipped a condom on and they joined together, moving slowly in rhythm, seeking ever more erotic sensations. They were so familiar with each other's bodies they were able to delay the ultimate pleasure until they were totally sated. If life were a wave, they were at its crest!

When Natalie was sobbing with pleasure, Charlie relented and drove into her, allowing her to follow and reach the crescendo she had been holding back. She screamed. Charlie sighed and they collapsed in each other's arms.

Natalie rested her head on his chest, put her leg over his body and snuggled as close as she could. He held her tight against him and like this, they fell asleep.

Several hours later Natalie felt chilled and pulled the sheet up over them. Charlie awoke and asked if it was time to get up. Hearing that it was not, he leaned over and kissed her on the mouth. The magic of the night reasserted itself and once again they made love.

The next morning Natalie got up and made breakfast for them. Charlie joined her and after the night of love, even Natalie had a hearty appetite.

"Charlie, I have to buy a bathing suit. If we're going to be at Wasaga Beach, we may as well enjoy all of it. Do you have one?"

"Yes, but I better try it on, because I've gained some weight recently and it may not fit now," Charlie said with a chuckle.

He got his trunks, pulled them on and found they were a little snug. "Do you think they're okay?"

Natalie laughed. "Only if you want to drive all the ladies wild. They're too small. You should come with me and we'll both get bathing suits."

When they got back from the store Natalie studied the road map.

"It looks like it'll take at least two hours to get there. Does that sound right to you?"

"It's been a long time since I was there, but considering how far Wasaga Beach is from downtown Toronto, two hours doesn't sound unreasonable."

"Okay, so that means we'll have to leave here about eight o'clock. I'll be here before then so you better be up and dressed. We'll pick up some breakfast on the way and eat it in the car to save time."

"Why don't you stay here tonight," Charlie said longingly. "That way you don't have to get up so early."

"No, tonight is my seniors' night and I won't disappoint Mae."

"But you could come back here after visiting the seniors," Charlie persisted.

"Yes, that's true, but don't forget, I'm staying over on Friday this week. Besides, you have to call Tom and give him your good news. He'll probably want to come over to celebrate with you."

Natalie made dinner. While they ate, they talked about the trip to Wasaga Beach and Charlie told Natalie what he remembered about his trips there with his family.

After Natalie left, Charlie called Tom.

"Charlie, how goes it?" Tom asked.

"Very well. As a matter of fact, yesterday I started seeing light. I think that means my sight is coming back."

"Charlie, that is the best news you could have given me. We must celebrate."

"That's exactly what I was thinking. I'd like to take you and Sara out for dinner next week. It'll be a celebration of my returning sight and a thank you for being such a great friend. I know I can never thank you properly for saving my life, but I can do this. Just name the day and place."

"Dinner next Thursday sounds wonderful, but let me take you. I'm working and can afford it better than you.

"That may be true, but that doesn't change the fact that I want to take you," Charlie insisted. "What's your favourite place?"

"There's a place downtown called Far Niente that Sara always talks about. We could go there. I'll make a reservation for seven."

"Seven it is. Anything else happening?"

"Not much. Harry keeps asking about you. Should I tell him your good news?"

"Yeah, that would be great. As soon as I can see a little more, I'll call him myself. Natalie is taking me parasailing tomorrow at Wasaga Beach. And Paul and I are going fishing on Sunday. I'm so fortunate to have so many people who care about me."

"You are, indeed, a fortunate fellow," Tom agreed. "So what's with this Natalie? Are you two an item? When do the rest of us get to meet her?"

"No, no, it's nothing like that. It's just that we spend so much time together. Parasailing was just something she wanted to do, and wondered if I might like to as well, that's all."

"Well she sounds like a great chick. Why don't you bring her to the pub on Tuesday?"

"No, she visits her grandmother or someone on that night."

"So, bring her next Thursday," Tom persisted.

"No, that's special for you and me and Sara. Just forget Natalie. She isn't our type."

"It's just that her name keeps coming up, and when you say it, it sounds like more than just a housekeeper relationship. Remember, I've known you for over twenty years, and I think I can tell when you are soft on someone."

"Well, you're partly right," Charlie admitted, knowing he couldn't lie to Tom. "I do like her, but she has her own life and doesn't want to get involved."

"Well, okay," Tom said, laughing. "But I don't know how she resists a hunk like you."

"I can assure you that I'm quite resistible. Anyway, I'll see you on Tuesday."

Friday morning Natalie arrived at the apartment at seven forty-five, only to find Charlie just getting out of the shower.

"Hurry and get dressed. I'll get the beach towels out. Do you have an extra blanket we could take? Oh, and just in case there aren't any change rooms, you may want to wear your trunks under your shorts."

"Good point," Charlie said. "I'll do that. I don't have an extra blanket, but there's a tablecloth in the cupboard that I never use. It could work as well."

"Great thinking. I'll get it out. I'll get an extra pair of underwear for you so you can change if we go swimming. We'll take my car today."

When Charlie was ready, they set off.

"I brought some of my CDs along to keep us company," Natalie said. "I have Bette Midler, John Denver, and the Kingston Trio. Some of these are pretty old. They were my mother's but are my favourites, too. What would you like to hear?"

"You're right, some of them are pretty old. Let's listen to the Kingston Trio. My dad used to sing some of their songs like, "Hang Down Your Head Tom Dooley" and "Lemon Tree". It'll be fun to hear them again."

Natalie found the right CD and put it into the player. Music filled the car and Charlie reclined his seat and closed his eyes. Natalie concentrated on her driving and sang along with the music. Since Charlie appeared to be sleeping, she didn't bother stopping for breakfast. They made good time and found the para-sailing area a short drive from Wasaga Beach. There were people already milling about so they immediately went to the kiosk to find out what to do, and to pay for a ride.

"How does it work?" Natalie asked the attendant. "My friend is blind. Is it safe for him? Do we need to be wearing bathing suits?"

"Hold on, let me tell you about it," the attendant said. "First of all, it's very safe. You're attached to the sail with a body harness, but you have to lift your feet for the landing. So, you'd have to tell your friend when to do that. You never go in the water, as everything is done from the boat. You are aloft for about ten min-utes. Right now the wait time is an hour."

Natalie turned to Charlie. "So, do you want to wait an hour?" she asked.

"Sure, I want to do it," Charlie assured her. "That's what we came here for."

When it was their turn, a crewman guided Charlie, and helped him get onto the deck of the boat. Natalie climbed on board after them. The crewmen helped them into the body harnesses, and made sure they were secure, and tight enough to hold them in place. He explained to Natalie how they should land and to watch for the flag when it was time to raise their legs.

He gave the signal and they took off. As the boat picked up speed the sail rose into the air and Natalie felt the wind on her skin.

Charlie burst out into uproarious laughter.

"What is so funny?" Natalie shouted above the sound of the boat engine and the wind in her ears.

"It just feels so great! Nothing like I imagined," Charlie shouted.

Natalie gave herself over to the feel of the ride, and looked out over the landscape. Mostly she saw water, but there were also houses, and she could see the highway as a ribbon winding through the countryside.

When their time was up, the sail descended back to the boat. She told Charlie when to lift his legs and the ride was over.

It was so much hotter on the ground without the wind.

"That was marvellous!" Charlie raved.

"I liked it a lot, too," Natalie said. "Let's go back to the beach, have some lunch and then go for a swim."

"Hurray! Food! Charlie shouted. "I'm starving. You forgot to get breakfast."

"I didn't forget, but you seemed to be sleeping."

"Yeah, I guess I was dozing off," he admitted.

Back at the beach Natalie found a restaurant with a patio and read the menu board. "The specials today are: nachos, Portobello burgers, hot dogs, and spinach salad. Does any of that turn your crank?"

"One of each for starters," Charlie said patting his stomach.

Natalie laughed. "Get serious. I'm sure they have a regular menu as well, if none of the specials appeal to you."

"Okay, let's share an order of nachos," he suggested. "And I'll have a hot dog with fries."

"That sounds more reasonable. I'll have the spinach salad."

When the waitress came, Natalie gave the order and included a draft beer for Charlie.

After lunch they went to the beach. Natalie spread out the tablecloth and stripped down to her bathing suit. Charlie did likewise. She took his hand and they ran into the water. The water was very warm because it was so shallow, and they had to continue wading for quite a long way before the water reached up to Natalie's waist.

She let go of Charlie's hand and ducked down until only her head was above water. Grabbing Charlie around the knees she tipped him over. He landed on his back with a splash and quickly jumped up, groping with his arms for Natalie, in order to pay her back for her treachery. She knew he would try something, so she moved away from him. As Charlie turned around with his arms out, searching for her, she was able to admire his fine physique. How lucky she was to have these moments with him! If only they didn't have to end.

"Natalie, you vixen," Charlie shouted. "I'll get you for this."

Natalie laughed. "Yes, but you'll have to find me first, and it's a mighty big lake."

Charlie turned in the direction of her voice, but she quickly swam to a different spot and called his name.

"It really isn't nice to tease a blind man," he yelled.

Natalie relented and went back to Charlie. "You're right," she said. "But how are we going to swim together and not get separated?"

"Yeah, that's tricky. Why don't we walk out as far as we can and then swim back to the shallow area," he suggested. "That way if we get separated we are at least heading for the safety zone."

"Okay, let's try that."

They held hands and continued walking out into the deeper water. When the water was up to Natalie's armpits, she stopped.

"This is it for me," she said.

The water only reached halfway up Charlie's torso, but he turned around and started swimming back to the beach. Natalie watched him for a minute to make sure he was going straight, and then began swimming to the beach herself. The water was so refreshing. It was years since she had swum in a lake and she was glad they had made the trip.

Being a stronger swimmer, Charlie reached the shallow water first and stood up. He waved his arms, trying to find Natalie, but when he couldn't touch her, he began calling her name.

"Be there in a minute," she called and after a couple of moments, she swam up beside him.

"That was fun, let's do it again." Natalie said.

"Yeah, a little exercise would be good for my out-of-shape body."

They did the swim a few more times and then walked back to their tablecloth. Natalie stretched out, closed her eyes and dozed in the hot sun.

On the way home Charlie monopolized the conversation. "Today was absolutely perfect. I wouldn't change one single moment. If I died now and could only keep one memory, this is the one I'd choose."

"I'll not have any talk about dying," Natalie scolded him.

"Okay, I'm not planning on dying. I'm just trying to tell you how much I loved this day. I've had so many good days since you came into my life but this one is the best. I definitely will come back and do the para-sailing again. The feeling of flying is amazing. Didn't you feel that too?"

"Yes, but I was so busy looking around I didn't concentrate as much on the flying," she replied. "I think that's where your lack of vision gave you an edge."

"You know, I believe you're right. I was totally able to enjoy the sensations without any distractions. I'll do it again when I can see and then I'll know for sure. But, besides the flying, I thoroughly enjoyed the swimming. I wish Lake Ontario would get as warm. One day I'll buy a cottage on a small lake and swim every day. Wouldn't you love to have a cottage?"

"It's not something I've ever thought about, but it could be fun."

They drove on and after a while he asked, "How close are we to home?"

"Probably about an hour away."

"The sun made me sleepy and I didn't doze on the beach like you did. I'm going to close my eyes. Wake me when we get home."

"I notice something about you is different," Natalie said one day a few weeks later. "Somehow you seem more light-hearted. Is something going on?"

"I think so," Charlie responded. "I'm feeling very optimistic. Every day my sight is improving. The changes are so imperceptible I can't describe them, but the haze that was around for the past six months seems to be lifting."

"How wonderful is that!" Natalie exclaimed. She hoped for his sake he wasn't fooling himself because she hadn't noticed very much improvement in his confidence level when he was eating or moving around his apartment. His actions didn't clearly indicate that he could see better than before.

But a few days later as she was vacuuming the living room by the window, she looked up and saw Charlie watching her. That was strange. Could he see her or was he just focusing on the noise of the motor? She continued vacuuming around the room.

"Natalie, would you please walk back to the window for me?" Charlie asked.

She did and then turned to face him.

"Now wave your arms in the air," he requested.

Natalie looked at him quizzically. "Are you messing with me?"

"No. I was looking in your direction when you were working at the window, and I thought I could see your form. But then you came back toward me and I couldn't see you anymore. That's why I asked you to go back to the window. And eureka! I can see your shape and movement again. Now come back toward me."

She obliged.

"There, stop there. That's the point at which I lose you again. Why do you think that's happening?"

"Let's see. So you can't see me here, but if I walk back to the window you can see me. Is that right?" Natalie asked and walked back to the window.

"Yes, that's exactly what's happening."

Natalie started to panic. Her heart pounded like a jackhammer. Could Charlie really see her? Oh no! Had she left it too late? Would he see how ugly she was and realize that she has deceived him? No, this couldn't be happening. She had planned to be out of his life before his vision returned. This would spoil everything.

"So if you can see me, what am I wearing?" she asked cautiously.

"No, it's not like that," Charlie said. "I can only make out your shape and I see the motion of your body when you move. But only at the window."

Natalie breathed a deep sigh of relief. He could not see her birthmark. "So you only see my shape against the light. Can you see any colours?"

"No, not yet."

"What do I look like?" she continued to probe.

"I can't tell that. I just see a shape." He drew a form in the air with his hands. "There are no details at all."

"Walk around the apartment and see what else you can see," Natalie suggested.

Charlie got up and walked into the kitchen. The light was on. He stood in the doorway and looked around. Natalie stood behind him and apprehensively waited for him to speak.

"I see the black burners on the white stove. I see the fridge, but I can't see the table or the cupboards. I know they're there, but they don't show up."

Natalie turned off the kitchen light and asked him what he could see.

"Nothing. I need light to see anything," he replied.

They repeated the experiment in the bathroom. Again, with the light off he had no vision, but with the light on he could see the dark towels against the lighter coloured walls. In the bedroom he could see the laundry hamper because it was sitting right under the window.

"It's pretty clear you're able to see things when there's lots of light and contrast. Charlie, this is momentous news!" Natalie exclaimed. "Don't you see, in only a couple of weeks you have gone from only seeing light to seeing form when there's contrast. Soon you'll be able to see everything." She gave him a big hug. "I'm overjoyed for you. You'll soon have your life back. Isn't that marvellous?"

Charlie took Natalie's hands and danced around. "Oh Natalie, I'm so happy. Soon I'll be able to see how pretty you are. I'll be able to get around again, and even drive my own car. I'll be able to get back to work and to the gym and get back in shape. It's like I died and now I have a second chance at life. Let's get married!"

Natalie laughed nervously. "Whoa there! Everything up to the married part sounded good. Get your life back first, before you start making major decisions."

"But I thought the only reason you didn't want me

was because I was a cripple. I know you love me, though you refuse to say so. And I adore you. And now that I'll be whole again we can be together forever."

"Charlie, you're such a dope," Natalie chided him. "How could you think I'm so shallow that your blindness would be a barrier between us. But my plans for the future don't include marriage. I'm sorry Charlie, I've tried to be honest about this with you throughout our wonderful relationship, but I see I've failed because you keep insisting that we should be together. Please don't expect more from me than I can give."

Charlie looked so crestfallen, it made her heart ache. "Oh Charlie, please don't be sad. It was never my intention to hurt you. I only ever wanted to make you happy because I really believed that would bring your vision back." She had to remain firm or she would simply crumble. "You weren't supposed to fall in love with me, and now you're miserable."

Charlie took her in his arms, "I'm sorry but I can't help loving you and wanting to be with you, and I don't understand why you couldn't go to school and be with me at the same time."

"If I did that, I'm afraid I wouldn't be able to devote enough of my time to the relationship."

He took her in his arms. "Natalie, my love, I will take whatever you can give me."

Holding tightly to each other they both cried.

"Perhaps it would be best if I stopped coming," Natalie whispered.

"No!" Charlie shouted. "I want you to come as long as you can, until you start school. It's only a few weeks more anyway."

Natalie reached up and kissed him. "Okay, I'll stay as long as I can. When I finish vacuuming let's go to the patio where we were the other night and have a drink before dinner. I think a Caesar is the perfect way to celebrate your progress."

"Forget the vacuuming!" Charlie cried. "Let's go now!"

As they were enjoying their drinks at the patio, Charlie asked hopefully. "Are you staying tonight?"

"Yes I am. And I promise to keep you awake all night," Natalie said with a wicked little smile.

Charlie laughed. "Promises, promises. We'll see who keeps who awake."

That night when they made love, for Natalie it was both wonderful and sad at the same time because she felt the imminence of their parting.

Chapter Thirteen

As their daily routine continued, Natalie grew increasingly more stressed. She constantly asked Charlie about his vision, and although she expressed great happiness for any improvements, there was a strong undercurrent of tension and relief she couldn't manage to hide.

"Natalie, why are you so tense these days?" Charlie asked one day as they were walking in the park. "You seem ready to shatter into a million pieces. You say you're happy my sight is coming back, but I also sense something else. It almost sounds like a note of relief in your voice that I can't see perfectly. Please tell me what's going on."

"Oh, Charlie," Natalie wailed. "I'm sorry I've been such a mess these last few days. I'm thinking about how little time we have left, and it's making me tense. I just want to store up good memories for when I don't have you anymore."

Natalie hated lying to Charlie but didn't know what else to do. Already he could see most objects as long as there was light. And although he couldn't read yet, he was able to follow baseball and some programs on TV by himself. There were also signs his night vision was improving. How long would it be before his colour vision returned and exposed her ugly birthmark?

She had originally planned to stay until the end of August but Charlie's returning vision made her getaway more urgent. Today was Wednesday. She decided she would stay until Friday but let Charlie believe she would be back for one more week.

She knew she wouldn't have the courage to say good bye to him directly, so she would have to do it in a letter. Oh, dear, this was going to be the hardest thing she had ever done.

Maybe she should stop being afraid and let Charlie see her? No! He would look at her, see her ugly face and feel that she had betrayed his trust by taking advantage of his blindness. More than likely, being such a hunk, all the women he had dated were beautiful. Although she had tried to tell him she was not pretty, he had never responded to that. If he were to see her ugly face, he would shun her and she would feel like she did when the kids called her names and wouldn't let her play. No, it was better like this.

Natalie could see by Charlie's frown that he wasn't totally accepting her excuses. Her constant questions about his sight were obviously arousing his suspicion. She knew the mystery only increased his curiosity, but that couldn't be helped. She had to keep her secret!

Charlie stopped and took Natalie in his arms. She buried her head into his chest and they stood like that for several minutes, disregarding the other people around them.

"I love you so very much," Charlie whispered. "You've saved my life and given me hope for the future. I want you to believe me there is nothing you could tell me that would change my feelings for you."

Natalie hugged him tighter. "You are a true sweetheart," she said kissing him. "I shall never forget you, Charlie Weaver. You'll always be my most cherished memory. Now let's just enjoy being together."

"Cherished memory!" Charlie responded. "That's not my idea of our future, but I don't want to fight with you. I agree, let's just enjoy being together."

Natalie was so relieved at Charlie's acceptance she almost felt weak in the knees. She prayed fervently this was the last time she would have to lie to him. Oh, please, let the next few days be happy ones!

"Tomorrow is Thursday," she said. "I'll do all the chores now so we can just have fun after that. Where would you like to go?"

"I think I'd like to go to Centre Island for a picnic," Charlie said. "It seems like a nice romantic place to me."

"That's a great idea," Natalie said. "I haven't been there for years. I wonder how much it's changed."

That evening Natalie tried to be playful to reduce the tension that had begun growing between them. She didn't want their last night together to be sad and emotional. She wanted to remember Charlie happy and looking forward to a bright future.

But she couldn't help feeling guilty because he didn't know that this would be their last night together. They would have Thursday and Friday, but of course she never stayed over on either of those nights.

Natalie sat on the couch and started reading the personal ads in her romance magazine. This always created a conversation between them, and as it was about other people's situations, they could make up whatever stories they wanted. It was a game they both enjoyed.

Recognizing Natalie's attempt at lightening the mood, Charlie responded by being even more provocative than usual. Natalie fought back with the most outlandishly romantic scenarios leaving them both laughing.

"Twenty-five-year-old, non-smoking curvaceous blonde seeks long-term relationship with thirty something athletic male," Natalie read in one ad. "Hobbies are cooking, running, tennis and sex."

Charlie laughed. "Sure, even volleyballs are curvaceous. She's probably forty, looking like the back end of a bus, and her idea of running is to catch the bus when she is late for work. As for sex and cooking those are trigger words to get guys interested. If she's so hot, why isn't she already in a relationship?"

"Oh, Charlie, you're so jaded," Natalie scoffed. "If she is what you describe, why would she waste her money on the ad. She wouldn't be able to hide her age and her shape, so she would be caught instantly. What would be the point of that?"

"So she could laugh at all the suckers who bothered to respond to the ad," Charlie replied, chortling.

"So you think she's a bitter woman who just wants to humiliate men?" Natalie persisted.

"Yeah, something like that," he shot back. "I figure if she truly is a curvaceous blonde, she could meet a partner anywhere. Why the ruse of a personal ad?"

"Perhaps she's not being totally truthful," Natalie said, while reflecting on her own guilty situation. "After all, if everyone was totally truthful about themselves, how many relationships do you think would ever get started? She's probably tired of going to places and being inspected by males who have no intention of forming a relationship. Besides, the responses she gets will probably be just as full of lies as her ad may be. I say, give her a chance. She's probably just a busy woman who doesn't have time to go and look for someone, but doesn't want to be alone either. And I bet she's a very good cook with a heart as big as all out-doors."

"Oh, Natalie," Charlie scoffed. "You're so naive. But enough about other people's problems. Let's dance!" He jumped up and went to the CD player, found a CD and put it on. As soon as he heard the opening strains, he ejected it and found another one.

"What are you looking for?" Natalie asked. "Can I help you?"

Charlie started the second CD. "No thanks. I found it," he said and presently they heard Johnnie Mathis singing, "Chances Are". He took Natalie's hand and pulled her up into his arms and began dancing.

Natalie melted into him and gave herself up to the music and the moment. She had made up her mind to enjoy every aspect of their time together tonight, because she knew how the night would end. She would tantalize and tease him and he would arouse the most sensual pleasures in her. She knew their relationship had deepened and matured and was so much more fulfilling now. Gone was her urgent need to be satisfied but the heat was still there, bringing the closeness she craved.

"I feel so alive when I'm with you," Charlie whispered as they moved slowly to the music. "I've never felt like this before. I didn't know it was possible to feel so wonderful."

"Yes, I feel wonderful being with you, too," Natalie

responded. "But for the past five months, we've been living a fairy tale existence with no real responsibilities, no real contact with the outside world and no stress. When you get back to your normal life, things will be very different. I love the time we've had together and wouldn't trade it for anything, but I know it isn't real."

Charlie shook a finger at her. "You can be such a wet blanket sometimes," he scolded.

"Sorry, but one of us has to be realistic. But let's not talk anymore. Let's just enjoy the music and the moment."

When the song ended, Charlie drew Natalie toward the bedroom. "I want to lay in your arms all night," he murmured.

They undressed and got into bed. Natalie snuggled into Charlie's body while he stroked her face and kissed her neck. She relaxed, totally open to his caresses. Gradually Charlie worked his way down to Natalie's breasts, and instantly her nipples hardened. She began lightly stroking his thighs, teasing and caressing all around his penis, but not touching him there.

Charlie moaned and thrust himself into her hand each time she came close.

"Not so fast," she giggled.

Charlie, responding to her playful mood, joined in the teasing. He brushed his fingers over her mound until she, too, began thrusting toward him.

"Now whose anxious?" he gloated.

Natalie laughed softly and increased her teasing. Charlie was hard and ready but Natalie continued to hold him off. Finally he didn't want to wait any longer. Rolling on a condom he pinned her down on the bed. When he moved between her legs she rose up to meet him. They joined together, rocking gently, neither wanting this moment to end. They sighed and moaned and kept each other tantalized as they swayed together.

Increasing the tempo and the fire between them, Charlie drove deeper into her and they came together. Spent and satisfied, they lay back on the pillows.

Charlie soon fell into a light doze and Natalie, conscious of his body so close to her, snuggled against him. Knowing this was her last night with Charlie she was determined to stay awake. Never had she been so happy and so sad at the same time. How desirable and cherished she felt when she was with him.

If only she could tell him about the birthmark—but she was so afraid. She wanted to trust him but where had that got her in the past? No, he was a man and didn't all men want beautiful women? He was so handsome he could have anyone he wanted, so why would he pick an ugly duckling like her? He would hate her for deceiving him.

Oh God, how was she going to live without him?

How she would miss her dear, sweet, wonderful Charlie. She would have to live on the memories of their time together, stored in her heart. It was all she would have for the rest of her life. With these sad thoughts she fell asleep.

Very early Thursday morning Natalie roused Charlie with a kiss.

"Whoa, what's up with you this morning?" Charlie asked with a surprised laugh.

"Nothing, I woke up and couldn't go back to sleep. It's still very early and I didn't feel like getting up so I woke you instead. Why? Do you want to go back to sleep?" she asked playfully.

"No way! I'd rather stay in bed with you all day."

"All day may be a bit of a stretch, but another hour or so could be fun. Do you have any ideas?" she asked coyly.

"Only one at this moment," he said, reaching over and pulling her to him.

They enjoyed their sleepy love making, dozed for a while and then Charlie got up, went to the kitchen and began making coffee. Natalie joined him and started frying bacon. Soon they were eating delicious bacon and tomato sandwiches.

"I've got a pretty full day cleaning and shopping," Natalie told him. "So just relax and keep out of my way."

The day flew by in a flurry of activity for Natalie but dragged for Charlie who had been left to his own devices. He still couldn't see well enough to read but thank goodness there was an afternoon baseball game to amuse him.

Natalie prepared a tuna salad for dinner and they ate in silence. Charlie pouted because Natalie had refused to give up her evening at the seniors' residence. Natalie was thinking about the letters she had to write for Paul and Charlie.

On Friday Natalie arrived early to take Charlie to his favourite café for breakfast and to put the letters she had written for him and Paul in the usual spot on top of the fridge.

Hannah greeted them warmly when they arrived. "My favourite couple," she chirped. "Will it be the usual today?"

"Yes," they replied in unison.

When Hannah brought the breakfasts to the table she asked, "Did you two have a fight? You both seem so sad."

"No, we haven't been fighting, but a lot of different stuff is going on," Charlie said.

After breakfast they walked back to the apartment. Natalie gathered up the beach towels, the tablecloth they used for a blanket, and packed some cold drinks in a cooler, while Charlie put on his bathing suit.

"I don't think the water in Lake Ontario will be as warm as Wasaga Beach, but it should be okay for swimming," Charlie said. "After all, it's had two months of sunshine to warm it up."

"I hope you're right," Natalie replied. "I'm wearing my swim suit, just in case. There won't be many more days warm enough to go swimming, so we might as well enjoy what's left."

They arrived at the Toronto Island ferry docks and Natalie was amazed at how many people had the same idea they did. Keeping Charlie amused while they waited in line, she described all the different hats and costumes folks were wearing.

"I know Toronto is a multi-cultural city," she said. "But seeing and hearing so much diversity all in one place really brings it home."

When the ferry arrived, Natalie gripped Charlie's hand as everyone surged forward. They were among the first to board and were able to get a good spot to stand by the forward rail.

Charlie laughed. "You'd be good to have at a general seating concert. You seem to be very good at using your elbows."

"Thanks. It's one of the tricks my mother taught me," Natalie said laughing.

They enjoyed the short ferry ride and were soon on the path heading to the beach on the far side of the island.

"This sure is a busy place," she noted. "Everywhere you look there are families picnicking and kids playing. Some have even brought their barbeques. Smell the hamburgers cooking?"

"Yeah, sure smells delicious," Charlie said.

Continuing to stroll in the hot sun they reached the flower gardens and Natalie described the flower beds they were passing. She drank in the heady perfume of so many blossoms growing close together and even Charlie seemed to enjoy it.

"Oh good, we seem to be leaving some of the crowds behind," Natalie observed.

They passed the fountain and soon reached the pier on the other side of the island. There were a few fishermen with lines dangling in the water and other couples like themselves, meandering along. Holding hands they strolled out to the end of the pier and sat on a bench to enjoy the breeze.

"Coming here was such a great idea," Natalie complimented Charlie. "I had forgotten how relaxing and peaceful this island could be."

"Yeah, I'm glad we came," Charlie agreed. "When I was a kid, coming to the Island was a real treat. We went to the cottage most weekends and only occasionally did things around the city. Those trips are some of my best memories."

"I came with my mother four or five times a summer," Natalie said. "The best part for me was always the ferry ride and playing on the beach. So what do you say, are you ready to try the water?"

"Sure. I don't think I ever went to the beach on this side. Where is it?" Charlie asked.

"It's just a little way along the shore to the right," Natalie told him.

They walked back to the front of the pier and continued along the path to the beach. There were lots of people out, but the beach wasn't crowded. Finding a quiet spot far from everyone, they laid out the tablecloth and Charlie put down the small cooler he'd been carrying.

"Well I'm ready to try the water," Natalie said, removing her shorts and t-shirt.

"Me too," Charlie said and stripped down to his swim trunks.

Hand-in-hand they walked into the water.

"Doesn't feel too bad here," she commented.

"Wait for it!" he warned.

As they continued walking they could feel the water getting colder.

"I'm getting cold," Natalie said. "Let's swim out to the buoy and back a few times. That will help to warm us up. Can you see the buoy?"

"Not from here," he said. "Perhaps when we get closer."

"Don't worry about it. Just stay with me and you'll

be fine."

They dove into the water and were soon swimming side by side toward the buoy. The cold water was exhilarating and Natalie found herself enjoying the exercise. They touched the buoy together and turned back.

When they reached shallower water she stood up. "That was great! Let's do it again."

They repeated the swim to the buoy and back several more times and then went to dry off and warm up in the sun.

As the afternoon wore on, folks started to pack up and leave the beach. Even the lifeguard called it a day.

"There are only a few other couples on the beach now," Natalie whispered. "Do you think we could make love without being seen?"

"What a deliciously indecent idea," he whispered back. "It'll have to be quick though, and I don't have any condoms."

"That's okay, I do," she confessed.

"Natalie, I'm shocked at you, planning such a risqué adventure," Charlie said with a wicked grin.

Natalie giggled. "But doesn't it sound like fun?"

"It sure does, but I thought you were a more modest damsel."

"I am. Usually. But we have never made love outside and I want to do that. Besides, the idea of maybe being caught will add to the thrill."

Natalie looked around and saw that only three other

couples remained.

"Perhaps we could move our blanket further back," Charlie suggested.

"No, that would only draw attention to us," she said.

"Good point. So how do you propose we accomplish this . . . hmm . . . deed?"

"Well, that breeze that has come up is cooling things down. We could pretend we are cold and wrap the blanket around us. And if we don't move too much no one will pay any attention."

"Yeah, that could work."

They slipped out of their bathing suit bottoms, drew closer together and brought the edges of the tablecloth on top of them. They were fully aroused by their whispered conversation and the prospect of what they were about to do. Natalie lifted her knee up and put it on Charlie's hip, and as she did so he entered her. They rocked together, slowly at first and then faster, forgetting in the moment of coming where they were.

Keeping the tablecloth over them, Natalie peeked over Charlie's shoulder to see if anyone had noticed them. To her relief, it seemed that no one had. They quickly donned their shorts and T-shirts, and emerged from their hiding.

While packing up their things, Natalie looked at the setting sun and realized their time together was nearing the end. She was drowning in the overwhelming misery of her deceit. Poor Charlie! He had no notion of what she was about to do. She just wanted to wrap herself around him and never let him go. Just a couple of more hours—she must hold it together.

"I'm starving," Charlie said as they walked towards the ferry. "It's been a long time since breakfast."

"Yes, let's go to the restaurant beside the ferry dock and get us some dinner."

In the restaurant Natalie was so tense she was unable to eat most of her dinner. She tried to keep up a light banter about the other patrons but it sounded forced.

"Natalie, what is wrong?" Charlie asked, reaching for her hand.

"I'm sure it's nothing serious," she assured him. "But my stomach just feels a bit nauseous and I feel a chill."

"Okay, if you need to get home, we better get the bill," Charlie said. "I don't know when the next ferry is due but we may as well join the line."

Natalie paid the bill and they joined the line-up for the ferry. "I'm sorry," she said. "I didn't mean for today to end like this."

"It's okay, we have five more days together."

She hardly said a word on the way home. When they got to the apartment she told him she would not come up.

"Will you be okay from here?" she asked.

"I'll be fine," Charlie said, kissing her. "I'll see you

Monday." He turned and walked toward the door.

As Natalie watched him go, tears welled in her eyes and slid down her cheeks. "Goodbye my love," she whispered to his receding back. "I shall miss you. I'm sorry it had to end like this."

She stumbled along the street toward the bus stop, crying so hard she could barely see. As she passed the park, she sat on the first bench she came to. Her mind was in turmoil. Oh, God, what was she doing? It wasn't too late! She could run back, tear up the letters she had written, apologize to Charlie and promise to never leave him. How could she do this to him? What if this drove him back to drinking? Oh, Lord, it just didn't bear thinking about.

"Are you okay miss?" a male voice asked.

Natalie looked up startled. She hadn't heard the man approaching.

"I'm fine, thank you for asking," she replied, and stood up. She quickly walked out of the park, in a hurry now to just get home.

Chapter Fourteen

Saturday morning Paul arrived, as usual, with breakfast.

Charlie had been up early and was waiting for him. "Hey Bro, how's Ilene doing? Isn't it just about time for that baby to be born?"

"Yes, actually it's past due," Paul replied. "According to the doctor she's a week overdue. He says that's not unusual for a first baby and is nothing to worry about. But, of course, we worry." He sipped his coffee. "Ilene is totally fed up with being pregnant. She just wants to have the baby and be done with it. I can't say I blame her. It must be very uncomfortable in this heat with all that extra weight."

"Well hopefully it will happen soon."

As Paul and Charlie ate their breakfast, they talked about the past week.

Charlie excitedly told Paul about his improving sight. "The changes are gradual, but I keep thinking one day I'll wake up and my vision will be back completely."

"I sure hope so," Paul said. "How much longer is Natalie going to be here?"

"Just one more week. I've become so used to her, I just know I'm going to miss her a lot. She's helped me so much. Without her I don't think I could've made it this far."

As Charlie talked, Paul stood up and took the envelope from the top of the fridge. He sat down and tore it open.

"Whoa, this is a big one," he exclaimed. "It's full of money! And there are two other envelopes in it, one addressed to me and one to you."

"What's going on?" Charlie asked.

"I don't know," Paul said. "Why is this envelope filled with money?"

"What envelope? What money? I don't know what you're talking about," Charlie snapped, frustrated by the mystery. Something about it made him very uneasy. Somehow he knew it was not going to be good. His heart started to race.

"They're from Natalie," Paul told him. "What's going on?"

"How the hell should I know?" Charlie shouted. Dread filled him, and a sinking feeling filled his stomach. "Open your envelope and see what it says," he urged.

Paul opened his letter. He read it and whistled.

"What? What does it say?" Charlie asked, totally panicked now.

"I'll read it to you. *Dear Paul: Thank you for giving me the opportunity to help your brother. It has been the most rewarding endeavour in my life. Charlie is doing so well now, he no longer needs me.*"

At this statement Charlie groaned. "No!" he yelled and banged his fist on the table. He finally understood why Natalie had been so uptight and strange for the past few days. She was not coming back!

"What's the problem?" Paul asked in alarm.

"I thought we had one more week!" Charlie shouted. "I needed that week to convince her to stay."

"What are you talking about?"

"I love her," Charlie groaned. "I wanted to marry her, but she said we were living in a bubble, and that when life got back to normal I'd see things differently. But I won't! She truly is my world."

"Oh Charlie, what a mess, I don't know what to say. But I think she's probably right in that you should wait until your life is normal again before making such important decisions. I guess that explains the rest of the letter."

Paul continued reading where he left off. "*I am returning the past few months' salary. It was not a job to me, but rather a friend helping a friend. Good luck to you and your wife on the birth of your baby. Regards,*

Natalie."

Paul counted the money from the envelope. "There's over four thousand dollars here!! What on earth is going on?"

"We can't keep that," Charlie barked. "She earned it honestly. She did everything she was supposed to do and helped me as well. You have to give it back to her."

"I didn't say I was keeping it," Paul objected. "I'll have to try to find her contact information. I didn't get a resume from her, but I must have a telephone number at the very least."

"First before you look for that, please read my letter," Charlie said. anxiously.

Paul opened the other envelope and took out the letter. "*Dearest Charlie: I am so sorry to end our relationship so abruptly. You are the dearest, sweetest man I have ever known and I know you will have a wonderful life. Your full vision will return soon and you will be able to go back to your old ways. And you will find your Amy; she is out there waiting for you. Again, please forgive me for ending it like this, but believe me it is necessary. Please do not look for me, for my life must be as I planned it. Goodbye dear, sweet, wonderful Charlie. I do love you. Natalie.*"

"I knew she loved me," Charlie moaned. "Paul, I have to find her. I can't let this end this way."

"I'll call Ilene and get her number for you," Paul said, reaching for his cell phone.

Charlie sat in a daze, his mind a jumble of angry words he wanted to hurl at Natalie for hurting him so, and pleading words to make her come back. It was all such a mess!

Paul gave Charlie a piece of paper with Natalie's telephone number.

Charlie snatched it from him but, of course, couldn't read it. "Fuck!" he swore. He retrieved his cell phone and asked Paul to read the number while he dialled. The phone rang twice and then an automatic message intoned, "The number you have reached is not in service."

Charlie couldn't believe his ears. He handed the phone to Paul. "I must have misdialed. Could you dial it for me."

Paul tried the number with the same result.

"Are you sure you wrote down the right number?" Charlie asked, running a trembling hand through his hair.

"Yes, it's the right number. I remember it from when she first started taking care of you."

"Don't you have an address for her?" Charlie asked, getting more and more frustrated.

"No, I never did get her address, and as she was so reliable it was never an issue."

Charlie was getting desperate. "Can't we call the police to find her?"

"What would you say to them? My girlfriend left me

and I don't know where she lives. Could you find her for me? The police would politely tell you that they are not a service for the lovelorn."

"Well, don't you have any other ideas how we could find her?"

"Where's your phone book?" Paul asked and Charlie got it for him.

"Her last name is Munroe. With u or an o?" Paul asked flipping the pages.

"I don't really know," Charlie said.

Paul spent the next half hour calling all the Munroes and Monroes, asking for Natalie, only to be told he had the wrong number. Two numbers didn't answer and he made a note of them for Charlie to try later.

"When I go to work on Monday, I'll try to find her on the internet," Paul said. "Do you know if she used a computer?"

"I don't think so, because she never talked about anything like that."

"That's too bad. I might have been able to trace her through Facebook. I'm sorry, I can't think of any other ways we could find her. We just don't know enough about her. Do you know what school she's planning on going to in September?"

"No," Charlie groaned. "She never talked about her school. I wish I'd asked more questions and been more persistent, but who could know it would end like this.

Oh Paul, what am I to do?"

"For the moment, nothing, but don't give up hope. The internet is an amazing source of information. It may turn up something. In the meantime I must get home to Ilene. She'll be wondering where I've disappeared to. Will you be alright?"

"Don't worry, I'll be fine," Charlie said. He just wanted to be alone with his anger and his grief.

After Paul left Charlie banged the table and cried out, "Natalie, Natalie, where are you? Why did you leave me like this? I need you! I can't live without you. Please come back to me!" He laid his head down on his arms and sobbed.

A while later he went into the living room and found the Johnnie Mathis album. He played it over and over, thinking of their time together. Finally he could stand it no longer. He called a cab and he went to the liquor store where he purchased whiskey and beer. Tonight he would get drunk.

He arrived home, went into the kitchen for a glass but, realizing that the breakfast remains were still on the table, he stopped to tidy up. Natalie wouldn't be happy that he had left a mess for her. Then he remembered she wasn't coming back anymore. Sobbing, he got a glass, picked up the whiskey bottle and headed for the living room.

He downed the first glass of whiskey and a beer very quickly, achieving a slight buzz. After two more glasses of whiskey he found himself feeling very angry and extremely sorry for himself. After all, hadn't he treated Natalie like a queen? How dare she throw his love back in his face! If that was the kind of person she was, he was well rid of her. He didn't need her. He'd find his Amy and show her!

As these thoughts coursed through his mind, the telephone rang. Hoping it was Natalie, he jumped up and grabbed it.

"Hey Charlie, it's me, Tom."

Slurring his words slightly, Charlie said, "Tom, it's good to hear from you. What's up with you and Sara?"

"That's why I called. Sara's out at some ladies' event tonight and I wondered if you'd like some company?"

"Sure, if you're in the mood to get drunk, cuz that's what I'm doing tonight."

"Sounds like you're half in the bag already. I'll pick up some pizza and be right over."

Tom arrived with pizza, chips, pretzels and beer.

Charlie hadn't realized he was so hungry until he smelled the pizza.

They ate in silence and when the pizza was gone, Charlie opened the chips and continued eating.

Tom sat back and waited for him to finish.

Finally Charlie said, "Thanks Tom, I didn't realize I was so hungry." The food had sobered him up a little and he was ready to talk.

"So, Charlie, why are we getting drunk tonight?"

Tom asked.

"Oh, Tom, I told you Natalie and I were just friends, but that wasn't true. We were lovers, and in love with each other, and now she is gone, and I still love her." Charlie blurted without stopping to breathe.

"Gone? Gone where?" Tom asked, perplexed.

"She's left me," Charlie responded in a hopeless tone.

"Why did she leave?"

"She doesn't want to be with me. She wants to go back to school and become a nurse. She said marriage wasn't for her and she was going to dedicate her life to helping others. I told her she could do all that if we were together, but she didn't agree. I always sensed that she was hiding something, but for the life of me I couldn't begin to guess what. To her it was something very bad, like she had two heads or something. Of course I couldn't see her but she sure felt good all over."

"Did you ask Paul about her?"

"Yes I did, but he didn't say there was anything wrong with her."

"So maybe it's something else, like she's schizophrenic or bi-polar or something," Tom said helpfully.

"No, it can't be anything like that. We were together five days a week for six months. If she had mental problems, it would've come out in that time. No, it's something else. Anyway, whatever it is, doesn't matter now. What matters is, what am I going to do? I know she loves me, she said so in her letter, but she's convinced our relationship couldn't work. I don't know how to fight that."

"Then it seems obvious that you just have to go on without her."

"But I can't do that!" Charlie shouted."She has taken over my heart."

The friends lapsed into silence. Charlie kept drinking whiskey and beer, becoming more morose with every glass. Tom refused the offer of whiskey and got up to put on some music.

"Johnnie Mathis?" he said as he pulled out a CD. "Well, no wonder you're so bloody morose."

"Put on a Boz Scaggs then!" Charlie yelled. When the music started, he began to sing along drunkenly.

Soon he was fast asleep. Tom thought about putting him to bed but decided to leave him in the chair. Sleeping was probably the best possible thing for him, he reasoned.

He let himself out and prayed Charlie wasn't going to let the booze take over his life again. Whoever this Natalie was, he wanted to throttle her. How could she have led Charlie on so? He hoped there was a very special hell for women like her.

Charlie woke up a few hours later. His mouth tasted like a sewer and there was a jackhammer pounding in his head. It was pitch black out, and his watch told him it was four twenty-seven a.m. In the bathroom he drank a glass of water with three aspirins, brushed his teeth and went to bed.

He woke up at nine-thirty and headed for the shower, still feeling lousy, but not as bad as he had earlier. After getting dressed he prepared a large breakfast of bacon, eggs, toast and coffee, all the while musing that he was seeing things very clearly today.

Finishing his breakfast, he cleaned up and went into the living room where the pizza box reminded him of the night before. He hoped he hadn't said anything to Tom that he would regret. After tidying up he thought he would go to the park and went to the window to assess the weather. When he looked out he realized that he could see the traffic and the buildings across the road very clearly.

"What the hell," he said out loud. "Is my vision back?"

He grabbed his keys and left the apartment, looking around everywhere. Everything was as he remembered. He ran to the elevator and waited anxiously for it to arrive. Again, everything, including the button panel, was perfectly clear. He ran all the way to the park, where he could see the kids playing, the flowers and their colours.

He could see everything!

"I can see! I can see!" he shouted, running through

the park.

Parents and kids watched him and some of the kids mimicked him, shouting, "I can see!"

Charlie didn't care what anyone thought, he only wanted to share this with Natalie. This thought sobered him a little, but could not quench his exuberance. He had his life back!

At home, he called Paul.

"Great news, Paul!" he whooped. "My vision is back! I can see everything again just like before."

"That's super!" Paul cried. "Now you can get back to normal. Why don't you come here for dinner?"

"Sure. Now I'll be able to drive myself. It'll be so strange to drive again after all this time. Can I bring anything?"

"No, just your big smiling self. See you about five."

Next he called Tom. "Thanks for babysitting me last night."

"No problem, but I wasn't babysitting you. I was on my own and needed some company, is all. How are you feeling today?"

"Now that you ask, I am flying!" Charlie shouted. "My vision came back, sometime between last night and this morning. I can see everything again. I'll be able to go back to work and get back to the gym. This is the best thing that's ever happened to me."

"Thank God! I can't tell you how relieved I feel and how happy I am for you. Why don't you come over here for dinner today? Sara's making her special lasagne and it's quite edible. I'll get some champagne and we'll celebrate in style."

"It's a great idea, but I've promised Paul I'd go there. I like the idea of champagne though, so I'll take some to Paul's. It's going to be strange driving again. I just hope I remember how."

"I'm sure you'll be fine, but I'm not busy right now, so I could come over and go with you until you feel comfortable."

"You're such a stand-up guy, but I think I'll be okay. Tell Harry that I'll call him this week. I'm going to make an appointment with my eye doctor and make sure everything is okay and then I'll be back on the job, if Harry has any space for me."

"He'll take you back as soon as you're ready. He asks about you all the time, and has taken on a couple more projects so he's very busy."

"So I'll see you at the pub on Tuesday. Look at that, you don't have to chauffer me anymore. Perhaps I could take you instead?"

"I'd like that," Tom said. "It'll be just like old times. See you Tuesday."

Charlie couldn't contain himself. Grabbing his car keys, he hurried to the garage. He was relieved that the space beside him was empty, so exiting would be a lot easier. The engine needed a good run after sitting idle for so long, so he headed for the highway. He hadn't realized how much he'd missed this. He had always loved driving, the feeling of the road beneath the tires, the sense of power he felt behind the wheel, and the freedom driving offered him. Yes, life was good. The only flaw was that Natalie wasn't there to celebrate with him.

That evening Charlie grabbed the bottle of champagne and went to Paul and Ilene's for dinner. After the meal Charlie told Ilene to stay put and relax because he would do the clean-up.

While he was working in the kitchen, Charlie heard Paul and Ilene talking excitedly. He couldn't make out the words but hoped it was good news.

He finished up quickly and joined them in the living room. "So, what's happening?" he asked.

"It's started, Charlie," Ilene trilled. "I'm going to be a mom soon. We're going to the hospital now."

"That's great!" Charlie said. "I'll go home, but call me as soon as you have any news."

Paul and Ilene left for the hospital and Charlie went home to wait. He sat up hoping for news from Paul but eventually gave up and went to bed.

He woke early on Monday to a ringing phone. He lunged for it. "Hello," he shouted.

"Charlie you're an aunt!" Paul yelled. "I mean it's a girl, Uncle Charlie!"

"Congratulations!" Charlie whooped. "That's great!

How's Ilene doing? Did everything go okay?"

"Ilene and the baby are both doing well," Paul said. "We actually got to the hospital a little too early. Her labour really didn't start until later. Charlie, watching a baby being born is a miracle. I know it happens millions of times, but for me this was so precious. You can't believe how exciting it is to watch that tiny baby come out."

"Better you than me, brother. I don't think I'd have the stomach for something like that," Charlie said. "Does she have a name yet?"

"Yes, Wysteria Ann Weaver," Paul said.

"That's an unusual name, but very pretty," Charlie said. "When do I get to meet her?"

"Ilene's resting now, but if you come this afternoon she should be up for visitors."

"This afternoon it is. Will you be there?"

"Yes," Paul replied. "See you later."

Chapter Fifteen

Saturday morning Natalie woke up thinking about Charlie, and wondering if he had read her letter yet. She went into the bathroom and looked at herself in the mirror. What a sight! She was puffy around the eyes and her nose was red. She got a face cloth, ran it under the cold water and placed it over her swollen eyes.

And started to cry again.

She had to stop feeling sorry for herself. What about Charlie? Poor Charlie would be devastated. Why did life always have to kick you in the teeth!

Natalie wondered what to do to distract herself from her sorry thoughts. Wanting to talk to someone she decided to visit Mae at the seniors' home. Mae was always happy to see her and was a good listener who gave very good advice.

She arrived at the seniors' home and found Mae outside enjoying the sun.

"Hi Mae," she called. "Would you like some company?"

"Oh my dear Natalie, how nice to see you on a Saturday," Mae said happily. "Get yourself a chair and sit by me. You look kind of beat up today," Mae noted. "What has happened?"

"Oh Mae, I've made such a mess of things," Natalie wailed. "You recall Charlie, the blind man I was helping?"

"Yes, you seemed to be very happy with him," Mae said. "What has he done to upset you?"

"He has done nothing, but I have," Natalie admitted. "I wanted so much to have a relationship that wasn't warped by this ugly birthmark. With Charlie I was free. I was the person I always wanted to be. He thought I was beautiful and with him I let myself feel desirable. We had a wonderful time for three months, and we fell deeply in love. Now his sight is coming back and I had to leave him without telling him why. I'm sure he's as miserable as me. I pray this doesn't drive him back into a depression and to alcohol," she finished, tears forming in her eyes.

"That's quite a story," Mae said. "But why did you have to leave him?"

"Because he would see how ugly I am," Natalie sobbed. "And he would hate me for using him the way I did."

Mae reached over and patted Natalie's hand. "My

dear, you are entirely too much focused on that birth-mark," she admonished. "I know how hurtful the kids were when you were growing up, but kids are like that. When we grow up and mature a little, those kinds of things are not so important. If Charlie truly loves you, that mark will not matter. From all the things you told me about him, I think you are selling him short. I'm sure he's a much better person than you think. You should go back and apologize and see what happens after that."

Yes, the kids had been very mean and had teased her, which had been hurtful. But that was nothing compared to the way those boys in high school had treated her. Hadn't they told her she was ugly and only good for sex?

"I wish I could believe what you say, but what if he's not such a noble person and will hate me? Then I won't even have good memories. I just can't take that chance."

"Then I'm afraid, my dear, sweet Natalie, that you will just have to live with what you have done."

"I'm afraid you're right. I just hope Charlie's not feeling as sad and lonely as me."

Mae patted her on the knee, "I should think he probably is, but when his vision returns he'll have lots of things to keep him occupied. That'll give him some time to get used to you not being there."

"I hope so," Natalie said, wiping her eyes. "He does

have some good friends who'll help him. Before he lost his sight, I think he had a pretty full life. That should help him. I just hope the break-up doesn't drive him backward into depression and alcoholism."

They sat in silence for a while and when it was lunch time Natalie helped Mae into the dining room.

"I'll come and say good-bye before I leave," she said and then went to help feed some of the more disabled seniors.

On the way home Natalie shopped for groceries. For the past few months she had eaten most of her meals at Charlie's but now her larder needed restocking. This memory brought tears to her eyes again. She had to stop weeping at every thought of Charlie and get her emotions under control. This was so much harder than she had anticipated. How to keep herself busy until school began? She would go through her whole house and clean it from top to bottom. Heaven knew she hadn't spent much time there in the past six months and so many things definitely needed doing.

Between spring cleaning, visits to the seniors' residence and long walks at the conservation area, the next two weeks went by quickly. Natalie tired herself out most days and usually managed to sleep at night. When she couldn't sleep she went back and read some of her favourite stories in her romance magazines. This didn't stop her from thinking about Charlie, but it gave her hope that one day he would be okay.

The first day of school arrived and Natalie went with high expectations. It turned out to be a small class of about twenty students who were all high school drop-outs like herself, and were there to get their high school equivalency diploma. There were a couple of older people but everyone else was quite a bit younger than Natalie. The mix of males and females was about even.

The first day, to her disappointment, was short. All that happened was they received their schedule of classes and a list of the supplies and books they would need. The school had some texts that could be borrowed for those who couldn't afford to buy them, but Natalie wanted her own and spent the rest of the day in the bookstore getting what she needed.

At home she started looking through the texts and found that she was quite excited at the thought of learning their secrets. The math text looked impossible but the English literature books thrilled her. This was going to be a fine year.

As the semester progressed, Natalie found she loved the challenge of learning again. She had always enjoyed school and it was only the kids she had hated.

Not having much of a social life, she found the homework assignments were welcome, keeping her busy and her mind off Charlie. She was always prepared for the lessons and, except in math class and computer science, her hand was the first one up to answer questions.

One day in early November, as she was eating lunch in the cafeteria, Natalie was surprised when a fellow student asked if she could join her.

"My name's Marsha," the woman said after sitting down. "And I know you're Natalie. I've been watching you and I noticed you're very good in most of the subjects, especially English, but not so good in math and computers. I'm good in those two subjects, but not so good in English. Perhaps we could help each other by studying together. What do you think?"

Natalie, totally taken aback by this onslaught of words, looked Marsha over. What she saw was a girl in her mid-twenties with spiked red hair, green eyes, an open, confident expression and a large happy smile. She thought the suggestion was a good one. She certainly needed some help in those two subjects, and she knew Marsha was good at them.

"Okay, but why did you pick me?" she asked.

"Because you're serious, and so am I," Marsha stated. "Most of the other students seem to be here because their parents insisted on it, or because it's better than hanging out at the mall all day. There's a math quiz coming up next week. Would you like to come to my place to study for it?"

Natalie felt a little nervous at this proposal. She had

never been to anyone's home before, except Charlie's.

"Where do you live?" she asked.

"I have a tiny little basement apartment in the Broadview and Danforth neighbourhood."

"Okay, when do you want me to come?" Natalie asked.

They settled on a date and time and finished their lunches in a friendly conversation.

On Saturday Natalie drove to the address Marsha had given. She was surprised at how small the basement apartment really was.

"You sure weren't kidding when you called it a tiny little apartment," she said, smiling. "How do you live here with no view of the outside world?"

Marsha shrugged. "Oh, you get used to it. Besides it's all I can afford and since I don't have too much stuff, it works okay for me. Anyway, let's get started."

Marsha was a good teacher and Natalie found she was beginning to understand the math better. She was glad she had come.

"So, Marsha, why are you in this program?" Natalie asked as they stopped for a coffee break.

"Because I left home when I was sixteen, dropped out of school and lived on the street for a few years," Marsha responded, sounding almost nonchalant. "Then I discovered that I didn't have any qualifications for getting a job. So I shacked up with an older guy for a few more years."

Natalie listened in shocked amazement as her new friend continued her story.

"Then I came to my senses. I wanted more from life than just playing house. So I got a government loan and here I am. How about you, why are you in the program?"

"Well, my story's a little different," Natalie began. "My mother had breast cancer and my father insisted I quit school to take care of her. I didn't mind because school was a misery for me. After my mother died, I was going to go back to school but my father had a debilitating stroke. So instead I looked after him for nine years, worked as a cashier for a couple more years and then, like you, decided that just wasn't enough for me. And here I am. I want to get my high school diploma and then I'm going to pursue a nursing career. But why did you leave home at sixteen?"

"It's a sad, miserable story which I may tell you one day," Marsha said.

Natalie detected a note of disappointment and resentment in Marsha's voice.

"So, how can you be so sure you want to be a nurse?" Marsha asked. "I don't know what I'm going to do yet. I hope by the end of this year I'll have a better idea."

"You're really good at computer science, so maybe you could do something with that," Natalie suggested.

"But to get back to your question, I thought about nursing because I want to do something useful and I realized how important caregivers are when I took care of my dad. I also volunteer at a seniors' residence and enjoy helping the ones who need it. Mae is my favourite person there and she's like a grandmother to me. I often ask her for advice."

"It looks like you have the right temperament for a nursing career," Marsha agreed. "I'm not sure what I'm suited for. I've toyed with the computer idea, but I'm not there yet."

After they finished their coffee they continued working until Natalie's stomach began to growl. "Sorry about that. I didn't have time for lunch so I better go home and make some dinner."

"I'm hungry too," Marsha admitted. "There's an inexpensive Chinese restaurant on Danforth, would you like to go there?"

"Chinese food?" Natalie said. "I don't think I've ever had that."

Martha was astonished. "Never?"

"I can't remember ever having any."

"Well, you're in for a treat," Marsha promised.

At the restaurant Natalie perused the menu. "You better order," she said "I don't have a clue about any of this."

"No problem. Is there anything you're allergic to or that you don't like?" Marsha asked.

"No, go ahead with whatever you like."

Marsha ordered some of her favorites. "I didn't order anything very exotic as this is your first taste. If you like it, we can get more adventurous next time. Have you ever eaten Thai or Indian food?"

"Oh, gosh no. My mother was a very traditional English cook and we didn't go to restaurants very often. I guess the most exotic thing I ever ate was pizza."

"Boy, you sure have lived a sheltered life," Marsha said in amazement. "Well, you have a lot of catching up to do. Many experiences in life can be very pleasurable."

"I'm not sure that life's pleasures are all that meaningful," Natalie stated. "My life as a nurse will be service to others, and that will bring me pleasure."

"Oh, but that's not enough! " Marsha exclaimed. "We're here on earth to learn and experience life. Just because you are going to be a nurse, doesn't mean you can't enjoy yourself."

Their food was delivered and Marsha served Natalie and herself. Natalie tried each of the different dishes.

"This is delicious," she said. "I don't think I've ever tasted anything quite like this chicken before and, believe me, I've eaten a lot of chicken."

Marsha smiled. "Well, I can see it's going to be a lot of fun introducing you to the flavours of the world. That is, if you're up for it."

"Yes, I believe I am," Natalie said. "I've lived such a

sheltered, closed life I think I'm ready for some adventure."

"That's the spirit, "Marsha enthused. "And as we're going to be spending a fair amount of time together studying, we might as well be friends."

"Friends?" Natalie murmured. "I've never had a friend before, except my mother."

"Really?" Marsha exclaimed. "How could that be?"

"Simple," Natalie said. "My mother protected me from the taunts of the other kids by keeping me at home. And then when I went to school I was too shy to approach anyone and my birthmark stopped them from coming to me."

"Wow! I'm surprised you turned out so normal," Marsha stated, a forkful of chicken halfway to her mouth.

"Thanks for that," Natalie said. 'I think I'm going to enjoy our friendship. And with your philosophy on life you'll help me broaden my horizons."

"Well, I'll certainly enjoy trying," Marsha replied.

They finished their food to the last morsel, and Marsha signalled for the bill.

"That was so good," Natalie said. "Thank you for bringing me."

The bill arrived and they split the payment.

They walked back to Marsha's place.

"See you on Monday," Natalie called.

She drove home, very excited about all the firsts

today.

The girls began hanging out at school and studying for all the tests and quizzes together. Natalie found this relationship very helpful and she enjoyed Marsha's acerbic wit, especially when they were talking about the young men in their classes. But most of all, the friendship helped Natalie to stop obsessing about Charlie. She wanted so badly to know how he was doing and a few times came close to calling Paul, but she always talked herself out of it, afraid of the reception she would get.

Christmas was approaching and Natalie wanted to do something special for her friend. She knew Marsha lived on a very tight budget and had noticed her winter jacket was very worn out. She had seen that Marsha was often cold when they waited for the bus, so she decided to buy Marsha a new winter jacket for Christmas.

One day in the school cafeteria, a few days before Christmas break, Natalie said, "Marsha, will you come to my place for Christmas? I'd love to do a traditional turkey dinner but it wouldn't be any good alone."

"Oh wow! I'd love to," was Marsha's enthusiastic response. "I wasn't looking forward to the holidays but now I think it'll be fun!"

And so on Christmas Day in the afternoon Marsha

arrived at Natalie's home.

"I had no idea you lived in a house," she said as she entered. "No wonder you find my place so crammed."

"This was my parents' house and I didn't see any reason to sell it. Have a seat in the living room. I'll put the tree lights on and get us a glass of wine."

Natalie returned with the wine and they wished each other merry Christmas, touching the glasses together.

"I'm so glad you came," Natalie said, smiling.

"I'm glad I did, too," Marsha responded. "I brought you a present." She handed a gift bag to Natalie.

"How wonderful, thank you so much," Natalie responded. She opened her gift and exclaimed, "What a beautiful scarf. I love the colours. It will brighten up my dull winter coat."

"That was the idea. I'm glad you like it," Marsha said.

"I have a gift for you as well." Natalie retrieved a large gaily wrapped package from under the tree.

Marsha frowned. "Hey, what is this?"

"Open it and find out," Natalie said with a big smile.

Opening the package, Marsha cried, "Oh, Natalie, I can't accept this gift! It's way too much money for you to spend."

"Of course you can accept it. You need a new jacket, and it doesn't break my budget, so please don't make me feel bad for giving it."

"You didn't tell me you were rich."

"I'm not rich. However my father was an amazing investor. He left me this house and some investments that allow me to keep it, with enough left over to live on. I certainly couldn't live in luxury, but my needs are small."

"Oh Natalie, I don't know how to say this," Marsha said, blushing to the roots of her hair. "It's not my style. I would never wear anything like this. This is more your style."

Natalie laughed. "Hey, that isn't a problem. You can exchange it for something you like."

"You are the sweetest friend I've ever had," Marsha said. She got up and hugged Natalie.

Natalie froze at this intimate contact.

Marsha sprang back. "I'm sorry, I didn't mean to offend you."

"You didn't offend me. It's just that I've never been hugged by a woman." She stepped forward and hugged Marsha. "Thank you so much for this beautiful scarf. I've never owned anything so colourful before."

"Yes, I noticed that you wear very somber colours. You also dress like a matron. You're young and beautiful, and have a wonderful figure. Why don't you show it off more?"

"I never want to draw masculine attention to myself. I figure if I look frumpy and unappealing, men won't be interested in me. I had a couple of bad experiences when I was in high school and don't want them re-peated."

"What happened?" Marsha asked quickly.

Since she had told Charlie about the rapes she found she could tell about them to Marsha without embarrassment.

"Since then I can't bring myself to trust any man," Natalie concluded. "I know I'm unattractive and so the only reason a man would be interested in me is for sex."

"Curse the entire male population!" Marsha cried. "Don't you know that young boys are beasts. Their hormones are raging and they haven't lived long enough to care about people's feelings. Only their own needs count. And, unfortunately, sometimes boys never grow up. But you can't give up because of that. If you do you'll always be alone. Don't you want to have a husband and children?"

"Yes, but those things are not for me." Natalie's tone was emphatic.

"You're making me very angry, my friend!" Marsha exclaimed. "You're a beautiful, intelligent, funny, gen-erous person, and you have so much to offer. Didn't your mother tell you that? She did you a disservice in protecting you so much. You never developed cal-louses over your heart to protect yourself from the stu-pid, ugly things kids say. Yes, a lot of people are insensitive and they're the ones you have to watch out for. Your birthmark sets you apart, but it doesn't make you ugly. As a matter of fact it makes your face and eyes very interesting. It makes them appear to be different colours. Anyone who would reject you because of that birthmark is a fool. But if it bothers you so much, why don't you have it removed?"

"As a matter of fact, after my father died I went to a plastic surgeon to have that done. He said he could remove it entirely from my cheek but not totally from the eyelid. He was concerned it might cause damage to my eye. I decided it wasn't worth the risk," she concluded.

The smell of the roasting turkey wafted through the house.

"I have to get the vegetables cooking," she said. "Would you like another glass of wine?"

"Yes, thanks," Marsha said. "I'll set the table in the dining room if you tell me where everything is."

Natalie needed to be alone for a while. The holidays, a time to be with people you loved, brought on thoughts of Charlie. She didn't want to spoil the day for Marsha so she kept herself busy with meal preparations and her mind off the might-have-beens.

When the dinner was ready Natalie asked Marsha to sit down and proudly carried the turkey into the dining room.

Marsha clapped with delight. "What a truly magnificent feast you've prepared. I've never had such a fine Christmas dinner. It sure beats the turkey sandwich I had planned for myself."

"I'm so happy you came. The last couple of years I was on my own and it made Christmas a misery for me,'" Natalie said as she sliced the turkey. "When my parents were alive we always followed the same tradition. My mom made cranberry porridge for breakfast and while we ate we listened to Christmas carols on the radio. Then we opened our presents. In the afternoon I would help with the dinner and my dad would have a nap. Around six we would have dinner and we would watch a movie. How about you? Do you miss your parents more during the holidays?"

"No," Marsha replied vehemently. "My memories of Christmas aren't happy ones. My parents were drunks and the holidays just escalated everything. By dinner time they were baiting each other and screaming. It often turned physically violent. I would grab something to eat out of the fridge and go to my room to escape the unhappiness. I hated Christmas!"

"Was it your parents' drinking that made you leave home so young?" Natalie asked.

"Sort of," Marsha responded. "I had planned on leaving as soon as I finished high school, but one night my father came into my room. Nothing happened because he was too drunk but I knew he would come back. I got out the very next day!"

"Oh, Marsha, I'm so sorry," Natalie commiserated.

"It must have been dreadful for you."

"Yes, it scared me pretty badly," Marsha said.

While Marsha was talking, Natalie had filled two plates with turkey and the fixings. She placed one in front of Marsha.

"Please start. Don't let it get cold," she said. "I know I've prepared too much food but it's the only way to be traditional.

They concentrated on the food for the next few minutes.

"Natalie, this is absolutely delicious," Marsha raved. "You must teach me how to cook."

"Sure," Natalie said. "But I'm not really a very good cook."

"Well, you're certainly better than me," Marsha said. "So, what did you do after your father died? You must have felt very alone."

"Yes, I did," Natalie replied. "I started volunteering at the seniors' residence and working as a check-out clerk at the local grocery store. That's where I saw the ad to take care of Charlie."

"Charlie?" Marsha repeated. "Who's Charlie? Why don't you take care of him anymore?"

Natalie laughed nervously and kept her eyes down. "You certainly have a lot of questions."

"It's just that you've never mentioned him before, and that makes me wonder why not," Marsha admitted.

"Oh, he was just someone who needed help," Natalie said blushing.

"Hey, girlfriend, you're blushing! Come on, out with it! What's the scoop on this Charlie?" Marsha badgered.

"Okay," Natalie acquiesced. "I'll give you the Coles Notes version. I didn't like my job at the grocery store and was looking for something more meaningful. Charlie's brother had posted an ad for a housekeeper for Charlie. He had lost his sight in an accident and needed someone to cook and clean for him. I took the job and looked after Charlie for five months before going back to school."

When Natalie fell silent, Marsha prodded her with a smile. "That's not the whole story. I told you my sad story so now it's your turn. I'll keep bugging you till you tell me."

"We fell in love," Natalie whispered. She turned her head to blink away the tears. "That's all."

"That's all!" Marsha shouted. "You tell me you fell in love and that's all you'll say?"

"I made a mess of everything and left poor Charlie in a lurch," Natalie sobbed.

"I'm sorry." Marsha reached over and patted Natalie's hand. "I didn't realize how difficult this would be for you. You can finish this another time."

"No," Natalie said. "I want to get it all out now." And she proceeded to relate the whole sad story.

Marsha whistled. "So you are still in love with him?"

"I'm afraid so," Natalie wiped her eyes. "But I feel a little better having told you about it."

"Yes, talking helps. But for now let's talk about something more cheerful. So, what are you going to do for New Year's Eve? I think we should go out and celebrate. It's time for you to stop being a hermit."

"I've never celebrated New Year's," Natalie said. "My parents thought it was a waste of money."

"Well, I can't deny that. Your parents were partially correct," Marsha agreed." However, I was thinking more about going to Nathan Phillips Square and joining the madness there. It doesn't cost anything and it beats sitting at home. Are you game?"

"Sure, that sounds like fun, as long as we stay together."

When they finished eating Natalie gathered up the excess food and went to the kitchen. Marsha brought out the dirty dishes and together they cleaned up.

Retiring to the living room, Natalie picked up the newspaper. "I was thinking of buying a computer and there seems to be a lot of really good sales on Boxing Day. Would you come with me and help me to choose the kind of computer I need?"

"What a wonderful idea," Marsha exclaimed. "But you realize we have to get to the store by eight o'clock or all the best deals will be gone."

"That's fine with me. But if we have to get there so

early, why don't you stay over tonight?" Natalie suggested. "As a matter of fact, why don't you stay here
for the entire week? We could go shopping, study for
the exams, go to the movies, or anything else we feel
like doing!" The prospect of having a friend to do things
with was almost making her giddy.

"What an awesome idea!" Marsha responded enthu-
siastically. "We could be like sisters. I never had a sister."

"Neither did I," Natalie said. "It'll be so much fun."

So all that week they spent in each other's company. Natalie even took Marsha to the seniors' residence and introduced her to Mae.

Marsha convinced Natalie to buy some new outfits
that fit her properly and were very modern and becoming.

"I like the way I look in my new clothes," Natalie said
as she was paying for her purchases. "But I think I'd
be embarrassed to wear them to school."

"Why on earth would you be embarrassed?" Marsha
asked in amazement. "What's the point of having them
if you don't intend to wear them?"

Natalie laughed. "You're right. I just have to get
used to the new me."

One day in late January Natalie arrived at school
early. She was sitting quietly reading in the classroom
when, through the open door, she could hear several

boys talking in the hall. She recognized the speakers as Gus and Sam, a couple of the young students in her class.

"Hey Gus, have you checked out the chick with the eye patch lately?" Sam said.

"Oh, you mean the brain? Yeah, she's really looked hot lately," Gus replied.

"Yeah, I always thought she was pretty sexy with that eye patch, but with her new duds she's quite a knock-out. Are you going to ask her out?" Sam asked.

"I'm not sure. She is pretty old. But her friend, the red head is pretty foxy. Have you noticed how she moves? I can just picture her between the sheets," Gus said.

"I know what you mean. Let's talk to them at lunch," Sam replied.

Well, how about that! Natalie smiled. Perhaps Marsha was right when she said her birthmark wasn't such a bad thing. Could there really be a chance for her and Charlie after all? She shook her head. No. He would hate her when he saw that birthmark, thinking that she had taken advantage of his blindness. She had to forget him and concentrate on school.

In the lunch room, later that day, Natalie told Marsha about the conversation. The girls had a good laugh.

Presently Gus and Sam approached their table.

"Hello ladies, mind if we sit down?" Gus asked and

without waiting for an invitation, he sat down.

Sam, leering at them, leaned against the table and asked, "Would you two lovelies like to go to the movies with us on Saturday?"

"Sorry," Natalie said. "I already have a boyfriend."

"How about you," Gus asked Marsha.

"Sorry, I only date older guys," Marsha said flippantly.

Sam got up. "Well, if you change your mind, we could show you a good time."

Natalie and Marsha giggled softly as the boys went back to join their own group.

"You know, it would be fun to have a date again," Marsha said. "Maybe I should have taken Sam up on his offer."

Natalie laughed. "Oh Marsha, you don't want to do that! What about that fellow you met on New Year's Eve?"

"He hasn't called. Maybe you and I should go to a club and see what's out there."

"I'd go to a club with you, but I'm not interested in meeting anyone. I still think about Charlie a lot."

"Natalie, my dear friend, you cannot carry a torch for Charlie forever. That way lies loneliness and madness. Remember Miss Haversham in Great Expectations?"

"Oh, I'm not going to go crazy!" Natalie scoffed. "I'll get over Charlie." Yes, perhaps when she was dead.

"This year I just want to concentrate on finishing all the credits I need for university. I know Gus thinks I'm old, but I really do believe I have a few good years left."

"You have lots of time left, but you know you have hermit-like tendencies, so don't leave it too late to go out and enjoy life," Marsha advised.

"Yes, I have spent a good deal of time by myself, but now that you're my friend I don't enjoy isolation nearly as much as I used to."

Marsha crumpled up her sandwich bag and aimed it at the waste basket. "Oh, I haven't told you, but last night my landlord called and said he's selling the house and wants the basement empty. I don't know where I'll be able to find another apartment as cheap, and I really can't afford anything much more. I know it isn't much of a place but it has worked for me."

"Don't worry. If you can't find anything you can always stay with me," Natalie offered. "We get along all right and I have way more space than I need. Having a room mate might be kind of fun. We'll just move the furniture out of the main bedroom to the basement and paint the room for you."

"Wow, Natalie! That's really wonderful. Thank you so much," Marsha said and reached over to touch Natalie's shoulder. "I think we'll enjoy living together."

"Yes, it'll be a welcome change for both of us," Natalie said. "And with the final exams looming, we'll be able to study together."

Chapter Sixteen

One Saturday in late April, Charlie was standing in line at the check-out of the local hardware store, when he noticed that the woman in front of him had short, dark brown curly hair. His thoughts immediately went to Natalie. Although he had never seen the colour of her hair she had told him it was brown and he had felt the curls. He had to resist the urge to run his fingers through the hair of the woman in front of him, and stopped just short of bending down and smelling it. He chided himself for being an optimistic idiot.

He saw the woman's profile as the cashier keyed-in her purchases. He noticed that she had a large dis-colouration around her left eye. It looked so much like a black eye, Charlie hoped she wasn't involved in an abusive relationship. As the woman was rooting for change in her purse, she laughed at some comment the cashier had made.

A siren went off in Charlie's head. Natalie! He could

never forget that laughter!

"Natalie?" he blurted out.

The woman's head whipped around. "Charlie!" she whispered.

Before he could react she had grabbed her bag and charged out of the store.

Coming to his senses he took off after her.

"Sir, sir! You must come back and pay for your purchases!" the cashier shouted.

At the door the security guard stopped him, and by the time he had paid and hurried to the parking lot Natalie was nowhere in sight.

Cursing his luck he kicked the tire of his SUV and slammed his fist down on the roof. Totally crushed, he got inside and pounded the steering wheel in his frustration. To have been so close to her, and not known it was Natalie, was more than he could bear.

"Damn you and all those rotten kids who bullied you," he shouted. "Natalie, I love you!"

For a long time he sat with his head in his hands against the steering wheel.

"Fuck!" he growled, and drove home.

Natalie's heart pounded as she raced from the store. She reached her car, jumped in and drove off, narrowly missing a pedestrian.

"Look out, you crazy fool!" the man shouted after her.

"Charlie, oh dear God! Charlie," she whispered over and over as tears filled her eyes.

Her panic receded as she increased the distance between herself and the store, only to be replaced by an overwhelming sense of emptiness and loss.

Tears were falling freely as she pulled into her driveway. She ran into the house and charged upstairs, totally ignoring Marsha's cheery greeting. She slammed the bedroom door shut and flung herself face down on her bed, sobbing uncontrollably. So engrossed was she in her own torment, she didn't hear Marsha's knock on the door.

Soon Marsha was sitting beside her on the bed, rubbing her shoulders soothingly. "Natalie, what is it? Are you ill? Are you in pain? What do you need?" Marsha's questions bubbled out in a panic.

"Oh Marsha," Natalie sobbed, turning her tear-streaked face up. "I saw Charlie at the store. Somehow he recognized me. It was awful." And she cried harder.

Marsha continued to soothe her. "Okay, just take a deep breath and tell me what happened."

Natalie sat up and blew her nose. She related the events at the store, including the fact that she had almost killed someone in her panic.

"When he called my name I didn't know who it was so I turned around. Marsha, he saw my face," Natalie wailed. "That's exactly what I didn't want to happen. Now he'll always remember our time together with horror." And her heart-broken sobs began again.

"Stop crying and get hold of yourself," Marsha admonished. "You're allowing yourself to believe your own story. You have no idea what he thought, or saw, or will remember. He must have been just as surprised as you were. Probably more, if you think about it, because, after all, he'd never seen you before."

"Yes, I guess you're right. And it's good to know that he has regained his sight. I'm really happy about that. And from my brief glimpse he looked even better than I remembered."

Taking Natalie in her arms Marsha said, "You are such a ninny. Hasn't this past year taught you anything about yourself and other people. You've become a self-assured woman who knows what she wants and is prepared to go out and get it. Don't be miserable for the rest of your life. Go and find out what kind of guy Charlie really is. You know his phone number and where he lives. Why don't you call him?"

"I can't do that. What if he has met someone else?" Natalie asked, her voice quivering.

"So what if he has?" Marsha quipped. "What is the worst that can happen? All he can do is swear at you and call you names."

"I'll think about it," Natalie said, knowing she would never call him.

All the way home Charlie cursed himself for being

an idiot. Natalie had been right there! As soon as he recognized her voice and heard her laugh, he should have reached out and taken her in his arms and never let go. Fuck! What was he going to do now? She knew he'd seen her face and knew her secret. He knew she was mortified. Had she not run away to avoid him seeing her in the first place? She would never call him now. He had to find her.

"Natalie! Why did you run away?" he shouted and furiously pounded the steering wheel.

Damn and double damn! He'd forgotten that Sara and Tom were coming for dinner and to watch the Blue Jay game on TV.

At home he gulped down some beer and busied himself making chili and garlic bread. But all the while he couldn't get Natalie out of his head. Seeing her like that brought back all the loneliness, anger and frustration of the past year without her. Oh, Natalie, where are you?

When Tom and Sara arrived, Charlie ushered them into the kitchen. "Dinner's ready so we may as well get started," he said, pouring their drinks.

As they settled down to eat, Charlie couldn't contain himself a moment longer.

"You'll never guess what happened," he blurted out. "I saw Natalie today." And he told his friends all that had happened at the store, including about the birthmark he had seen. "She's beautiful and I love her more now than ever. The birthmark is obviously the cause of all her anxiety and the reason she ran away. I must find her," he concluded.

"Sounds pretty immature to me," Tom said. "I would've thought she'd have gotten over that a long time ago. After all, she's not a kid anymore."

"You don't understand," Charlie groaned. "She thought she was ugly because all the kids at school teased and bullied her. And instead of helping her grow a thicker skin, her mother sheltered her so she never learned to trust anyone."

Sara held out her glass for more wine. "I understand her totally. You guys have no idea how cruel teenagers can be. Especially girls. They call you names, they never choose you for their team, they make fun of everything you do, and say, and wear. They could drive a genie back into his bottle."

Tom looked at Sara and frowned. "You sound like you have personal experience."

"Yes, thank goodness it was only one semester," Sara said. "The 'queen' of the class decided that she didn't like me and the rest of the girls followed her lead. My mother transferred me to another school and that was the end of it. I was lucky." She turned to Charlie. "Have you thought of how you're going to find her?"

"No, I don't know yet. I'm still trying to get my head around the fact that I actually saw her today."

After the three had finished eating and had retired to the living room, Sara began to flip through the over-full magazine rack, checking the dates of the newspapers. "Charlie, some of these magazines are over six months old," she commented. "Are you saving them for any special reason?"

"No, I've just been too lazy to clear out the rack," he said. "I'll have to dump them in the recycle tomorrow."

Sara continued looking. Suddenly she started to laugh. "Charlie, I didn't know you were a romance magazine aficionado!"

"What are you talking about?"

"At the bottom of this mess I found three romance magazines," she said holding up one of them.

"Sara, you are a genius!" Charlie whooped, snatching the magazine from her hand. "Those are Natalie's. She and I had a lot of fun with the personal ads. I know she reads them religiously. If I put an ad in that magazine she'll be sure to see it. I'll do that tomorrow. Thank you so much for finding them."

The next day Charlie placed the following ad in the magazine.

"*For Natalie. You are the one true thing in my life. You are my Amy. I love you. Please call. Charlie.*"

He watched the news stand for the next edition. When it arrived, he purchased a copy and quickly flipped to the back. There was his ad.

Now it was time to wait. And pray.

Armed with the newest edition of her romance magazine, Natalie walked up the path of the seniors' residence. It was a very warm June evening and several of the seniors, including Mae, were outside sitting in a circle, talking.

"May I join you?" Natalie asked. "I have this month's magazine. Would you like me to read a couple of the personal ads and then we can talk about them?"

To a chorus of yeses, she sat down to read. After listening to the ad they all discussed the merits of the wording and tried to guess if the writer was sincere. She was about to read another one when suddenly she stopped.

"What is it?" Mae asked.

Natalie sat frozen, staring at the magazine. "It's nothing," she finally managed to blurt out.

"It is something, isn't it?" Mae whispered to Natalie. To the seniors she suggested, "It's getting cool, perhaps we should go inside."

They agreed and went in, leaving Mae to sit with Natalie.

"What is it, dear?" Mae asked again.

"Listen to this ad," Natalie said and read the ad.

Mae gripped Natalie's hand. "Oh, my dear sweet Natalie, this is your Charlie, isn't it?"

"Yes, I'm sure it is," Natalie said quietly. "What should I do?"

"That is not for me to tell you," Mae said. "You must listen to your own heart and act accordingly."

"But I'm so confused. I told you about meeting him when I was shopping and I was so sure that he was horrified at my face."

"My dear child, you have no idea what he was thinking. You have beat yourself up for so long about that birthmark that you think everyone believes as you do." Mae squeezed Natalie's hand and continued. "This past year, I thought you had got over that. Hasn't your friend Marsha convinced you yet that you are a wonderful, beautiful person?"

"I don't know that I'm wonderful and beautiful, but yes, I do accept myself more easily than I used to," Natalie said.

"Then follow your heart," Mae's repeated.

In bed, later that night, Natalie thought about Charlie and the wonderful times they had enjoyed together. She wanted desperately to call him after having read his ad, but knew she could never summon up the courage to do so. Charlie had only glimpsed her face and couldn't possibly have seen how ugly she was. She knew he would reject her if they ever met. He was so perfect and she was not, so why would he want her? Oh, what should she do?

The next day Natalie showed Marsha the ad.

"It's a sign from heaven. Call him!" Marsha exclaimed.

"I can't," Natalie sobbed.

"What are you afraid of?" Marsha asked.

"That he will reject me."

"I have a solution. Phone him in the middle of the day when you know he's working. You can leave a message, and ask him to meet you some place. That way, if he just wants to get back at you, he doesn't have to show up."

"Yes, that could work, Natalie agreed. "I'll call and leave a message tomorrow." She desperately hoped that his ad was sincere.

Every night Charlie checked his phone for messages. Five days after he had seen his ad in the magazine, he came home from work to find the message light blinking.

"Oh please let this be Natalie," he whispered.

His hand shook as he picked up the receiver and punched in his password.

"Hello Charlie, if you truly believe in the sincerity of the writers in the personal ads, meet me at our favourite bench, on the Saturday before Father's Day, at three o'clock."

Charlie forgot for a moment he was listening to a voice message, and shouted, "Natalie, I'm here!"

Feeling foolish he shut up and once again listened to her message. He had placed the ad but had been sceptical about whether it would actually work. Now he was overjoyed to hear her voice but most of all, her message. He listened to it over and over, just to hear her voice.

When was Father's Day? Not this Sunday, but next Sunday. Only ten days to wait. He immediately called Tom.

"Tom, Natalie called!" Charlie shouted. "She wants to meet in the park next weekend. Isn't that wonderful? I'm so happy, I can't sit still!"

"Okay, I'm happy for you, but let's just wait and see how the meeting goes before we start celebrating," Tom advised, sounding less than enthusiastic. "She might screw you again, you know,"

But Charlie refused to be drawn into Tom's negativity. His Natalie wasn't like that.

The days dragged on endlessly. For him, time seemed to have stopped. He practiced what he would say to her. He would tell her how much he'd missed her. He would tell her how beautiful she was and how he was never going to let her go. And—above all—he would tell her how much he loved her.

Finally Saturday arrived. Charlie got up earlier than was his usual Saturday habit, shaved with care and checked out his wardrobe. He wanted to look perfect for Natalie. He finally selected a blue golf shirt that matched his eyes and a pair of off-white chinos. He finished off with a tan belt and sandals. He was ready long before it was time to go, and decided to have lunch in the park, just in case Natalie was early.

He made himself a ham and cheese sandwich, grabbed a ginger ale from the fridge and headed for the park. Thankfully their favourite bench was empty so he sat in the middle to discourage others from coming to sit there.

It was a gorgeous day. The park was full of kids and families and Charlie was on cloud nine. Today Natalie was coming back! But as he thought about the meeting, he began to get nervous. What if she was only coming to tell him that she hated him, or that she had found someone else? Then he chided himself for being an idiot. Of course she was coming to be with him, or she would have simply ignored his ad. Wouldn't she? Oh please let her come soon!

Natalie was apprehensive about the meeting. She wanted to look special for Charlie so she let Marsha talk her into a complete make-over. But when she looked at herself in the mirror she was horrified. The woman staring back at her was not her. Immediately she washed her face and applied only a bit of lipstick. She donned the pink mini skirt and flowered blouse she had worn the first time she made love with Charlie, hoping he would recognize it and be pleased with the hidden suggestion.

She had planned on being early and so just after two o'clock she was walking toward the park. As she reached the path to the bench she spotted Charlie there. Her heart lurched and she almost lost her courage. She didn't know what his reaction would be to her birthmark. Despite Marsha's and Mae's reassurances, she still didn't believe the mark would be unimportant to him.

Then Charlie was running toward her, laughing and calling her name. She ran to him and jumped into his arms. He swung her around kissing her on the lips and whispering her name over and over.

"Oh, Natalie, my darling, I'll never let you go. I've been so miserable without you. Natalie, my life! Please say you'll marry me and be mine for all eternity."

"Oh, Charlie, I'm so sorry for putting both of us through a year of misery," Natalie said as hand in hand they walked to the bench. "How could I have so misjudged you? Can you, will you, ever forgive me?"

"Natalie, my darling, I'll forgive you anything. I know now why you left. I knew after I saw you at the store, but you ran away from me again. You really must stop doing that. Don't you know how beautiful you are, what a wonderful person you are, and how much I love you? I want you beside me for the rest of my life."

"Those words are music to my ears," Natalie said, reaching up and kissing him on the cheek.

They sat on the bench, marvelling at the miracle of their reunion.

"I've learned so much this past year," Natalie said.

"I met a girl at school and she has helped me to grow up. Her name is Marsha and though she's younger than me, she's so much wiser about life. It's because of her that I found the courage to come here today," Natalie confessed. "The world is so much better than I had ever imagined. And now that I have you back it's perfect."

"So you're obviously still planning to get a degree. Four years is a long time to wait," Charlie groaned.

"We'll work it out," Natalie assured him. "Just because I'm going to school doesn't mean we can't be together.

She had a question she really didn't want to ask, but knew if she didn't, it would torment her forever. "Did you date anyone this past year?" she whispered.

"In the past couple of months I had a few one-timers," Charlie confessed. "I took women out for dinner and then took them straight home. The dates were difficult for me because all I did was think of you. I wouldn't have dated at all if Tom hadn't nagged me so much. I'm so glad you're back." He laughed. "I won't have to be a monk anymore. How about you, did you date anyone?"

"You already know the answer to that. I never dated before I met you, and had even less desire to do so, after," she said.

"I have another question for you. Why did you leave that money?"

"Because we were lovers, and lovers do things for each other without getting paid," Natalie replied.

Charlie kissed her finger tips. "Yes, I know, my little pirate."

Then he looked at her with a huge grin on his face. "Is your pink outfit saying what I think it's saying?"

"I was hoping you'd recognize it," she replied with a twinkle in her eye.

"So, you'll stay with me tonight?"

"Yes, of course I will. And then we'll go see Hannah for breakfast."

"But let's go home now. I just want to hold you and feel you next to me without an audience."

"My thoughts exactly!" she replied, giggling.

Hand in hand they walked out of the park and back to Charlie's place.

Home.